# *BAHALA NA*

## (Come What May)

# *BAHALA NA*

## (Come What May)

A WORLD WAR II STORY OF LOVE, FAITH, COURAGE, DETERMINATION AND SURVIVAL

## ROSALINDA ROSALES MORGAN

# *BAHALA NA*

## (Come What May)

A work of historical fiction

ISBN-978-0-9890017-0-0

Kobbe Books 2013

This book is for Mom and Dad and for all those brave Philippine and American soldiers who defended my country in WWII.

With love and gratitude

# Table of Contents

# AUTHOR'S NOTE

About ten years ago, I was trying to document the life of my parents for my children, my nieces and nephews and cousins and the future generations of both my parents' families. Everyone seemed to be doing their genealogy and I felt compelled to do ours. How my parents met is so unique and quite special and then I heard during the later part of my father's life about my parent's lives during World War II. It was heartbreaking to hear about the hardship that they and their fellow countrymen endured during World War II. I felt a deep animosity toward the Japanese who destroyed my country whenever I heard their stories. My parents never talked about the war until near the end of my father's life. I believe he did not want to relive the sad experience. When he finally did, I tried to put the pieces together like a big puzzle. I should have written down their stories sooner.

In Oct. 2006, when my parents both got very sick in the Philippines and I was summoned to their hospital bed from New York, I felt the urgency to put all the stories in writing even in bits and pieces. I felt the time was running out. When both of them were released from the hospital and recuperating at home, I was grappling with the idea to write a book about their love story and their life during World War II. During the two weeks I spent with them in the Philippines while they were recuperating, I tried to question my father about the past and he obligingly answered my questions. That's when I decided I should write a book about the people of Batangas. I don't think he knew what I was thinking of doing and I never told him. I just listened to his stories. During the early hours of the day when I could not sleep, I would sit down and jotted down some notes. When he passed away, I continued questioning my mother when she was visiting me in South Carolina in 2011. We talked most of the morning and I wrote something down in the afternoon. The stories came in fragments. Some events she could not remember when it happened. She was 89 at the time.

I did not change the location in the book because I felt it a tribute to my town. This book will serve as a piece of its history that the children in my town will remember and their future grandchildren will cherish. It is part of their history and will become a legend in time. This book is a tribute to the men and women of Batangas which embodied the true Batangas and Filipino ideals. It is a book about the spirit and resiliency of the people of Batangas amidst the chaos that was not of their own making.

I researched some events and how things fit together. They gave credence to the story. Some of the people I wrote about I invented. Some names I changed. The historical figures and events that shaped their lives are based on my research. All the things that happened in Batangas during the Japanese occupation are stories my parents told me. Some things are works of my imagination blended in with historical facts. The events that are real and imaginary are intertwined.

This book is considered a work of historical fiction. However, the war events in Batangas happened where my parents lived, and there are actual scenes of which my parent had first-hand knowledge and personal experience. The long journey from Mankayan to Alitagtag when the war started is a glimpse of what my father endured at the start of the war. It was an undertaking that my father would not forget. The fire in Taal and the massacre in Bauan were the most heartrending events that affected my mother since it concerned some of her relatives. They can never be found in history books yet it actually happened.

I also realized while writing the story that most of World War II books are written about the Atlantic side of the conflict. Very few are written about the Pacific theater yet they suffered as much damage and sufferings as the Europeans. They felt like abandoned children which in essence they were since President Franklin D. Roosevelt regarded them as a lost cause. Maybe those soldiers who died for my country did not want to relive the atrocities of the Japanese and so my only reliable source when I started to write was my father when he was still alive and then my mother took over after he passed away.

R. R. M.
Feb. 2013

# Acknowledgments

My heartfelt thanks go first and foremost to my husband, Matthew for acting as my copyeditor and proofreader. I trust him more than anyone else for his good command of the English language.

Special thanks to my dog, Jake, a pointer who even close to his dying days was always by my side while I was pounding the computer late at night.

I also want to thank all those here in the United States and in the Philippines especially my parents who provided me with materials, inspiration and encouragement to make this novel possible.

# Cast of Characters

## Maranan Family

Benjamin
Enrique, Benjamin's father
Barbara, Benjamin's mother
Ramon, Benjamin's eldest brother
Manuel, Benjamin's brother #2
Francisco, Benjamin's brother #3
Delfin, Benjamin's brother #4
Antonio, Benjamin's brother #5
Luis, Benjamin's brother #6
Dolores, Manuel's wife
Teresa, Benjamin and Adelaide's daughter
Delfin, Benjamin and Adelaide's son

## Buendia Family

Adelaide
Regina, Adelaide's mother
Marta, Adelaide's eldest sister
Isabel, Adelaide's sister #2
Esmeralda, Adelaide's sister #3
Lucio, Adelaide's eldest brother
Rodrigo, Adelaide's brother #2
Cayetano, Adelaide's brother #3
Julian, Adelaide's brother #4
Nicolas, Adelaide's brother #5

## Others

Alex Montenegro, Benjamin miner's friend
Elias, Benjamin's cousin #1
Felipe, Benjamin's cousin #2
Zenia, Adelaide's cousin
Aling Ana, a storekeeper next to Benjamin's store
Mang Selso, Aling Ana's husband
Jacinto, Adelaide's cousin
Rolando, Jacinto's friend
Tio Dominic, Adelaide's uncle
Mang Sylvestre, bread vendor
Isidro, a restaurant owner
Felicia, Benjamin's childhood friend
Pedro, Benjamin's old friend
Aunt Genoviva, Adelaide's aunt
Judge Cordero, Benjamin and Adelaide's wedding sponsors
Cecilia, Teresa's godmother

"Courage and perseverance have a magical talisman, before which difficulties disappear and obstacles vanish into air."

John Quincy Adams

# BAHALA NA

(Come What May)

# PART I

# CHAPTER 1

"**I** want to meet her. I must meet her," Benjamin said to no one in particular. For reasons he could not understand, he took a pair of scissors and cut out one of the pictures, the one with the green gown. Funny why he did that but he felt something he could not explain. He wanted to meet this beautiful lady. He looked at the picture again, then carefully folded the picture and placed it inside his wallet. "Who is she? Why do I have this urge to meet her? I have to find out where she lives." He thought to himself.

How unpredictable life could be. One minute, you had nothing to do. Then with a stroke of fate, life threw a curve ball and your mind was in a tizzy. A few minutes ago, Benjamin was getting extremely bored, sitting at his store in Baguio in Northern Luzon, about 450 kilometers from where the picture was taken, doing nothing. The day seemed to stop. It was too slow for him and he was getting antsy. There was hardly anyone around. The market was too quiet. There was no one to talk to so he went to the next store which was selling newspapers and magazines. He wanted to do something to occupy his mind. He thought maybe he could read instead of just sitting idle, doing nothing. It helped passed the time more quickly.

Benjamin looked at the stand of magazines and newspapers. There was *The Philippine Free Press*, the oldest news weekly established in 1907; *Manila Times,* the oldest daily national newspaper featuring daily headlines, business, provincial and world news established in 1898; *Manila Daily Bulletin,* the second oldest newspaper established in 1900; *Liwayway* magazine; *Bulaklakan* magazine and some comic books. He started reading the headlines from the newspapers. The most notable news was the bombing of Alicante, Spain with 313 deaths in the Spanish Civil War. He could not care less about that. So what? Spain was too far from Baguio and it had no consequence to him. Maybe it had to some Filipinos whose ancestors came from Spain but not him. Nothing in the newspapers interested him at all. He picked one of the comic books and flipped through the pages. He seemed disinclined to buy that one either. He put that down. Then he saw the *Liwayway* magazine, the oldest weekly magazine published since 1922 featuring short stories, poetry, serialized novels, serialized comics and news and the *Bulaklakan* magazine, a fairly new magazine with the same format as *Liwayway*. He thought the magazines usually had beautiful pictures, articles and advertisement. Maybe he should buy the magazines. First, he could not make up his mind on which one to buy. He liked the cover photo of the *Bulaklakan* magazine better than *Liwayway*. But *Liwayway* had the Kenkoy comic strip so he decided to buy both.

Benjamin went back to his store carrying the magazines. He sat down in front of the store and started flipping through the pages of *Liwayway* magazine. He read the amusing adventure of comic hero Francisco "Kenkoy" Harabas. He was a funny man, irreverent, hilarious and a fashion plate and everyone loved his antics. Except for his hairstyle which was slicked back and flattened out and his most recognizable trademark, Kenkoy fashion style changed with the times. Kenkoy was the most popular figure at that time and his picture was more recognizable than the leading politicians.

Kenkoy was the first pop-icon of the Philippines and his comic strip was sure to make one laugh every time. His trademark dialogues were an irreverent adaptation of a mixture of Spanish, English and Tagalog languages like *Halo, how is yu*?, *watsmara* (what's the matter), *dats oret* (that's all right), *nating duwing* (nothing doing), *okidoki* (okey dokey) and *bay gali* (By golly!). Kenkoy certainly made the day go by quickly. Benjamin enjoyed reading Kenkoy's adventures or rather misadventures and it was always hilarious and true to life. There was nothing like Kenkoy and his dramatic life.

When Benjamin was done reading the hilarious misadventure of Kenkoy, he picked up the *Bulaklakan* magazine next. He thumbed through the pages, not bothering to read the stories but just looking at the pictures and the ads very quickly. He was looking at the pictures of a *Flores de Mayo* of a town. He noticed it was from a town close to his hometown. It said Sambat, Bauan, Batangas. He glanced at the pages and was about to turn onto the next page when a couple of pictures of this young beauty caught his attention. He took a second look. In one picture, she was wearing a beautiful green gown holding a fan and in another picture she was wearing a simple flowered dress with round neck and short sleeves and her long black hair was braided and draped over her shoulders down to her waist. She had the most beautiful smile, accentuated by her two dimples on both sides of her face. She had a lovely deep-set pair of black eyes with thick eyelashes. Her eyes seemed to speak to him in volumes that he could not fathom. Benjamin had met several ladies in his roving days but he was taken aback by the simple beauty of this girl. She looked different. Something in him stirred as he looked at her picture. The look in her eyes was captivating. She had that regal bearing in her and looked quite confident about herself.

In Bauan, Batangas in Southern Luzon, where Adelaide was at that time, the fragrance wafting from the tropical plants was filling the air. The gardenias were in full bloom in front of Adelaide's house. Adelaide touched the white bloom and inhaled as she and her cousin passed the gardenia plant lining the walkway. Adelaide was about to stick her nose on the white bloom but stopped short when her cousin, Zenia tagged her arm and asked her excitedly.

"Did you see your picture?"

Adelaide turned sharply to her cousin and asked, "What picture? What are you talking about?"

Looking at her cousin with that perplexed look, Zenia had a suspicion Adelaide didn't know anything about it.

"Your picture as Reyna Elena last month," Zenia said, smiled and waited for a reaction.

"What? What about it and where may I ask did you see it?"

"In a magazine," Zenia said. "There was a whole page article about the town fiesta."

Adelaide opened her mouth in disbelief upon hearing it and stared at her cousin.

"Are you kidding me?"

"No. I'm not kidding."

Adelaide tried to digest the news. She hesitated for a brief moment, then said, "I would like to see it. What magazine is it in?"

"In the *Bulaklakan* magazine."

*Bulaklakan* magazine coined from the word *bulaklak* meaning flower was impressed with the pictures and decided to do a feature article on their town and its Flores de Mayo. In the month of May, most towns celebrated "Flores de Mayo and Santacruzan", a tradition dating back to the Spanish regime. Adelaide had been a part of it every year in her hometown as Reyna Elena.

"Do you know who sent the pictures to *Bulaklakan*?" Adelaide wanted to know, her curiosity getting the better of her.

Zenia started walking away from her trying to ignore Adelaide. She was debating whether to tell her the truth or not. Adelaide grabbed Zenia's arm, turned her around and asked again, "Who did it? Please tell me."

"I heard Jacinto, our cousin did it," Zenia blurted out.

"I have to talk to him. He should ask me first."

"He's probably playing a joke on you and did not realize it would get published."

Adelaide could not help smile. "He is such an idiot sometimes."

Zenia shook her head. "No. Look at it this way. Our town now is famous. And so are you. It made the magazine and now you're famous. You should be happy."

"No, I am not. I don't like it one bit. Wait till I see him."

At the time Adelaide's picture appeared in the *Bulaklakan* magazine, Benjamin, a dashing young man from a nearby town, was residing temporarily in Baguio, the summer capital, built by the Americans at the turn of the 20th century and used by the rich and famous Filipinos and Americans alike to escape the oppressive summer heat in Manila and its suburbs. Hot, humid days during the long summer months sent wealthy Filipinos and Americans to the cool, dry climate of the Mountain Province especially the resort town of Baguio. It was considered a summer retreat with its cool mountain breezes amid towering pine trees and lovely surrounding vistas. Baguio became a town in 1900 and a chartered city in 1909. Before the American occupation, the area was a small settlement, a hamlet of about 20 homes known as Kafagway. The Americans conscious of the cool mountain air beneficial to their health chose the site and built a town whose layout was modeled after Washington, D.C. Its name was changed from Kafagway to Baguio from the word *begjiw*, an *Igorot* word meaning moss which was in abundance in the Burnham Lake area.

Benjamin went home in early December with great anticipation. Since Adelaide lived in the next town from his hometown, he was hoping he would bump into this girl on one of those days when he was home. He inquired about her among his friends from Batangas who lived in Baguio but nobody seemed to know her. That alone intrigued him for how can such a beauty be unknown to so many young men. "Where did she come from? Is she really from Sambat? Maybe not. Maybe she is from another barrio. I have to find out."

He planned to go to Bauan first thing. He would start his search at the market which he believed was the perfect place to begin. It stood to reason that everyone shops and he had a good chance of seeing her in the market. Her face is imprinted in his brain and he would know her if she was ever near him. He was so certain he would see her in town. "Maybe I will hang around the market long enough and I will see her there," he told himself. "I'll sell in their market if I have to. Maybe she'll come by." He promised himself. But the first day produced no positive result.

The next day, he approached his father, Enrique, with his new idea knowing if he put in the right word, his father might not even suspect his real motive. He tried to sound enthusiastic and convincing. "I was at Bauan market yesterday and they were busy. There was a big crowd and I heard there were lots of rich people shopping and business looked much better there than anywhere else based on my own observation. I would like to try selling there, maybe till Christmas. It's worth a try."

Enrique looked at his son and thought for a moment. Benjamin waited as his father tried to digest what Benjamin was saying. Enrique nodded his head, "That's a great idea. Do it."

9

"Thank you sir."

Benjamin hired a *calesa* (horse-drawn carriage) and took his wares to Bauan the following day. He found a stall and rented it for the rest of the month of December. As he predicted, business was better indeed. He sold a lot of his merchandise. As the days went on, he kept his eyes on the lookout for the mysterious lady in his wallet. But she did not appear the first day or any other day. He was crushed but he did not give up. He could not give up easily. He wanted to meet her.

Everyday he went to Bauan to sell his goods. His father was wondering why all of a sudden he wanted to go to Bauan and no place else. Benjamin kept on telling him, "Business was more lucrative there." It was true in a way because he sold more but when he got home he suddenly felt empty. He did not want to do anything. He was getting depressed. His brother would ask him to go out and joined them playing softball with the guys after dinner but he did not feel like doing anything. His mind was elsewhere. He could not stop thinking of the lady in his wallet and his obsession to meet this lady.

It was almost a month and he had not seen her. He tried to look for her everywhere but after several days, there was still no sign of her.

"Does she ever go shopping?" Benjamin began to wonder.

Time was running out. He was leaving the following week and he still had not seen the lady in his wallet. He had to go back to the Mountain Province. This time he had to go to Mankayan, a mining town near Baguio, where they now owned a store.

When Lepanto Copper Mining started operation again in Mankayan in 1936, Enrique found an opportunity there and decided to open a store in Mankayan. Business was picking up there with all the miners moving in. He did not want to lose that opportunity and so he assigned Benjamin to manage the store if he was not there. Benjamin had no choice. Copper mining was known to have taken place at Lepanto as early as the Ming Dynasty when Chinese traders bartered their wares for copper ingots. When the Spanish explorers arrived in the 16th century, the natives attracted their attention to the extensive use of copper. However, hostile natives kept the district blockaded for many years. The opposition to the Spaniards was very much like their encounter with the Ottoman Turks in the "Battle of Lepanto" in 1571 and so the Spaniards named the place Lepanto. At the turn of the 19th century, the Americans started prospecting in the Lepanto area. Various prospectors pooled their holdings and in September 1936, the Lepanto Consolidated Mining Company was born.

Mining had been practiced in many lands for centuries and copper was the first metal mastered by man. Copper was interwoven closely with the history of every advanced nation of modern times. The Egyptians were the first miners and used copper 5,000 years before Christ and the copper mines of Sinai were the most ancient mines in history.

Copper had been regarded first of all as the electrician's metal. Without it the amazing progress in electrical science would have been impossible. Most places in the world ran a network of copper wires transmitting electricity to carry cable, telephone and telegraph messages, to furnish light and power, to run street cars and trains. In addition, cooper had many other important uses, in peace and war, on land and sea.

Man learned early to work copper, for like gold and silver it was found locally in a pure state and could be beaten into shape even when cold. The metal was easier to work than iron, for it could easily be hammered into a desired shape or cast, or drawn out into fine wire. Alloyed with tin, it gave us bronze, and so widespread was the use of bronze in early history that the period was known as the Bronze Age.

In Mankayan, Benjamin became acquainted with a few miners. A few of them played basketball with Benjamin during his off hours. After some games, Benjamin would go out with some of them to have dinner and a few beers. Curious as always, he asked his friend, a mining engineer, about the condition down in the mine as they were having dinner at an eatery.

"So how do you like it down there?" Benjamin asked his friend, Alex Montenegro, one day.

"Not bad at all. It was scary when I started but you get used to it."

"So tell me what is it like in the tunnel?"

"Why do you ask?" Alex started scratching his head and wondering why all of a sudden Benjamin was asking about his job.

"I am curious to know, that's all," Benjamin answered.

"Well, let's imagine a room approximately 5 by 8 meters (approximately 16 by 26 feet), walled with brick and cement and extending down nearly a mile below the surface of the earth. That is called the shaft. It is divided into six compartments, up and down," Alex began.

Benjamin raised an eyebrow. "Did you say a mile deep? How do you go down there?"

"Yes, you heard me right. A mile. 1.6 kilometers." Alex took a gulp of his beer and continued. "At one end are two elevators with double-deck cages for men and materials, and at the other end are two more cages, each provided with a nine-ton self-dumping bucket, hanging below it. These buckets are used to bring the ore up from the tunnels below, where it is mined. In the two compartments in the center are large cylindrical steel bailers through which the abundant water in the mine is brought to the surface. The elevators travel at a dizzying speed, much faster than the elevators in skyscrapers."

Benjamin's eyes lit up in amazement. "Do the elevators go all the way down? Is that where you work? Way, way at the bottom?"

"There are various levels. I work at one of those levels. At various levels the elevators pass horizontal tunnels which run in various directions, and in which men work digging out the rock or ore which contains the metallic copper. Each of these tunnels is equipped with little railway tracks and electrically operated cars to haul the ore. Each has an elaborate system of water pipes and hydrants, with fire hose and chemical engines for use in case of fire, an electric alarm system, and telephones."

"They have an alarm system and telephones too?" Benjamin repeated not comprehending what he was hearing.

"Oh yeah, just in case there is an emergency. You know accidents happen. We just hope it will not happen. It is a scary thought but you live with it."

"What else is happening there?"

"At the ends of the tunnels…"

"You see the light," Benjamin interrupted and waved to the waitress to bring another beer for him and Alex.

"Where was I?"

"You were at the end of the tunnel." They both laughed.

"Yes, at the end of the tunnel, the miners are loosening the copper ore by powerful hydraulic drills. A vast ventilating system is constantly forcing the air from the surface into the mine, for the temperature increases so rapidly that at the bottom of this deep shaft, which goes down nearly a mile as I mentioned before, the temperature would be something like 32°C (90°F) if it were not artificially lowered."

The waitress came back with two more San Miguel beers. They both raised their bottle and clicked.

"How do they turn the ore into metal?" Benjamin asked. He was wondering how that was done.

"Copper ore is reduced to metal by various processes, depending upon the nature of the ore. The "dry" process consists of roasting to eliminate certain impurities. The "wet" process, used with ores containing low percentages of copper, consists of dissolving out the metal with acids, or converting it into a water-soluble salt by roasting with reagents. Special processes, including electrolysis, are also used.

"In order to get all the copper from the ore, the copper smelter's first object is to reduce the ore to a fine powder of 'concentrate.' The screen separates small pieces and sends the large lumps only through the jaw crusher. In the same way the rolling screen or 'trommel' and the cone-like screen sort the ore and send only pebble-like pieces through the roll crusher. 'Jiggling tables,' meanwhile sort out all particles that are fine enough and send them direct to the furnaces. In the 'desliming cone,' worthless earthly material is thrown to the top, dissolved in water, and overflows as waste, while the valuable portions go through to the 'Wilfley table.'

13

This table developed by Arthur Redman Wilfley in 1896 sorts out 'concentrate' ore for immediate roasting and sends the rest to a 'ball mill', to be reduced to sand. The sand then goes to the 'flotation machine,' where it is mixed with oil and pumped into rising water. The oil clings to the metallic portions and carries them up, while non-metallic earth sinks to the bottom. The metallic sand thus obtained contains the last of the copper in the ore, and goes to be roasted together with the 'concentrate' previously obtained." Alex finished and took another gulp of his beer.

"Whew... That's a long process and tedious. At some point, you lost me. It went over my head." Benjamin picked his bottle and gulped another sip too.

"Maybe it is too technical for a non-miner."

"It is," Benjamin said.

"The most important copper ores are native or pure copper, sulphides, and oxides." Alex continued. "Let me put the process simply. The first step in the preparation of the ore when it comes from the mine is to crush it as finely as possible. The ore is then mixed with water and run over tables, called 'jiggling tables,' that are in constant vibration. The bits of rock containing copper, being heavier, sink to the bottom, and the waste is washed away. The concentrated ore is then smelted, that is, melted, and the copper is separated from the impurities. Sulphide ore, which is called 'copper glance,' is first roasted to drive off the sulphur. After two smeltings the metal is sufficiently pure for ordinary purposes, and is known as 'blister' copper. To make the purest copper, blister copper is refined by electrolysis."

"What is electrolysis?" Benjamin asked.

"Forget it. Maybe next time I see you you'll have another lesson. Why don't you be a miner?" Alex suddenly asked.

"Oh no. Thanks. It is not for me. I like to stay above ground. I'll stick with my business." Benjamin paid the waitress for the meal and the tip and two of them left the restaurant.

"Thanks for dinner," Alex said.

"You're welcome. I'll see you at the basketball court next week."

"See you."

When Benjamin reached the house that he was sharing with his brothers and two cousins, his thought went back to Adelaide. He made the decision to write her as a pen pal and see what happen. "*Bahala na.*" Come what may, he told himself.

He started to write "Dear Adelaide," but he did not know what else to say. He crumpled the paper and threw it out in the waste basket. He stood up and looked outside the window. He stared out looking at the trees. There was a verdant landscape outside. He felt the breeze coming his way. He inhaled deeply and went back to the table and sat down again. He picked up his fountain pen and started again.

"Dear Adelaide, I saw your pictures in a magazine." Then he stopped. He still could not proceed. He crumpled the paper once more. He picked up another sheet and with his fountain pen hanging in his hand, he could not think what to do. "What now? What can I tell her? I have to think. She might think I'm too forward. What would she think of me?" He was at a loss. His mind was swirling and he did not know what was happening. "Why do I have this urge to know her? This is so weird." He put his fountain pen on the paper and started all over again.

*Dear Adelaide,*

*I saw your picture in Bulaklakan magazine. I almost missed it but I turned back the page and looked at you. You have the most beautiful smile I have ever seen. I would like to be a pen pal with you if you don't mind.*

*I live in Baguio and it is a beautiful place. I can write you about it if you like.*

*Your new pen pal,*
*Ben Rose*

When he finished, he read and reread the letter. It was a very short letter and he thought it was harmless. He basically said he wanted to be her pen pal. He hoped she would agree. He put the letter in an envelope, addressed the envelope, sealed it, put a stamp and brought it to the post office. After he mailed it, he kept on thinking if he would get an answer. "What if she did not answer? What should I do? Shall I write her again?"

A week passed and he decided to send another letter. After that, he got braver and sent Adelaide another letter the following week, and then the week after that and another one after that. It seemed every weekend, it became part of his Sunday routine. He would sit down and write her something. If he could not write something, he would pick up a postcard and sent it to her. He kept on writing and waiting for a reply but nothing arrived.

After three months of weekly letters, he became despondent. He knew he would never get an answer. He was losing hope but somehow he still kept on writing her. He figured she might notice him if he kept these letters coming.

After Adelaide's pictures appeared in *Bulaklakan* magazine, Adelaide became so popular, she started getting fan mail. She got lots of young men from everywhere in the country writing to her as far away as Northern Philippines. She not only attracted the attention of Filipino men but also the attention of some American men who lived in the Philippines. She got letters from American G.I.s. She even received some letters from a couple of Japanese men. She was not sure if they were soldiers. They did not say. Adelaide read all her fan mail but she never answered anyone. She was fascinated at the volume of fan mail she was getting but she had no inclination to answer any of them.

As the weeks passed, she began to know the mailman. He came with bundles of letters all tied up for her. At first, it was so exciting but got a little tiring after a while. As she read her mail, she noticed some men continued to write every week but slowly dropped out. But there was one particular fellow who would not quit writing. For several weeks, this particular fellow just kept on writing. He wrote and wrote and wrote and sent postcards and pictures one after another. The letters and postcards kept coming from this same fellow. As her mail built up, she finally got friendly with the mailman who came every week. "Here's another letter from Mankayan," he would announce. Then she also got an anonymous gift subscription to *Bulaklakan* magazine.

Finally, Adelaide got curious and decided to answer him back. She was also feeling guilty and rude by not answering all these letters. Maybe it was time to find out who this man was.

Benjamin was beginning to get weary and told himself. "Forget it. If she does not want to answer me, I am just going to her town and inquire about her next time I go home. But that means not till the end of April when I go home for the town fiesta." It felt like eternity. He decided to keep on writing.

Everyday his hope was vanishing slowly. Then one day when he least expected it, he got a letter in the mail. It was stamped "Bauan". His heart jumped. He was so ecstatic. His hands were trembling when he opened the letter. It was a short note, just saying,

*Dear Ben,*

*I got all your letters, pictures and postcards. I'm sorry I was not able to mail you an answer right away. I had difficulties getting to the post office.*

*Sincerely,*
*Adelaide*

Benjamin could not believe it. After all this time, he finally got what he wished for. He was now looking forward to meeting her in person. He continued his correspondence, now with more intensity and anticipation for her reply. Adelaide did not write as often as Benjamin did but she wrote every other week. The postcards from Baguio kept on coming. She was fascinated about the place where he lived. They exchanged pictures and a steady stream of letters ensued. She began to like her new pen pal and putting his pictures and some postcards in picture frames and displayed them on the living room wall. She had no illusion of meeting him in person since he lived too far away. She did not know his hometown was just a few kilometers away from her hometown. Benjamin never mentioned that in his letter. She always thought he lived in Baguio all his life.

Benjamin went home for the town fiesta in early May the following year. He was determined to meet Adelaide in person. He went back to the Bauan market the week after he got home. He inquired about her but got nowhere.

By the end of May, there was a procession for the Flores de Mayo in his hometown of Alitagtag and also at the next town. Benjamin wanted desperately to go to the procession at the next town hoping to see the lady in his wallet but unfortunately he was invited to be an escort to one of the young ladies in his hometown. He had no choice but to say yes without being rude. His parents told him he had to do it. He knew they were playing matchmakers.

The young girl, Felicia, was from a family that his parents had been friendly with for many years. He knew Felicia all his life. They were good friends. They grew up together. At some point in time, he thought he would marry her someday. But then as they grew older, his attention wandered everywhere. He had no intention of getting married to her now. He was enjoying his bachelorhood. He was not in the mood for marriage. Now, he had his mind set on this girl whose picture was still hiding in his wallet. He was gracious to accept the invitation to escort Felicia though he would rather be in Bauan and see the Flores de Mayo there. He was cold to her all evening. He did not want to encourage her. Felicia was very nice to him and so were her parents.

Benjamin missed his chance to see the lady in his wallet. Adelaide was at the procession of the Flores de Mayo in her hometown. He began to realize he was wasting his time but by then it was too late. It was useless to convince himself that he should forget his attraction to her and move on to greener pastures. But he could not turn his back now and pretend he had never seen her picture. He had to go on looking for her. His obsession was utterly irrational but he could not rid himself of it. He knew he was making a fool of himself, and he knew that every time he visited her town was yet another step down a blind alley, but he simply could not stop looking for her. Visits to other women, a useful diversion in the past now made little difference to his peace of mind. He remained obsessed. In love, he called it, maybe. An infatuation? Not really. It was a combination of admiration, longing and a desire to possess and love her. He could not get her out of his mind. He knew he was falling in love with a mysterious girl.

# CHAPTER 2

It was a fine morning in early June. All the May festivities were behind them. Talks of the Flores de Mayo were dissipating although the May flowers were still in bloom. The florists were still coming up to the market and arranging their daily stock. Although May was gone, June was also a month of festivities. However, it was not as big as the May events. They celebrated the Feast of the Sacred Heart of Jesus through the whole month of June. However, there were only two barrios involved in the June festival but there were also parades on June 30 but not as elaborate as the ones on May 31. As the years go by, the June festival was losing popularity. The reason partly was because June started the rainy season and also the start of the school year.

Students with their school bags went by, going up to the school just behind the market. There was an eager look on their faces. The street in front of the market was packed with cars and carriages with people coming to town. Benjamin picked up a newspaper and went to his stall. He passed the florist in her stall. He bent down and put his nose on a pot with white flowers and started talking with the florist. It was still early and no customers were around.

"What a lovely scent!" Benjamin muttered. "Is that *sampaguita*?"

"Yes, it is," the florist said.

"I thought they only have one row of petals. This almost looks like a rose."

"The plant bears either a single flower, a row of petals, or flowers with doubled petals, bundled at the top of the branches and look like small white roses and are exceptionally fragrant."

Benjamin put his nose again on the bloom and asked, "Do they bloom year round?"

"The single flower of sampaguita blooms year round, has white, small, dainty, star-shaped blossoms, which open at night and wilt in less than a day and has a distinct sweet fragrance. It does not bear seed, so it is propagated through cuttings. The Philippines have different domestic species of jasmine growing wildly."

"How long have they been around? I always remember seeing them everywhere I go."

"Sampaguita was believed to have come from the Himalayan region during the 17th century. Sampaguita has taken root in the Philippine folklore and religious rites."

Sampaguita or *jasminum sambac,* the Philippine's national flower, is a subtropical evergreen creeping vine reaching up to 2 to 10 ft tall and very fragrant and is used extensively at Flores de Mayo as a garland and in arrangement. It is mentioned in many legends, stories and songs. It symbolizes a whole series of virtues: fidelity, purity, devotion, strength and dedication.

Benjamin looked around, seeing there were no customers around, put on his beguiling smile and asked, "Isn't there a legend about sampaguita?"

"Yes, there is and it is fascinating."

"Tell me. I would love to hear it." He looked around again and still there was no customers yet except him.

"Gladly. Since we are not busy yet, why not."

The florist began......

*There was this young beautiful princess called Lakambini and after her wise father died, she had to take over his kingdom. But she did not know how to govern and there was a danger that the kingdom would be invaded by the neighboring rulers. She fell in love with a young unselfish prince, Lakan Galing, from another kingdom who was ready to defend her kingdom against the invaders. On a hill above the sea when the moon was bright and full, they both embraced each other and promised to love thru eternity. "Sumpa kita." I promise you.*

*Lakan Galing was not satisfied with just watching and guarding the kingdom of the princess. He wanted to pursue the enemies. "If the enemy does not come, then I will seek them." He left with his men on his ships and looked for the enemies. Lakambini was anxious for his return. Every day she went to the hill looking out to sea to find if her love was coming back. However, she waited and waited in vain. Lakan Galing never returned.*

*A short time later, she died of a broken heart. On her deathbed, she asked to be buried on the top of the hill where she always waited for him. Shortly thereafter, a vine with small white, pearl-like blossoms grew on her grave with a very sweet fragrance. When the moon was full, the leaves rustling in the wind echoed the word of the princess, "Sumpa kita." The flower was then called sampaguita. This is what the people saw ever after during the month of May.*

"That was very sad but totally romantic. I love it. Thank you for telling me about the legend." Benjamin sighed and bent his head and smelled the flower one more time. He thought of the lady in his wallet.

"You're welcome. Maybe you might want to buy your girlfriend a plant."

"I wish I can. I'm sorry. I have no girlfriend. None yet anyway."

"I can't believe it. You better get to work on that one."

Benjamin smiled and waved goodbye.

Countries have adopted flowers as national cultural symbols. The United States has the rose; the Netherlands, the tulip; Japan, the chrysanthemum; Austria, the edelweiss and Ireland the shamrock. The Philippines have several national symbols: the *carabao* (water buffalo), the *narra* tree and sampaguita. Sampaguita or *kampupot* was adopted by the Philippine government as its national flower in 1934 by the then American Governor General of the Philippines, Frank Murphy, through Proclamation No. 652. Filipinos string the flowers into leis, corsages, and crowns. In warm climates, the flowers bloom all throughout the year and are produced in clusters of 3 to 12 blooms at the ends of the branches. The species name "sambac" seems to derive from "zanbaq," the Arabic word for jasmine. The name sampaguita evolved in turn from "sambac" through the Spanish colonizers of the Philippines, where this name was common.

Since he missed the procession in Bauan, Benjamin decided maybe he should stay another month before he returned to Baguio. He was able to extend the lease on his store in Bauan. As the month progressed, he became very friendly with the couple at the next store. They must have been watching him all the time.

One day, Aling Ana said to him, "We have been watching you for a while and for a young man, you are so intense in your business." She glanced at her husband. He winked. She then continued, "Do you have a girlfriend? Any plan for marriage?"

Benjamin was surprised at these questions but said politely, "No to both of your questions. There is nobody in particular," he replied, then hesitantly added, "Someday, I might find her."

"Oh, that is a pity. You are much too involved in your business. You have to find time to socialize," Mang Selso advised him.

"I have no time. I'm always here at the market and when I'm done at the end of the month, I will be leaving for Baguio."

"Why Baguio?" Mang Selso asked.

"My father has a store there and my other brothers and I manage it throughout the year except when we go home for Christmas and the town fiesta. Actually we are supposed to be home only for the whole month of May. This year, I decided to stay another month."

"That must be exciting, seeing other places." Aling Ana's eyes brightened up.

"Oh, it is," Benjamin said.

"Where do you live?" Aling Ana and Mang Selso wanted to know where he was from.

"Alitagtag *po*." Alitagtag sir.

"Where do you live? Do you live here in Bauan?" Benjamin asked in return.

"Yes, but not in town. We live in the barrio of Sambat, not far from here."

"Sambat?" His heart started pounding heavily. "Didn't you have a Flores de Mayo there recently?" Benjamin was hoping this will lead to something.

"Yes," Aling Ana answered. "It was great. Why do you ask?" Aling Ana gave Mang Selso a questioning look, then waited. They still could not read his mind. Why was he interested in their Flores de Mayo. Every town had their own. It was the same everywhere. Benjamin pulled his wallet. Aling Ana and Mang Selso looked at each other and didn't know what to make of it. What was in his wallet?

Benjamin eyes lit up. "Maybe I should confess," he thought to himself. His hands were shaking a bit and he was trying very hard to control himself. Luckily a customer interrupted Aling Ana.

Benjamin waited until the transaction was over and then he said, "Before we got interrupted I was about to show you this picture that I saw in a magazine last year. Do you know this girl? She intrigued me," Benjamin lied and did not tell them that he and Adelaide had been communicating for a year now without meeting each other.

Aling Ana took a glance at Mang Selso who winked at her and said, "We know her. I don't blame you. She is the prettiest girl in town. She's the youngest daughter of Aling Regina. Her grandfather was the *Cabeza de Barangay* during the Spanish time. Aling Regina is now a widow and Adelaide, that's her name, is very much protected by her three older brothers. You cannot get near her without passing those boys. At the rate they are guarding her, she will end up an old maid or in a convent. Such a shame! She's the most beautiful girl you will ever see, nice personality, very kind and gracious."

Aling Ana handed him back the picture and he put it back in his wallet. Aling Ana and Mang Selso looked at each other and watched him as he carefully inserted the picture back in his wallet. They had the feeling of love in the air but wondered how it could be possible. This young man obviously had not met the girl yet, but he seemed to be very interested in her and the look on his face really betrayed his feeling for the girl. Why would he keep her picture in his wallet? It did not make sense one bit. It was fascinating how love can affect man's behavior.

Without even thinking, he said almost pleadingly, "I would like to meet her. Will you help me get an introduction?" Aling Ana looked at Mang Selso again and he nodded.

"Of course. I don't blame you. If I were your age, I probably would go after her too." Mang Selso winked at Benjamin. He smiled and they understood.

"I know somebody who is very friendly with her cousin and I'll introduce you to him. I'll ask him tomorrow," Aling Ana said.

"Thank you. I appreciate it very much."

"You're welcome. We want you to find the right girl and she's a good catch if you know what I mean."

Benjamin just smiled. Now he had the funny feeling that he was on the right track. He would finally meet the elusive girl in his wallet.

Benjamin left the market that afternoon in a good mood. He was in seventh heaven. He would meet his pen pal soon. He could not wait for the next day.

The next day was bright and sunny and it reflected the same sunny disposition Benjamin had that morning. He was whistling a tune as he entered the market place. He passed the florist and saw the sampaguita plant again in front of the florist shop. He could smell the fragrance as he walked past the florist shop. He thought of buying a garland for Aling Ana but decided against it. That would look too obvious. He wanted to downplay the importance of his request.

Aling Ana was true to her promise. Aling Ana's friend, Rolando came by. She introduced Rolando to Benjamin. He was about his age, though small built and had very dark brown skin. He was wearing a brown slack, blue plaid shirt and brown leather shoes. He was holding an unlit cigarette in his right hand. He put it in his left shirt pocket and shook hand with Benjamin.

"*Kumusta*. I'm Rolando."

"*Kumusta*. I understand you know someone who knows a lady named Adelaide from Sambat."

"Correct. I know her cousin. His name is Jacinto."

"I just told Aling Ana yesterday I would like to meet Adelaide and she suggested your name. She said you know one of her relatives. I understand it is very difficult to meet her because of her brothers."

"That is a known fact. They protect her at all times. She's a gem."

"Do you think Jacinto can help me?"

"We can try. Maybe he can take you to her house."

"How do I meet Jacinto?" Benjamin was determined to meet Adelaide's cousin.

Rolando suggested, "We can go see Jacinto at his home in Aplaya. He lives there near the beach."

"When?" Benjamin could not help being anxious.

Rolando saw the eagerness on his face and asked, "Why the urgency?"

"You see I have to leave for Baguio at the end of the month and will not be back again till Christmas. I don't have much time."

Rolando sensing the urgency asked, "Well, when do you want to go?"

"Anytime, I can always close my store."

"Is tomorrow OK?" Rolando asked.

"Yes, tomorrow is fine. Say around 1 o'clock."

"Good, I'll come by tomorrow at 1 o'clock."

"Thank you. I do appreciate it very much."

"You're welcome. I'll see you tomorrow." They shook hands again and Rolando left. Benjamin was thrilled.

# CHAPTER 3

There were times when the clock seemed to stop. This was one of those days. It seemed that the day stood still. It was also a slow day in the market which made it worse. Benjamin could not wait for 1 o'clock to come. It seemed like forever. The anticipation was killing him. He kept looking at his watch. Finally he saw Rolando striding toward his store.

He closed his store, hired a calesa and he and Rolando took a ride to Jacinto's house in Aplaya, a coastal town next to Bauan. From the market, they took the main road towards Bauan church where the street to Aplaya meets the main road. The road descends slowly towards the beach. Jacinto's house sat next to the road with marsh in back of it where crocodiles can be seen swimming on nice sunny days.

Upon reaching their destination, they alighted from the calesa and Benjamin paid the *cuchero* (coach driver). Rolando walked to the house, followed by Benjamin. Jacinto was in the back at the kitchen just finishing doing the dishes.

"This is Benjamin. He's from Alitagtag." Roland introduced Benjamin.

Benjamin extended his hand. "Pleased to meet you."

Jacinto smiled and shook hands. "Nice meeting you too. Have a seat. Can I get you something to drink?"

"No but thanks anyway," Rolando said.

"What can I do for you and your friend?" Jacinto turned to Rolando.

"Well, how do I put this?" He looked at Benjamin who nodded at him and proceeded. "Benjamin saw Adelaide's picture in

*Bulaklakan* magazine and he's eager to meet her. Aling Ana highly recommends him."

Jacinto gave him a friendly grin. He was thinking this guy should be a good catch for his cousin. He's good looking and looks well off. Not bad at all.

"Gladly, we can go any minute. I have some errands to do near there anyway so I'll drop you in front of her house. Her mother is a businesswoman and she will receive you with no problem. Her brothers will not be around so I can't see any difficulty in you meeting Adelaide."

"Are her brothers that protective of her? Aling Ana said the same thing." Benjamin wanted to know.

"You bet your life they are. But if I were you, that wouldn't stop me. You'll do fine," Jacinto said. He was beginning to like Benjamin.

"Do you know who put that picture in the magazine?" Jacinto asked.

"Who? I have to thank that person. If it was not for that person, I would never see it."

Jacinto started to roar with laughter. Benjamin looked at him puzzled. "What's so funny? Did I say something funny?"

"No. But listen. I did not know it will lead to this," Jacinto said and scratched his head.

"What are you talking about?" Benjamin asked.

"I sent the pictures to *Bulaklakan* as a joke. I didn't know someone would notice it. Apparently I was wrong."

"So you are the one who I should thank."

"Never mind. When she found out about it, she was mad as hell. She has been getting so much mail since then."

"Really?" Benjamin pretended not to know about it. "Well, before anyone rushes to meet her, can you tell me where she lives? I don't want to be the last in line."

Jacinto smiled. "Sure. I'll even take you there now. I'm going that way anyway."

They walked outside and looked for another calesa to take them to Sambat. They didn't walk that far to find one. Rolando sat in the front with the cuchero and Jacinto and Benjamin sat in the back seat. As the calesa rolled to town, Rolando said to drop him back at the market. He wished Benjamin good luck and waved them off.

The calesa went up north outside the market area then the road to Sambat changed to a gravel road. As the calesa moved along, a cloud of dust went billowing out following them. Jacinto was busy talking to Benjamin about life in the coastal town and Benjamin who was ensconced all year long in the mountains was fascinated with Jacinto's tale. When they reached the junction to the next village, they realized they missed the house. They were busy talking. Now, they had to go back. Benjamin got off on the street a few feet from the front of the house and paid the cuchero. The usual cost of a calesa ride from Aplaya to Sambat is 10 centavos. Benjamin felt generous and gave the driver 50 centavos. The cuchero was so grateful. He could not stop thanking Benjamin. He felt so lucky to find a very good customer.

Jacinto waved his hand and said, "Nice meeting you. Good luck." Jacinto knowing that Benjamin was off to a good start decided to leave him on his own. He looks confident enough and he can take care of the next move.

Just as Benjamin alighted from the calesa, he saw a young woman who happened to be a friend of Adelaide. Benjamin asked, "Excuse me, may I ask where is the Buendia's house?"

From where they stood, they could see the front steps to Adelaide's house which was located on the top of a hill. The young lady pointed in the direction of the steps.

"There it is. You see those steps. That is the front of her house." "I'm Zenia, a relative." Benjamin was so surprised but was quick to recover.

"Thanks so much. My name is Benjamin."

Benjamin proceeded to walk towards Adelaide's house. Zenia stood staring at his back, wondering who is this fellow and why is he looking for the Buendia's house. He does not look like he wants to be doing business with Aling Regina. This is quite interesting. "I have to talk to Adelaide tomorrow," she told herself.

Benjamin got in front of the house and he stopped. He did not know what to do next. Here, he was a total stranger knocking at somebody's door. What was he going to say when they opened the door and found a total stranger? He thought about it and froze on the spot.

The house was a two story Spanish style house located on top of a hill. To the right of the house is a small tree about 15 ft tall called *kalachuchi* tree, (frangipani or plumeria) whose fragrant flowers were permeating into the air. The tree was multi-branched and had thick foliage which was crowded at the terminal end of the branch, oblong in shape and reaching a length of 15 inches and a width of 2-3 inches. The tree had a green trunk and its stems were smooth and shining and the flowers, about 2 inches wide were arranged in 5 petals, waxy and very fragrant. The inner side was whitish with the outer petals turning yellow.

Kalachuchi flowers are known for their unique fragrant clusters of colorful, bright, waxy and long lasting flowers. During Flores de Mayo, Kalachuchi are used for making all kinds of floral arrangements. Sometimes, they are used to make leis also like sampaguita. The kalachuchi flower can be worn by women to indicate their relationship status - over the right ear if seeking a relationship, and over the left if taken.

Suddenly Benjamin got cold feet. He stayed on the street for a while staring at the kalachuchi tree.

Another neighbor saw him and asked if he needed help.

Benjamin asked, "Is this the Buendia's house?"

The neighbor said, "Yes, just go up and knock at the door."

Benjamin still could not move. He was a total stranger in town and knocking at somebody's door was bad manners to say the least. What would they say? As he went up the bamboo steps leading to the front yard, he was getting really very nervous. As he reached the top of the steps, the pleasant smell of gardenia in front of the house filled his nose.

He was standing at the top of the steps when he saw a man come out from the back of the house carrying two square cans on an abaca rope attached to a bamboo pole. He looked like he was about to get some water somewhere. He saw Benjamin and asked if he could help.

Benjamin asked again, "Is this the Buendia's house?"

He said, "Yes, just go up the stairs and knock at the door."

Benjamin turned left to the walkway. Adelaide was peeking through the window and watching him intently. She could not make anything out of this strange man loitering in front of her house.

Benjamin thought he saw an older lady who opened the window and peeked. He presumed she saw him. He swallowed hard and decided to just go and knock at the door. He wished he had asked Jacinto to accompany him. But it was too late now. Somebody had seen him from inside.

As Benjamin went up the walkway, he passed a four foot gardenia shrub by the front stairway loaded with white fragrant flowers. To the right was the stair leading to the living quarters upstairs. There was a big wide front window with five sliding capiz shell windowpanes.

*"Tao po, Tao po,"* he said as he crossed the walkway leading to the stairway. "Tao" means person and when a person comes to someone's house, he says "Tao po," meaning "A person is here sir" thereby announcing his presence.

*"Panhik po kayo."* You may come up sir. Benjamin heard someone said.

"Someone was telling me to come up," Benjamin told himself. With a little trepidation, he started climbing the steps. He reached the top of the stairway and knocked at the door.

A few minutes later, a middle-aged lady opened the door. He was ushered in to the entrance hall. It was a long hallway with a big bench that looked like a church pew stretched across the whole length of the hall next to a big wide window. There was a table flanked by two chairs on the other side of the hall. There was an array of family photos displayed on the wall above the chairs.

Benjamin introduced himself, "My name is Benjamin Maranan from Alitagtag."

The lady said, "I'm Mrs. Buendia. Welcome to our home." She was a beautiful smart looking lady in her late 40s, well dressed in a long flowered dress, a coral and gold necklace around her neck and diamond earrings on her ears. Her hair was pulled in a bun pinned on top of her head.

She looked Benjamin up and down and saw that he was a very presentable young man. He was wearing a white suit with a very conservative tie and holding his hat to his side. He had on his wingtip shoes.

Over the years, Benjamin had taken one bit of his father's advice to heart – to buy the best clothes and the best shoes. Though he owned only three suits, they were of the finest broadcloth and all were conservative white suits. He polished his shoes to a mirror shine every day. As he'd learned years before, he had to be as ready as any man to stand before any man of business or otherwise at any time of day to make a good impression. Benjamin felt and looked confident the way he was dressed looking like a big shot.

Mrs. Buendia extended her hand and Benjamin took it and shook her hand. She asked, "What brings you here?" She thought he was a businessman who wanted to deal business with her.

Benjamin looking embarrassed, could not think of any other way to say what he wanted to say so he just answered, "I saw your daughter's picture in a magazine last year. I have been trying to find out where she lives for almost a year. I was finally introduced to your relative, Jacinto from Aplaya by Aling Ana at the market and Jacinto showed me your home. I would like to meet your daughter if I may."

Benjamin waited for her reaction. She was taken aback as she didn't quite expect it. As soon as she recovered, she said. "You seem like a nice fellow. You know, she is only sixteen. She's a little bit shy but I'll go and get her. She's in the back room with her sisters and doing some embroidery. Have a seat in the *sala*."

Mrs. Buendia went in the back room and Benjamin was left in the living room. While waiting, his eyes started wandering around the room. He saw some pictures on the wall. He saw his pictures next to Adelaide's. There were lots of pictures from Baguio that he sent her on the wall. He was mesmerized looking at how she put his pictures side by side with her pictures that he did not notice when she came into the room.

Adelaide said hello and he said hello but never looked around nor introduced himself. He continued looking at the pictures. He glanced at her but she was not looking. At the first sight of her, he was dumbfounded, he could not speak. He lost his tongue. She was prettier than he thought, much prettier than the picture in his wallet.

Finally, Benjamin turned around and said, "I would like to introduce myself."

Adelaide said, "Wait, let me call my sister. She's in the next room."

To shake hands with a man alone at that time was taboo. It could lead to a big scandal and to save your face, you had to get married right away. Adelaide being brought up with proper decorum had to ask permission from her chaperone who was her sister in the next room to shake hands. She ran back out and got her sister. When she came back with her sister, Benjamin extended his hand and they all shook hands. Then her sister left the room and went to the next room within earshot. Benjamin decided to play some game on her. He knew she did not recognize him because he introduced himself as Benjamin Maranan, his real name. Her pen pal was Ben Rose. He knew she'd be confused.

Benjamin turned to the wall, pretending to be studying the pictures. He asked, "Where are those pictures from? The place looks beautiful."

"From Baguio," she said.

"Oh! You know someone from there?" Benjamin asked.

"Why, yes. My cousin lives there," she lied.

"And who is that man in the same picture frame next to you?" Benjamin asked, still not looking at her.

"That is my cousin who sent me those pictures from Baguio. Why do you ask?" He could sense she was getting annoyed with his questions.

"It just so happened I live in Baguio and sent some pictures, the same pictures to somebody who I wrote to often," Benjamin said and waited for her reaction.

"I don't understand. Mother said you are from next town, Alitagtag. But you just said you are from Baguio. So where are you really from? Is it Alitagtag or is it Baguio?"

Benjamin waited a while. He pretended he was still scrutinizing the pictures.

After a moment of silence, Benjamin looked at her but she was not looking. She was staring at the floor. Then she looked up. She stared at him and he knew she recognized him. He saw she felt embarrassed and started blushing.

He saw she was about to leave the room but Benjamin was quick and grabbed her arm. She shook his hands off of her.

"You look prettier when you are blushing. You don't have to lie to me because I know who that man is and who those pictures are from. My name is Benjamin Maranan, my real name. I'm happy to finally meet you." Benjamin extended his hand again. She took it. They both smiled.

They talked for a while. Then she said, "I forgot to ask you if you want anything to eat or drink." Without getting an answer, she left for the kitchen. She came back with a cup of coffee and a couple of rice cake on a tray and a spoon and fork. Benjamin noticed the spoon and fork on the tray. He did not say a word. In most houses in rural areas, people ate with their hands. Food was picked up with the fingers and put into the mouth. Only rich people used a spoon and fork. He got the impression that this family was different from everyone else he knew.

Adelaide's mother and three sisters were right behind her. Her mother and sisters were very interested about what Benjamin was doing in Baguio. They were so fascinated about the place being so far away from Batangas. Benjamin told them about the rice terraces and the native tribes there, the climate being so cool and the orchids. He did not stay too long. He promised he would be back the following week. However, he was back in four days. This time he brought Adelaide some everlasting flowers. As soon as she opened the door, he handed her the bouquet of everlasting flowers.

She put her nose on the flowers. "Thank you very much. I like them."

Then she put her nose on the flowers one more time. There was a faint scent on them. They were a muted color, light yellow and orange with a tint of brown. The flowers were 1 to 2 inches wide, daisy-like blooms. They were beautiful and looked fragile. She tried to think if she had seen anything like that in town but she could not think of any.

"I brought them all the way from Baguio. I carried them in my duffel bag. I didn't think they would make it to here but luckily they did. I wrapped them carefully with tissue papers," Benjamin told Adelaide.

"They are beautiful. I love them." She smelled the flowers one more time.

Then every three days, he was back again and this went on till he left for Baguio the following month. He became a regular visitor. He usually had *merienda* with her. Sometimes, her sisters would join them. He still had to meet her brothers. Somehow he kept on missing them. They came home very late in the afternoon and Benjamin could not stay too late.

# CHAPTER 4

May was a month devoted to fiestas. There were town fiestas everywhere. The weather was sunny and warm. School was out. The whole town was jubilant with big anticipation. During fiesta time, the frenzy climbed to its highest peak. People had been coming from all over. They came from the neighboring villages and far away cities. Everyone in the family who was away would make every effort to go home for the fiesta.

Going down the street in the morning, you'll see people on their way to go to mass in the church. After mass, people were coming into the plaza from all sides, and up and down the street the marching band paraded and played, the pipes shrilled and the drums pounding and behind them came the crowd marching along with them. The fiesta had started. It kept up day and night for four days. The merriment kept up, the drinking kept up and the noise went on. Everything became quite unreal. All during the fiesta you had the feeling, even when it was quiet, that you had to shout any remark to make it heard. It was the same feeling about any action. It was a fiesta time, time to be merry and it went on and on for four days.

In Bauan where Adelaide lived, the town fiesta was on May 3. Adelaide and her siblings would go to town and watch *Juego de Anielo*. It was the most exciting game you'd ever see. There were games, rides and all kinds of vendors in the plaza. The kids enjoyed themselves watching and playing some games. Some kids liked the rides but Adelaide and her siblings liked the games better especially Juego de Anielo. They would go early to find a good seat near the front of the ring. There would be a long line to get in to the ring.

After they bought the tickets, they would proceed to their respective seats. The whole place was in electric mood. Every year at fiesta time, people look forward to seeing the *genite* or *cavallero* come to town from other places and they participated in the game. It is a ring game introduced by the Spaniards.

The game began. Men called genites entered the ring with much fanfare. People were screaming with delight and clapping their hands. Some were whistling as the genites rode on those beautiful horses galloping at full speed. Around a circle there were rings hanging. The goal was to shoot the suspended ring with a pole. The genites went round and round around the ring and tried to aim their pole at the ring. The frenzy continued.

"Look." They stared as a genite came galloping with his pole ready. He tried to shoot the ring. The crowd watched.

"Nawh." He missed. The genite kept galloping. Another genite came charging in. He aimed his pole. The pole hit the ring. The music band started playing. The crowd roared. The music stopped. Another genite came forward right behind the other genite. He aimed and the pole hit it too. The music band started playing again. The crowd whistled and roared. Some of them stood up. Then the music stopped. The genites went round and round again. Then nothing happened and then one genite raised his pole and aimed. The pole hit the ring. Music played and then stopped. Another one did the same. Music played again, then stopped. And then another. The music band kept on playing and stopping. The crowd was now standing up. There was only one ring left. The genite aimed and it hit the pole. The crowd roared. All the genites made one more round around the ring and then took off toward the exit. The crowd was now clapping their hands and whistling. The noise was deafening. The crowd thoroughly enjoyed themselves. It was a great and exciting game to watch.

*Juego de Prenda* was another game that young people enjoyed. They sat in a circle and a handkerchief was passed around while the music band started playing. When the music stopped, whoever has the handkerchief lost and got penalized. Adelaide wanted to play the game.

She looked at her brother, "May I?"

Lucio nodded, "Go ahead. I'll just watch from the side."

Adelaide took her seat. As soon as all the seats were taken, the music started playing. The handkerchief was passed around. The music just got started and it stopped right away. The first victim was asked to sing. A young man got up. He stood and scratched his head.

"What song?" he asked.

"Any song." Someone yelled.

"Okay." Then he opened his mouth and sang "*Bahay Kubo*."

Everyone laughed. It was a song you learned at First Grade. He was also out of tune. It was so terrible but everyone was beginning to enjoy the game. After one verse, he sat down. The game continued. The handkerchief was passed around. The music played again. This time it kept on going. The participants were laughing and passing the handkerchief as soon as it landed on their lap. Then the music suddenly stopped. It landed on another young man. He was asked to sing too. He got up, took a bow dramatically, opened his mouth and belted "*Dahil Sa Iyo*." Because of You. It was lovely ballad and the crowd was mesmerized. He had such a nice baritone voice and so much expression put into the song and it was such a beautiful song to listen to. When he finished, everyone clapped heartily. As soon as everyone got settled, the music started playing again and the handkerchief was passed on once more. The music got louder, then it went soft and loud again and suddenly stopped. The handkerchief landed on another young man. He was stunned and tried to pass it on but too late. The penalty was to shake hand with a lady.

The announcer bellowed out, "You have to shake hand with a lady whom you don't know."

The young man knew whose hand he wanted to shake. He looked across the circle and his eyes focused on Adelaide. He was eyeing her all through the game. Everyone was watching. Adelaide saw him eyeing her. She got nervous. She wanted to get up.

"Come on. Let's go." The announcer egged him on.

The man boldly crossed the center and walked toward Adelaide's direction. He extended his hand when he reached Adelaide's seat. Adelaide shook her head. She looked at her brother on the other side of the tent. Her brother signaled for her to get up.

She got out of her seat at an instance, turned around her seat and walked toward her brother without saying a word. Her brother grabbed her wrist and they slipped out of the tent. The young man was stunned. He did not quite know what to do or say. He was embarrassed and felt humiliated in front of his friends. He was really looking forward to meeting this young lady whom he was watching all afternoon. He did not know Adelaide's brother was watching him eyeing Adelaide intently while the music was playing.

The young man looked after her as she was leaving the tent. Then he said, "I could not believe it. Why did she leave so suddenly?"

Someone said, "I guess you do not know who she is."

"No, I don't. Who is she?" The young man asked, feeling agitated. Why did she leave? Who is that guy with her?"

"That's her brother. She never goes to any event without being chaperoned by one of them. There are three of them. They look after her all the time."

The young man shook his head. He was furious. "What if I kidnap her?" He stared after her with a threatening look.

"No way Jose. You won't be able to get close to her if her brothers are around."

He looked at Adelaide who was now leaving the tent. She and her brother, Lucio hurried out, took a calesa which was parked outside and headed home immediately. Adelaide was relieved.

In the afternoon there was the big religious procession. In the procession were all the dignitaries, civil and religious. You could hardly see them because the crowd was too great. The procession was to start inside the church and there was a smell of incense and people filing back into the church. Then the procession went outside and the street was lined on both sides with people keeping their place at the curb to watch the procession. The town was crowded. Every street was full of people. Cars and buses kept driving up and down or parking around the plaza.

Then the next morning it was all over. The fiesta was done. Finished. The plaza was empty and there were few people on the streets. A few children picked up odd things in the plaza. Everyone was sweeping their yard and the streets in front of their house and sprinkling them with a hose to settle the dust.

Before the war, Benjamin would be out on the road for months. He would then be home for Christmas and then out again and then back home again around the end of April in time for his home town fiesta on May 7, right after Adelaide's town fiesta

The weather in Batangas in May was bright, sunny, hot and humid. It is the last month of the dry season, just before the start of the rainy season in June. In the small town of Alitagtag, the whole village was exuberant with joy and anticipation for the whole month of celebration. `There were eight areas called "buklod" and each area had a "tuklong", a small chapel where they worshiped the Blessed Virgin Mary through the whole month of May. Preparation was made a year in advance. Members of the committee would go around the area and asked each household to pick a date in May to sponsor. The best date to pick was May 1 which was the opening day and May 31 which was the big day. Some parishioners would pick up their children's birthday, their wedding day, the date of the death of a member of the family. Very few people wanted to pick May 31 because it could get very expensive. Some of the "buklods" did it differently. The committee would go around and let each household pick a number from the raffle box. That way, nobody could avoid May 31. Of course, superstition prevailed that it was lucky to pick up May 31.

The daily Hermana (sponsor) would supply refreshment that could run from simple coffee and snacks to an elaborate dinner. In the afternoon of the day the sponsor picked, the ladies of the "buklod" would come to the sponsor's house to make elaborate floral arrangements as *alay* or offering for the Virgin Mary. The Hermana supplied the flowers. The stalk from the banana tree is used as the display unit. It was the local version of the oasis used by modern day flower arrangers. There were no such things as vials for flowers. The flowers were good for one day because a new Hermana was in charge the next day and she had whole new sets of floral arrangements. The floral arrangements could be in the shape of a star, a heart, a circle, a square, a triangle and one with the word "Ave Maria" or if you had an artist in residence, he could design anything to his heart's content. The stalk of the banana tree was not that wide, usually about 6, maybe 10 inches wide. To make a wider arrangement, it would be joined with a sliver of bamboo strips. A long stick, maybe two feet long and served as a handle that would be inserted from one end to the other end in the middle of the convex flower arrangement. This was done because there would be a procession at 6 o'clock from the Hermana's house to the "tuklong", the chapel. The Hermana and her family joined in procession to the chapel holding the floral arrangements, followed by a group of singers singing hymns all the way to the "tuklong". Upon arrival at the "tuklong", prayer would begin interspersed with hymns. It was their version of Lessons and Carols only this was done in May instead of the Christmas season. While they were singing the hymns, the Hermana and her family would walk up a few steps to the altar and then kneel when they prayed.

Here is a verse of the hymn that the congregation sang and the English translation:

> *"Tuhog na bulaklak, sadyang salit-salit,*
> *Sa mahal mong noo'y aming ikakapit,*
> *Lubos ang pag-asa nami't pananalig,*
> *Na tatanggapin mo, handog na pag-ibig,*
> *Lubos ang pag-asa nami't pananalig,*
> *Na tatanggapin mo, handog na pag-ibig!"*

> *"Garland of flowers, we threaded,*
> *To your beloved forehead, we'll place it,*
> *Exceeding our hope and faith,*
> *And love, please accept it,*
> *Exceeding our hope and faith,*
> *And love, please accept it!"*

It could take three sets of kneeling and walking before they reached the altar where they offered the floral arrangements to the Blessed Virgin Mary. The length of the prayer service was contingent on how many floral arrangements had to be offered. For the wealthy members of the "buklod", it could be a lengthy affair. After the prayer service was done, some groups of young ladies and gentlemen would linger on and sing serenade to the accompaniment of guitars and banjos. This could go on till midnight. Everybody had a good time. None of the neighbors complained of the noise. Rather, they enjoyed it immensely.

May 31 is a little different. They have the *Tapusan* which literally means the end and it was celebrated in honor of the Holy Cross on the last day of May. The Hermano Mayor, for the most part volunteered and came from the wealthier and more prominent families in town and could not pass the opportunity for its prestige. He footed the bill for various fiesta features, from church decoration, church choir, meals at open house tables for the whole day of festivities. At times, he could go into deep debt to provide something extravagant for the feast since it could be *hiya,* (a shame of not living up to the standard of one's community) to have a small party. The 'takeaway' custom of sending guests home with extra food from the feast table could not be understood by Americans or other nationalities.

The Hermana would have a big gathering at her house starting late morning. She would serve lunch and dinner and snacks in between the day and everybody in the town was invited. They were also in charge for the big procession called "Santacruzan" (Festival of the Holy Cross) at night with floats, band and "Reyna Elena". There was a contest on who had the best float. The floats were made by each "buklod" in secrecy so the other area won't know what the design was. Nobody could spy because everybody knew each other in the whole town and no person from another area was allowed in the area where the float was being made. After lunch, the ladies were frantically busy making the floral arrangements that the young ladies would hold at the parade. Young girls from 5 to 15 would dress up in fancy long gowns to be in the parade. You had to be invited by the Hermana to be in the parade. The Hermana would be at the end, just in front of the float. Young children who were not in fancy clothes would tow the rope attached to the float. The young girls with fancy gowns would be inside the rope holding the floral arrangement with her consort holding a candle. The float was made to sit on top of a jeepney and driven slowly down the road, about one kilometer west of the 'buklod" and one kilometer east of the "buklod". Some "buklods" were more ambitious and would do two miles each way.

In Alitagtag, there was only one road in town, running east to west. Spectators usually went to the middle of the town to catch a glimpse of all eight floats. Everybody in the parade walked slowly as they said the rosary. The band would be playing behind the float after each decade of the rosary. It was a very moving and festive experience. The whole town was aglow with lights. The floats were always fabulous and garnered ohs and ahs from the crowd. It was a day in May that everybody was looking forward to.

In the month of May, town fiestas are very common in Batangas and different barrios celebrate their own respective fiestas. Alitagtag was probably the only town in Batangas or maybe in the Philippines that celebrated two fiestas, one on May 3 and another one on May 7. May 3 was the feast day of the Holy Cross in Binukalan. It was also the town fiesta of Bauan.

May 7 being the big fiesta, preparation was undertaken to really go all out to impress everyone. Every house in town started preparing for the big day starting on May 4. The people work hard to make their homes presentable, cleaning and scrubbing floors and windows, putting new curtains on the windows and have the whole house in a festive mood. Streets were decorated with bamboo arches and brightly colored paper streamers. The town plaza had vendors selling toys, trinkets and food. There were ferris wheels, carousel and other entertainment on the plaza near the church.

Batanguenos love to eat and they are great cooks and fiestas around the towns showcase their expertise in cooking delicious meals. Preparation for making *suman* was scheduled to have the ingredients for the recipes bought and be ready on May 4. Banana leaves were picked to be used in cooking suman. Suman is a desert or snack whose ingredients are *malagkit na bigas*, (a special sticky rice), coconut milk and brown sugar, salt and wrapped in banana leaves. It was mixed and then steamed to perfection. This desert was cooked on May 5. In Batangas, suman is usually eaten as a snack. The rice cake is also served for breakfast in most of the towns and served with hot *tablea tsokolate* (cacao chocolate). Aside from the hot chocolate, the Batangas coffee *"barako"* is also a favorite complement for the delicious snack. After a few days, suman gets gooey so they discovered another way of serving it. They unwrapped them, then fried them until golden brown under low heat and then dipped it in sugar. It tasted better this way.

On May 6, a pig was slaughtered. For several months before the feast, every house had one pig that they fattened and designated for the fiesta. If you could not afford to have a pig, you would ask one of your relatives if you could share their pig.

Few neighbors came over to help slaughter a pig. To persuade a pig to come out of its sty and be killed was a fascinating show to watch. The owner went inside the pen and attempted to cajole the pig to get out of the pen. He tried to pull the pig from the cozy darkness of its pit out into the glaring sunlight of a yard filled with men hooting encouragement, where a big cauldron of water was bubbling, hot fires were smoking and gleaming knives ready to do the job. Of course it was not that easy to cajole a pig out of his pen. The pig also weighed a good hundred kilos, most of it solid muscle. It would dig its trotters into the mud and refused to budge. Everybody knew this was going to happen. Yet everybody always knew better than everybody else what should have been done to prevent it. Eventually, with four men pulling the pig's legs and two behind controlling the tail, the pig was hauled into the open. The legs were tied with great effort and a long bamboo pole inserted between the legs and the poor creature was carried to the killing table.

The pig killing table was ready for the pig. The killer dragged the pig alongside the table and the men all gathered round. They grabbed the pig by the legs and tail and heaved it up onto the rough table with the pig kicking and squealing. Ropes lashed it into position where it subsided into a sort of despairing resignation. They tied the pig to the table. The man with the knife was standing by. An upward thrust and the knife jabbed in, deep into the underjaw. The pig shrieked and became powerless.

"Bring the buckets and wash the neck!"

There was a lull as the pig heaved quietly and the killer poked about under its throat to find the perfect spot for the knife thrust.

Then the knife went in and with a twist, the blood gushed into the bucket and stirred to stop it from clotting. The pig heaved and lashed out and whined, and the men who were leaning on the pig to persuade it to stay on the table look at one another with knowing looks as it went limp and the life passed from the body. Then one of them gave it a slap to signal that the worst is over.

"That's good and done."

It was terrible to watch but it had to be done. The town's fascination with the slaughter had the same mix of repulsion and excitement that you would find at cockfights. And then afterwards, the horror of the thing vanished and was forgotten. All of a sudden the living creature shrieking out its last breaths became an inanimate object. Then everyone relaxed with broad smiles. This was part of the tradition during fiesta. Then the pig was opened up and split. Each organ or piece of tripe was taken away to start the long process of transforming it into all kinds of great recipes – *langoniza, chicharron, tocino, relleno,* and so on. All parts of the pig were cooked into different recipes.

*Lechon* (roasted pig) was another important dish for fiesta or big events as turkey on Thanksgiving Day in the United States or ham for Christmas in European countries. Lechon as cooked in Batangas was different from the way it was cooked in other regions of the country to preserve the crispy skin of the pig. The sauce had a special ingredient which made the lechon a sumptuous delicacy in Batangas.

Then the chickens went next, jabbed, scorched, feathered, split and hung. Then the kitchen crew started drinking. Round and round went the *lambanog*, washing down pig-greasy dishes. Chicken was also cooked on the same day. Another food specialty that was cooked on May 6 was called *kalderetang kambing* which was essentially stewed goat's meat. It was cooked with tomato sauce, green and red peppers, potatoes and some spices. *Pancit* which is a kind of noodle recipe was cooked on the eve of the feast.

By mid morning, the men were in need of sustenance so a feast of *chicharron* was brought out, and washed down with beer. Chicharron is the fatty excrescences which appeared all the way along the long intestine. Fried in oil until the outside is crispy, they are absolutely delicious. While the men were relaxing after the hard work with the pigs, the women were busy washing all the dishes and utensils to be used on May 7. All these dishes and utensils had to be washed with charcoal ashes and soaked in hot water in a huge cauldron.

Besides food, there were also some local fiesta games in Alitagtag. *Palo Sebo* was a traditional game played at fiesta time. In Palo Sebo, a bamboo pole was greased from the bottom to the top and there was prize money in a bag placed at the top of the pole. Agile young boys and men in barefeet climbed the greasy pole and tried to get the prize money with the bamboo swaying as they climbed the pole. It was so greasy that the climbers kept on sliding down but they still kept on going. Another climber will follow him up the pole and they would both be sliding down. It went on and on until the climbers gave up or one was lucky enough to get to the top and retrieve the bag. As the bamboo swayed, the crowd got bigger and more vociferous. Some shouted and encouraged the climber to keep on going. It was fun watching them keep sliding down as they went up. When the climber reached the top and held the prize money, everyone cheered and then he slid back down triumphantly.

*Pabitin* was another popular game with children in many fiestas. Baskets of goodies were hanged and kids tried to reach them. These were very popular with the little ones. They jumped up and down to reach the goodies which were not hung too high, just high enough for them to be able to reach it. It was almost like a piñata except they don't use sticks.

In some towns, prominent members of the community organized a ball for charity. By tradition, the *Rigodon* dance opened the ball. Most of the invitees were dressed to impress. Those who could afford it showed off their wealth and tried to outdo their friends. Here you'll observe the distinction of the social classes in the Philippines. The rich and privileged were partying inside the enclosed area and the poor and less privileged are outside watching the spectacle.

Fiesta was homecoming time for Filipinos. Sons and daughters studying or working in big cities came home for their town fiesta and oftentimes brought some friends with them. Fiesta was instituted by the Spaniards in the Philippines to gather the people who were scattered all over the country to a central place in order to create a forum for Christianizing the population. Since fiesta revolved around the parish church it was easy to perform certain rites during fiesta time. One particular rite was the confirmation where the bishop came to town to perform the confirmation.

On the eve and day of the fiesta, marching bands went around the town, making the day joyous and really festive. On the night of the fiesta, there was a big procession starting from the church and went through the barrios and back to church. People holding candles in one hand and the rope on the other hand pulling the *carroza,* a float carrying the image of the patron saint joined the procession with the marching bands. They prayed the rosary and sang hymns as the carroza wound through the streets.

Benjamin invited Adelaide and her family to his town fiesta in May 1941. Since Adelaide was going to her cousin who lived in another village of Alitagtag, her mother consented and said they could go. Adelaide's entourage was going first to her cousin in Dominador and it was agreed that Benjamin would send for them in a *calesin* at around 1 o'clock in the afternoon.

The calesin came and Adelaide, her mother and two sisters boarded the calesin which took them to Benjamin's house. Adelaide was dressed in an ankle-length pink flowered dress. A lovely pearl necklace with matching pearl earrings complemented her outfit. Her mother wore a lovely *terno,* her standard outfit for special occasion. Her two sisters wore simple summer dresses. There was a festive mood at Benjamin's house. There were so many people, mostly relatives. They were curious to see and meet Benjamin's friend from another town. Food was plentiful. Beef *morcon,* goat kaldereta and pork lechon were complemented by huge plates of pancit, a noodle dish with cabbage and dried shrimp. A few of the men had *tuba* and lambanog, a fermented coconut wine but mostly people drank barako coffee and *salabat,* a ginger tea.

Enrique sat at the head table with his wife, Barbara, at the opposite end of the table. Regina sat on the right of Enrique with Adelaide to his left and Benjamin seated next to Adelaide. Benjamin's brothers scattered around the table with few aunts and uncles here and there. Everyone was in good humor. Benjamin was trying to show off Adelaide to his family and tried to win their approval. Adelaide was a bit nervous but Benjamin's father was easily charmed by the young lady and her mother. By the time they left, Benjamin knew that he wouldn't have any trouble asking his parents for their blessings when it was time to ask Adelaide to marry him.

After that visit, Benjamin kept up his courtship. When he visited Adelaide on Sunday, he usually hired a calesa and the cuchero would pick him up at 5 in the afternoon to take him back to Alitagtag. It was always a pleasant visit, with her family always gracious. He somehow knew that they liked him and he wouldn't have any problem when he was ready to propose. The visits went on until he left for Baguio in late June 1941.

Before Benjamin left for Baguio, Benjamin approached the subject of Flores de Mayo with Adelaide. Adelaide usually participated in the procession. Benjamin asked her not to join the procession the following year. He was getting nervous that somebody might take her away from him.

"Are you planning to participate at the Flores de Mayo next year?" Benjamin asked nervously. He did not know what her reaction would be.

"I hope so. I always do."

Benjamin took a deep breath. He knew the next question would be difficult.

"Don't you think it's time for you to stop?"

"Why?"

"Because I think you should. I think it is time for you to stop participating."

Adelaide looked at him, perplexed at his request. She said, "No. Why should I? Just because you said so?"

"Adelaide, please. Don't get angry. I just thought..."

Adelaide cut him off. "We are not engaged you know. I don't see any reason why I have to listen to you. I'll do as I please. You can't tell me what to do," Adelaide reasoned out, getting agitated.

"But..."

"I'm sorry. If I want to participate in it, nobody can stop me."

"Okay then. I'm sorry I brought it up."

They were outside under the shade of a lemon tree. Benjamin was leaning on the tree and Adelaide was just standing a foot away. They were quiet for a while. It was beginning to be uncomfortable.

Benjamin decided to change the subject and let it go at that. "I'm leaving tomorrow for Baguio. I do hope you're not mad at me."

She looked at his eyes and saw he was really sorry. "I'm not mad at you."

"Please forgive me." He begged. He extended his hand. Adelaide took it. Benjamin squeezed it lightly and their eyes met. Benjamin wanted to say something but he refrained. He released her hand and said instead. "I'll write you as usual and I'll see you when I come back."

On his way to Baguio, he could not help thinking why he asked her to refrain from participating in the Flores de Mayo. He hated that they argued about it. He knew the underlying issue was the fact that he was leaving again and wouldn't see her for quite sometime and it bothered him. His only consolation was when he looked into her eyes. He knew something was unspoken there. She cared about him too. He did not know how much but he knew just the same that there was something there. She did not have to tell him. "Oh Adelaide, I wish I had the courage to propose then and there. Now I have to wait until I see you again which will not be till December."

# PART II

# CHAPTER 5

Before the war, Americans enjoyed a life of ease and comfort in the Philippines. Most American servicemen loved to be stationed in the Philippines because of the lifestyle they heard from people who had been living there. Manila was then known as the "Pearl of the Orient" because of the beauty of its old buildings, the parks and broad thoroughfares. For men, there were the best entertainments Manila had to offer that no other place had. Domestic help was plentiful and cheap. Here you could have someone wash your clothes in the morning and be pressed and ready by the time you came home at night. There was someone to clean your home, cook your meals, shine your shoes and drive your car. It was an idyllic life until the morning of Dec. 8, 1941 when things abruptly changed. The world of the Americans and Filipinos living in the Philippines will never be the same.

On Sunday, Dec. 7 in Manila, there was a festive mood all around. It was the eve of one of the most holy days in the Philippine Christian calendar, the Feast of the Immaculate Conception. Because of International Date Line, it was Saturday, Dec. 6, 1941 in Hawaii. The Americans were holding a big birthday bash for Brigadier General Lewis Brereton, MacArthur's Army Air Force commander at the Manila Hotel given by 1,200 men of the 27th Bombardment Group.

While the party was going on in Manila, on the other side of the Pacific Ocean, some 320 miles north of Hawaii, Commander Kanjiro Ono of the Japanese aircraft carrier *Akagi* was listening to the radio. He was staff communications officer for Vice Admiral Chuichi

Nagumo, commanding a huge Japanese task force of six carriers, two battle ships, three cruisers, and nine destroyers that were racing quietly southward through the night. Admiral Nagumo was about to launch an all-out surprise assault on the U.S. fleet at Pearl Harbor. The Japanese fleet had moved across the Pacific Ocean under complete silence. He knew that the American had not the slightest idea of the upcoming attack. The radio showed nothing but some soft island music playing on the radio. Admiral Nagumo relaxed, confident that the plan will be carried out without a hitch.

Shortly before 8 am, five thousand miles away aboard the battleship *Nagato,* the Japanese Commander in Chief of the Combined Fleet, Admiral Isoroku Yamamoto carried out his plan of surprise attack at Pearl Harbor on December 7, 1941. *"Niitakayama nobore"* (Climb Mount Niitaka), a special code in a message by wireless was sent to the whole Japanese fleet which means war with America should proceed. It was a daring move and the surprise attack was very successful and there were heavy casualties on the American side.

*"Tora, tora, tora,"* was the code for the successful surprise attack. There was a saying in Japan that, "A tora (tiger) goes out 1,000 ri (2000 miles) and returns without fail." Even before the first bomb fell, the Japanese knew that the surprise attack was successful: "Tora..... Tora.... Tora..."

The first wave of Japanese bombers struck at 7:55 A.M. Hawaii time when the Army, Navy and Marine airfields were in a typical Sunday peacetime morning relaxation. They were not ready. The Americans thought that the attack would be someplace else but not Pearl Harbor in spite of warnings from Ambassador Joseph Grew in Tokyo reported as early as January 1941. Passengers on an incoming American liner were happy to witness what they thought was a realistic maneuvers. It was total surprise.

A second wave came over at 8:40 A.M. In less than two hours, more than 350 Japanese bombers, torpedo bombers and fighters attacked the U.S. fleet at Pearl Harbor and the U.S. Army and U.S. Navy incurred heavy losses, mostly aircrafts on the ground. The U.S. entire fleet stationed in Hawaii was badly crippled. Six American battleships – *West Virginia, Tennessee, Arizona, Nevada,*

*Oklahoma* and *California* - were either sunk or badly damaged. Three light cruisers were damaged, three destroyers were torn by bombs and four other ships were sunk or damaged, all unserviceable. Fortuitously, all four American aircraft carriers and five cruisers as well as most destroyers assigned to the Pacific were away on exercises or on missions away from Pearl Harbor. Thousands of servicemen were either killed or wounded and there were hundreds of civilian killed in the attack. The Navy lost more than 2,700 men either killed or wounded, over twice as many as in the Spanish-American War and World War I combined. The Army and Marine Corps lost more than 700 men either killed or wounded. Not only the huge naval base in Pearl Harbor suffered losses, Japanese high-flying bombers also wreaked havoc on the Army Air Force bases at Hickham Field and Wheeler Field.

In Manila, ten minutes after the first bomb hit Pearl Harbor, a startled radio operator at Asiatic Fleet headquarters intercepted an unencrypted Morse Code from Adm. Husband Kimmel, the Honolulu-based Pacific Fleet Commander: "AIR RAID ON PEARL HARBOR. THIS IS NO DRILL". He alerted his duty officer, Marine Lt. Col. William T. Clement, who in turn contacted Admiral Hart who failed to relay the message to anybody. An enlisted army signalman happened to tune in to a California radio station and heard it and immediately told his duty officer who in turn phoned Brigadier Spencer B. Akin, MacArthur Signal Corps chief who went directly to Major Richard Sutherland, MacArthur's chief of staff who then called MacArthur penthouse atop the Manila Hotel.

MacArthur could not believe it and supposedly exclaimed, "Pearl Harbor! It should be our strongest point." At 3:40 am, he got a call from Washington, DC confirming the news. Even after the attack was confirmed by Washington, D.C., MacArthur for some reason failed to act for five long hours. Maybe it was too much information coming all at the same time but nobody could figure out why the inaction on his part. Maj. Gen. Lewis Brereton, MacArthur's commander of the air force, wanted to launch an immediate attack on the Japanese airfields on Formosa but did not get an answer until 10:10 A.M. but only to launch a photo reconnaissance of Formosa, in preparation for an air strike which was the first step before an attack by the B-17s the next day. As a result, his aircrew decided to go to chow instead while his planes, eighteen B-17s, assorted fighters, mostly P-39 Air Cobras and P-40 Tomahawks were parked outside exposed to enemy fire.

Just a few hours later, on the same day Pearl Harbor was attacked, December 8 west of the International Date Line, powerful Japanese bombers, stationed in Formosa did a "Second Pearl Harbor" in the Philippines, five thousand miles west of Hawaii. The first Japanese bombs to fall on Philippine soil hit Camp John Hay in Baguio. The Japanese bombers stationed in Taiwan just north of the Philippines bombed Iba airfields destroying all sixteen P-40's on the ground or about to touch down. They also did great damage to Clark Air Base. Coming in several V-shaped formations, the Japanese pilots was surprised to find the sky clear and rows and rows of planes on the ground. They dropped bomb after bomb on the parked planes.

When the last Japanese planes left Clark and turned toward Formosa, they had destroyed eighteen of the 35 B-17s, along with fifty-three P-40s and thirty other crafts. The Boeing B17 Flying Fortress was a four-engine heavy bomber aircraft developed in the 1930s for the U.S. Army Air Corps. The P-40 was a fighter/bomber produced by Curtiss Aircraft in the 1930s and 1940s. Half of MacArthur's air force was gone within the first hour of the war and several men dead. The base was totally destroyed. Tank after tank blew up and flames could be seen as far away as Manila. The Japanese had bombed and strafed the key U.S. air bases on Luzon: Iba, Clark, Nichols, Nielson, Vigan, Rosales, La Union and San Fernando fields.

Not only did the Japanese forces attack Pearl Harbor and the Philippines, they also mounted simultaneous attacks on several American and British targets in the Pacific. The British sent *HMS Repulse*, a 32,000-ton battle cruiser and *HMS Prince of Wales*, a 35,000-ton battleship, their two most powerful ships in Asia to defend their territory. The Japanese forces sank them both on Dec. 11 together with the new Commander-in-Chief of the British Far Eastern Fleet, Adm. Sir Thomas Phillips. Landings also started in British Malaya accompanied by air strikes. Another group of

Japanese bombers destroyed the British air power in Hongkong. They also attacked two U.S. outposts in the Pacific which most American had never heard of before: Guam and Wake Island. The next day, they landed in Bangkok.

Shortly after noon on December 8, Washington, D.C. time, President Roosevelt appeared before a joint session of Congress demanding a state of war against Japan be recognized. *"Yesterday, December 7, 1941, a date which will live in infamy, the United States of America was suddenly and deliberately attacked by naval and air forces of the Empire of Japan."* He went on to tell the places that were attacked and the casualties. He then offered assurance that we would win the war – *"With confidence in our armed forces, with the unbounded determination of our people, we will gain the inevitable triumph, so help us God."* The American people were stunned.

The speech lasted only six minutes but in less than an hour Congress responded with only a single dissenting vote – Representative Jeannette Rankin, a pacifist from Montana who said she wanted to show that a "good democracy" did not always vote unanimously for war. The Senate passed, voted unanimously for an all-out declaration of war, eighty-two to nothing and the House passed it three hundred eighty-eight to one. "Infamy" was the word that touched a cord in the American hearts and unified the American people together in anger as they had never been before or since until the war was won. Roosevelt did not declare war against the other Axis power. However, four days after the attack on Pearl Harbor and The Philippines, Adolf Hitler, the German dictator who had conquered most of Europe the past two years and Benito Mussolini of Italy declared war against the United States. Congress in response passed a joint resolution accepting the state of war which had been thrust upon the United States.

Pearl Harbor was America's greatest military disaster. Still, the Japanese forces did not bomb the enormous fuel dump at Pearl Harbor, the submarine base or the naval repair shops. At Pearl Harbor, the U.S. Pacific fleet had been caught napping. It was the first attack on American soil by a foreign power since the British burned the White House during the War of 1812. The country moved from peace to war, joined together in unity and a desire for revenge never seen before in time of crisis. The United States had suffered the worst military disaster in her history in the Pacific. The war that started at Pearl Harbor was now extending its reach into the Philippines Islands and the rest of the Far East.

# CHAPTER 6

While Japan was waging war in the Pacific, there was still calm in a small town called Mankayan in the Mountain Province. The Mountain Province was later divided into the provinces of Benguet, Mountain Province, Kalinga-Apayao and Ifugao by Republic Act No. 4695 on June 18, 1966. Though Baguio City, the summer capital of the Philippines is only 95 kilometers south of Mankayan, people in Mankayan were still oblivious of what was going on. Baguio is 260 kilometers (160 miles) north of Manila and Benjamin's home town, Alitagtag, a small town in the province of Batangas is about 110 kilometers south of Manila.

Mankayan though small was a beautiful and peaceful place and was home to Inodey Waterfalls and Cabacab Plateau. Mankayan was a mining town. The area of Mankayan was loaded with gold, copper and other minerals. Copper ingots from Mankayan were used in exchange for goods with the Chinese traders as far back as the 12th century. When the Spanish came in the 16th century, copper was then used extensively as their main metal source. Saw mills were also sprouting everywhere near Mankayan. The government was letting lumberjacks into the area to establish settlements there in the 1930s. The place was a bit of a jungle and the government welcomed the entrepreneurs who were catering to the employees of Suyoc Mining Company and Lepanto Mining Company which started operation in 1936.

At the outbreak of the war, Benjamin, his brothers and cousins were in Mankayan in the southwestern part of the Mountain Province, up in the northern part of Luzon. Their hometown in Batangas was in the southern part of Luzon. The Mountain

Provinces occupied a big land mass in northern Luzon, bordering the provinces of Cagayan, Isabela, Nueva Vizcaya to the east, Pangasinan to the south, La Union, Ilocos Sur, Abra, Ilocos Norte to the west and the northern tip of Cagayan to the north. Mankayan was not that far from Banaue in the heart of the *Ifugao* tribe territory. Ifugao means "hill" and to the tribes-men who lived there, hill meant everything to their livelihood.

As the bright morning sun filtered through the trees, Benjamin was sitting in the kitchen mesmerized, watching the sunrise come up behind the mountain. The sight of the early morning sun peering through the mountain always gave Benjamin that feeling that a new day was dawning full of hope and adventure at the same time. Sunrise here in Mankayan was a glorious sight. Here in the mountain, there were incredible varieties of plant life ranging from ferns to giant trees. Several varieties of ferns and wild orchids grew in abundance. The diversity and abundance of the tropical vegetation made the scenery so beautiful. In the higher elevation, he could see large areas of pinetum. On the lower slopes, bamboos, coconut palms and banyan trees abound. The rain that had fallen for the last six months had made this area into a verdant landscape. The air here smelt so clean and fresh. He loved this part of the country. He was in the midst of Cordillera Central of Luzon. It was the most prominent mountain range in the Philippines. It consisted of three parallel ranges averaging 1,800 meters, about 5,900 feet in height. These ranges were mostly covered with dense forest. Lauan, Philippine mahogany comprised a large percentage of the forest.

"How lucky we are here to be alive in this part of paradise! Someday, I want to settle down and live here permanently," he told himself.

The kitchen where Benjamin was sitting was fairly large, measuring 6 meters by 9 meters. There was a mahogany table with two matching benches opposite each other next to a big picture window facing the mountain to the east. On the far end of the kitchen were the stove on the west wall and the sink on the south side. Benjamin always wanted to watch the sun rise in this spot in the kitchen of their rented farmhouse. He was always the first one to wake up among his group. As he was watching the sunrise, for no apparent reason his inner self was telling him that it was to be a different sort of day. He got that foreboding sensation in the air which he could not explain. A premonition perhaps. He could not pinpoint what made him feel that way but somehow it was there.

As he poured his second cup of coffee, he heard the hooves of the horse. The *caretela,* the horse-drawn carriage of the vendor who peddled some fresh baked bread every morning was near their rented farmhouse. The farmhouse was situated just behind the store where he was selling dry goods. This was in the middle of a small village in Mankayan where there was a village market. In the village market, there were a hardware store, a food store, a vegetable stand, and meat stalls. Benjamin's store was the only dry goods store in town. Most of the store owners were from the lowlands and were trying their luck with the miners. He called his store Batanguenos Dry Goods Store.

Life was wonderful. Some days, they only opened the store for half a day and the rest of the afternoon, they took off and enjoyed themselves. They played *sipa* behind the store or went bowling at a nearby bowling alley. Sipa is a simple ball game where the ball or sipa is made of rattan interwoven to form a ball and hollow inside and is about 4 inches in diameter. It is kicked backwards and forwards and kept going continuously, and cannot be touched with any part of the body except knees, legs, and feet. They had a great time playing it and they could play for hours on end.

As he heard the caretela approach, he put on his sweater and his hat. He walked to the front door and quietly walked across the front yard separating the farmhouse a few feet back from the store. There was a misty air and the fog was lying low. It was chilly outside and he could feel the cold air on his face. He buttoned his sweater all the way to the top. He got to the road just in time the caretela reached their place.

"*Magandang umaga po.*" Good morning sir, Benjamin said.

Mang Sylvestre (Mr. Sylvestre), the cuchero was not as jolly as he used to be. Mang Sylvestre, a man in his 50s, a short stocky fellow with dark olive skin, thick hair with thick bushy eyebrow, always had a smile on his face. His jovial disposition endeared him to his customers. This morning he was wearing brown pants with a striped shirt with long sleeves and his usual Panama hat. Benjamin noticed he had a bewildered look on his face. He looked worried. He did not return Benjamin's greeting which he usually did. Benjamin sensed something was amiss.

Benjamin asked, "Mang Sylvestre, what is the matter? Are you all right? Is anything wrong?"

"I'm fine. Nothing is wrong with me," Mang Sylvestre said. He looked at Benjamin. He suspected Benjamin did not know the latest news. Mang Sylvestre thought Benjamin did not look worried. Nothing showed in Benjamin's face that he knew something was going on. How was he going to break the news? Maybe he should just tell him outright. He could not break the news gently. It would be impossible.

Mang Sylvestre swallowed hard and in a soft voice asked Benjamin point blank, "Did you hear the news from the radio?"

Benjamin asked, "What news? I have been busy. I have not heard anything nor turned on the radio." His heart started pounding. He looked at Mang Sylvestre and waited nervously for what Mang Sylvestre had to say.

Mang Sylvestre fumbled getting the bag of bread. He took a deep breath and said, "You better turn on your radio. A terrible thing has happened." Then he stopped, seemed not to know how to proceed. Benjamin waited in anticipation and didn't know what to make of all this hesitation.

Then he broke the news.

"The Japanese bombed the U.S. naval base at Pearl Harbor in Hawaii the other night and there were heavy casualties. Wheeler Field and Hickham Field were also bombed. A lot of the fleet was damaged and planes on the ground were destroyed. There was an unconfirmed rumor that Clark Field was also attacked. There were also minor attacks on Tarlac, Tuguegarao and Camp John Hay yesterday."

Benjamin gasped. He felt short of breath. He felt dizzy all of a sudden. He tried very hard to steady himself.

"Am I dreaming? Am I hearing him right?" He heard himself asking. Mang Sylvestre got off the cart. Benjamin was trying to absorb the enormity of what he said. He tried very hard to calm down. He swallowed hard. Mang Sylvestre shook him by the arm trying to calm him down.

"You're not joking, are you?" Benjamin finally asked, shaking his head in disbelief.

Mang Sylvestre still looking distraught looked Benjamin in the eye and said, "It is true. I wish it weren't but it is true. It is all over the radio. There could be more. President Quezon who is visiting in Baguio is rumored to be preparing to leave for Manila if he hasn't done so. I believe a war between the United States and Japan has already started."

Benjamin was so stunned. "O my God," he was barely able to say. He was so shocked, he began to tremble. He was trying to digest what Mang Sylvestre had just said.

Finally, he said, "But why? Do the Japanese hate us so much to inflict such destruction? I thought the United States and Japan are talking. What happened? So we are at war now?" Benjamin asked as he began to regain his composure.

Mang Sylvestre thought hard looking for an explanation and merely said, "I believe it is for economic and political reasons. Philippines is the Pearl of the Orient and with so many resources here, it is a major prize for the Japanese. Our location is also strategic if they want to conquer the neighboring countries." He wanted to comment more but decided to cut it short otherwise he would go on a lengthy discourse with Benjamin and he had to get back on his route.

Then he merely added, "I don't know, my friend. All I can say is it does not look good."

"Thanks for the information. I do appreciate it. I have to tell my brothers. We have to do something."

"For your own safety, I advise you to leave this place as soon as possible. I know your hometown is in the south, in Batangas. This place is a long way from home. You do not want to be so far away from your family in case this war escalates. It is advisable that you, your brothers and your cousins wrap up your businesses here and prepare to leave town as soon as possible. I will be back tomorrow morning in case you are still around and tell you what news I can gather."

Mang Sylvestre handed Benjamin his usual order of a dozen *pandesal* (an oblong roll of bread about 8 inches long with indentation cut halfway lengthwise through the middle) and a dozen *boniti* (a crunchy buttery muffin). Benjamin paid him and went back inside. All of a sudden, he felt weary. He felt his legs were about to cave in.

As Benjamin walked back to the farmhouse, his mind was in such turmoil he could not think straight. He got back inside the farmhouse, sat down on the bench by the kitchen table and turned on the radio. There was static so he played around the volume knob and then turned the volume at full blast.

His oldest brother, Ramon, who was asleep at the next room jumped up from the mat where he was sleeping and ran into the kitchen yelling.

"Benjamin, what is going on? What do you think you are doing? Why are you playing that radio so loud at this time of day? Everybody is still asleep."

"Quiet!" Benjamin yelled.

Benjamin put his index finger on his mouth as if to silence his brother.

Ramon getting indignant continued to ask, "Do you know what time it is? It is only 5 o'clock. It's way too early in the morning. You'll wake up even the dead".

Then the radio blurted and Ramon heard it: *"Pearl Harbor was attacked by the Japanese forces the other night. There were heavy casualties,"* the radio's blaring sound said. *"There were bombings also in Baguio, the summer capital of the Philippines and site of some military installations. At Clark Field, reports of enemy planes were spotted leaving the area amidst heavy black smoke after explosion."*

Ramon rubbed his eyes and tried to wake up. He thought he was dreaming. He looked at Benjamin questioningly. He felt his heart was pounding heavily.

"No! That's impossible," Ramon said in disbelief. "It's not true! There must be a mistake! It can't possibly be!"

Ramon felt weak all of a sudden and plopped down on the bench opposite Benjamin, looked him in the eyes for confirmation. Without saying a word, Benjamin just nodded his head.

"O my God," was all Ramon could say. He sat motionless for a while trying to grasp the severity of the situation. He knew deep down inside his heart that things would never be the same again. The world had suddenly changed.

"Yes, it's true. Mang Sylvestre just told me. That's why I have the radio on so loud so I can hear the news," Benjamin told Ramon.

Ramon still could not believe what he was hearing. He started shaking his head. Benjamin saw tears start flowing from his brother's eyes. He stood up, went across the room to the other side of the table. Ramon got up and the two brothers hugged each other. Benjamin patted Ramon's back and assured him they would be okay.

After a few seconds, Ramon still choking with emotion, sat down again on the bench opposite Benjamin.

Finally, taking a deep breath, he asked Benjamin, "What are we going to do?"

"I think we should go home," was all Benjamin could muster to say.

"Yes, we have to go home immediately," Ramon concurred. "*Inang* (mother) will be worried sick." As he began to get out of the chair, he extended his hand across the table and patted Benjamin hand and then said, "Let me wake up the guys."

As Ramon was leaving the kitchen, the radio announced:

"*The zero hour has arrived. I expect every Filipino – man and woman – to do his duty. We have pledged our honor to stand by the United States and we shall not fail her, happen what may,*" President Manuel L. Quezon's voice came through the radio. Benjamin turned the radio off, went back to the stove and poured himself another cup of coffee.

Ramon went back to the bedroom and one by one quickly woke up everybody. Manuel got up first, followed by Francisco, and then Delfin. All sat up still half asleep. Rubbing their eyes to get used to the dawning light, and wondering what the urgency was all about, they got out from underneath the mosquito netting and finally had all their senses at attention.

"Hurry up and go to the kitchen. Get yourself a cup of coffee and wait for me there. I have an urgent and important news to tell you," Ramon said hurriedly and about to dash off to the next room when Francisco asked, "Like what?"

"I will tell you in the kitchen. Just go."

Ramon then went to the next room. He poked through the mosquito netting and tried to wake up his two cousins, Elias and Felipe.

With bleary eyes, they slowly got up.

"What is wrong? Why are we getting up so early?" Elias asked.

Felipe started stretching his arms and yawning. "I was sound asleep. I can't believe you woke us up this early. I don't remember you telling us last night we have to be up this early today. Why?"

Ramon answered, "Just go to the kitchen, get yourself a cup of coffee and I'll tell you why. Hurry." He then left the room and headed back to the kitchen.

Ramon poured himself a cup of coffee, glanced at Benjamin who sat quietly at the other end of the table and waited for everyone to have their place at the table.

Delfin who always loved singing started humming a tune and then sang:

*"Sa kabukiran, walang kalungkutan,*
*Ang mga ibon ay nagaawitan."*

*"In the countryside, there is no loneliness,*
*The birds are singing."*

"Quiet!" Ramon told Delfin. "All of you. Get your breakfast and be seated," he commanded. "I have very disturbing news."

"Yes Boss," Delfin answered him sarcastically.

All piled in toward the stove, perplexed and they had that questioning look on their faces. They helped themselves to the coffee, pouring in a thin stream of canned evaporated milk. Elias who was still half asleep followed everyone to the hot stove, pouring the dark hot liquid into his cup and scalding him as he gulped it down, waking him up quickly.

As soon as everybody got their coffee and bread and got seated, Ramon started saying, "A terrible thing has happened." Everybody looked askance.

"Like what?" Everybody asked in unison.

"Did somebody important die?" Felipe asked.

"It must be really terrible, for you to wake us up this early. We are not due at the market for a couple of more hours. I'm in the middle of this fabulous dream, alone with this lovely negrita (tribal young girl). Now I will never know how to find her," Francisco joked.

Everybody started laughing.

Ramon gave Francisco a dirty look and without any preamble, Ramon broke the news. "The Japanese attacked Pearl Harbor the other night."

"What? No!" Everybody gasped, their faces turned white with disbelief. Then a brief silence.

Felipe was the first one to break the silence. He said, "You're joking. That's not true."

"It has to be, otherwise he would not wake us up this early," Elias interjected.

"But why?" Felipe asked.

"I knew something horrible is up in the air. You cannot trust those Japanese. I thought the United States and Japan were working on a peace treaty or something," Manuel ventured to say.

"What are we going to do?" Francisco asked.

"Are we staying here or do you think we should attempt to go home?" asked Elias.

Ramon answered, "It looks like the war is coming this way. They bombed Tarlac, Tuguegarao and Camp John Hay in Baguio yesterday. God knows what they will bomb next. They seem to be everywhere. I want you all to finish what you are supposed to do today. We are not staying here. We are going home. We might be leaving sooner than when we planned. We are not staying here for another three weeks. Keep your eyes and ears open today as you move around the town. Get rid of your inventory. We will need all the cash we can have to get home."

"What do you think will happen now?" Manuel asked.

"We don't know," Benjamin countered. "Mang Sylvestre said he will give me an update tomorrow." He pulled his necklace from underneath his shirt and held St. Christopher's medallion tenderly in his hand and quietly said, "Please take care of us and guide us in our journey."

On the day after Pearl Harbor, people started milling about in the street earlier in the morning than usual. There was a big commotion. The place was in an uproar. Newspaper's big black headlines across the front page blared the attack on Pearl Harbor. Some people were crying. Some people looked scared. Some people felt that this was an all out war and they started digging trenches. Some were carrying bags and bundles, ready to go back to the provinces where they thought they would be safe. Everybody was seeking news. A lot of people had their radio on listening for an update. However, in this part of the country, the reception was really bad because it is surrounded by mountains. The radio was full of static. The front page of *The Manila Herald* was screaming with headline "Japanese Attack Pearl Harbor!" Headlines on the front pages of other newspapers announced the same thing – the attack on Pearl Harbor. There were few newspapers around and they were being sold out very quickly. People started talking to each other and trying to find out if any recent bombings had occurred. Most of them were still in disbelief. From their faces, you could see they were horror stricken. People were stunned. Some were crying. They could not believe that a country with less military power than the U.S. and Britain, the great powers, would dare to attack them. It was incomprehensible.

Benjamin thought that they should really get out of there and fast. All day long, he was very anxious. He was moving about doing his business like a zombie. He was often distracted. There were more customers than usual. It seemed that more people were looking for bargains now. He wanted to get rid of most of his inventory so he decided to lower his prices without losing much money. By the end of the day, he only had a few things left to sell, half a dozen blankets, four mosquito nettings and five big *banigs*, straw mat. He believed people were stocking up on their supplies.

Benjamin got back into the house later than everybody else. Manuel was already preparing supper. Manuel was the one on duty that day. They always took turns on who cooked the meals. Since there were seven of them, they had just the perfect number rotation to have one person for each day of the week to prepare meals. Benjamin could smell the boiling vegetables and chicken as he entered the house. They were having *Sinigang na Manok,* boiled chicken with *malunggay,* a green leafy vegetable and rice for supper.

While Manuel was busy in the kitchen, Ramon was studying the map of Luzon. He was trying to figure out what was the best route to take to go south. Francisco and Delfin were busy reading the papers. Elias and Felipe were in the bedroom taking inventory of their merchandise nervously. They could not think of anything else to do.

When Manuel announced that dinner was ready, they sat down to eat in a somber mood. Nobody said a word for a while. Everyone was silent and preoccupied with their own thoughts. They still could not come to grips that the United States had been caught napping by the early morning Japanese air assault at Pearl Harbor and now the Japanese did a "Second Pearl Harbor" on Philippine soil which is five thousand miles away from Hawaii and nobody was ready here either. After they finished eating, everyone stacked their plates in the sink and quietly went in the living room without a word.

As they sat in the living room, Ramon asked Benjamin, "What do you think the Japanese are going to do next?"

"Who knows? I'm sure they will be landing soon. The air assaults are just preliminaries. They'll be landing on beaches next. I'm sure of that," Benjamin answered.

"I was thinking the same thing. What do you think we should do?" Ramon asked looking worried.

"There is only one thing we have to do. We have to get out of here," Benjamin said.

"How?" Everyone seemed to ask at the same time.

"We have to formulate a plan and we have to do it soon." Ramon looked at Benjamin. He could not figure out how they were going to get back to Batangas which was so far away. It seemed like it would be an impossible task.

"We could be stranded somewhere or worst yet encounter some Japanese soldiers on the way. We could be killed," Manuel, the worrier of the bunch made a point.

"We could. None of us even have a gun to defend ourselves," Ramon said matter-of-factly.

"Shall we buy one?" Francisco asked.

"I thought the same thing. But where?" Benjamin countered. The idea kept nagging his brain.

"I'm sure the army got them all," Ramon said.

"God, please helps us." Benjamin prayed in silence. As if God was listening, he heard himself say, "Keep the faith."

# CHAPTER 7

It was a sunny bright day on December 8 in Sambat, Bauan. There was not a cloud in the sky, not a hint of pending disaster. Adelaide and her eldest sister, Marta prepared to go to town and deliver the finished product to their distributors. With their bundles of goods, the two of them took a calesa to transport them. They got to town without any problem.

At around noontime, at a small barrio near Batangas, a couple of hundred miles from Manila, Adelaide and her sister just finished their deliveries of some textiles to their distributors and were heading out the door when someone came rushing into the shop and almost knocked them over. He breathlessly said, "The Japanese just bombed Clark Air Base and Baguio."

Adelaide and Marta turned around. The owner of the shop said, "What are you talking about?" The owner of the shop could not comprehend what the man was talking about.

The man said breathlessly, "I heard it on the radio. The Japanese bombed Clark and Baguio." The man repeated.

"O my God!" She made a sign of the cross and watching her, Adelaide thought the lady owner was going to faint. The lady owner sat down and asked for a glass of water. The man went to the back room to get some water from the earthen jar.

Adelaide looked at her sister who was as shocked as she was. The man came back from the back room with the glass of water. Marta signaled to Adelaide and she and Adelaide said goodbye and hurriedly headed toward the door. They walked a couple of blocks trying to find a bus to take them home to Sambat. They went to the bus stop. Few people were milling about. Marta asked one of the women who was standing nearby and talking to somebody else.

"Excuse me, when do you think the next bus to Bauan is going to be?"

"I don't know," the lady answered.

"I understand there is no bus service today," the other lady said.

"Why?" Adelaide asked.

"All the buses are taken by the army." The lady felt sorry for the two young girls. "Maybe you can find a calesa instead." She pointed in the opposite direction and said, "Go that way, sometimes there are some calesas standing there."

"*Salamat po.*" Marta said. Thank you, m'am.

Marta took Adelaide's hand and they walked in the direction that the lady pointed as fast as they could. They saw a couple of calesas about to leave. They were full and would not take another passenger. So they waited. And they waited. After half an hour, another calesa came by finally. There were seats available but it won't take them to Sambat. They would only go to Bauan market. Marta looked at Adelaide. Adelaide nodded her head. They took it anyway. They got into Bauan market and there was a big commotion around. They had to get another calesa to take them to Sambat. They waited and waited. But no calesa was coming.

Adelaide was getting nervous. Adelaide asked her sister, "Why don't we just start walking? It would probably be faster."

"Ok, if you are up to it. Let's go," Marta said.

As they were starting to walk, they saw a lot of people doing the same thing. There were very few calesas on the road. No buses at all. They kept on walking with Adelaide's braid swinging behind her. Then suddenly Adelaide stopped, pulled her braid over her shoulder, fingered the tip of it. Marta looked at her. "What's the matter?"

Adelaide blurted out, "The man said Baguio was bombed. I wonder where the bombing was in Baguio." She had been thinking about it ever since she heard the news but was afraid to ask Marta. Finally she could not keep it to herself anymore.

"We forgot to ask the man." Marta could feel the anxiety on Adelaide's voice.

"Benjamin is there." Adelaide was trying very hard to suppress her anxiety.

Her sister caught on quickly. "Yes, I know what you are thinking but we do not know exactly where the bombing was. The Japanese probably were attacking just the army bases. I don't think you should worry."

"I am not worried," Adelaide lied.

"Yes, you are. He'll be fine. Trust me."

"Do you think the Japanese will kill the civilians?"

"Hard to tell. If they were on their way, they could be killed."

"Benjamin is in Mankayan. I don't know how far that is from Baguio."

"I don't know either. Let's just hope he has the common sense to stay away from danger."

"I wonder how long this war is going to be."

"It's just starting. We'll probably be safe here in the province."

"I hope you're right. It's scary."

"It's so different from the previous wars. Grandfather said during those days, you can even watch them. They didn't have these new weapons that are supposedly more dangerous than those used during the previous wars."

"But still, look what happened with *Tio* Dominic. He didn't even fight till the last minute and he still died."

Tio Dominic was their uncle, their mother's only brother. He was a cavalier with the American troops and fought during the Spanish American War in 1898 when numerous battles were fought in many provinces between the Spanish and the American-Filipino forces. One of those battles was fought near the church in Bauan. Tio Dominic came in at the tail end of the battle and was spotted by the Spanish army. They accused him of killing the Spaniards and he was later shot by firing squad by the Spaniards.

"That was awful. I hate wars."

"So do I," Marta agreed.

Two days later on December 10, Lt. Gen. Masaharu Homma's 14th Army stormed ashore in northern Luzon and began driving southward towards Manila. The Japanese bombed Singapore and sank the battle cruiser *Repulse* and the battleship *Prince of Wales* which were on their way to Malaya. On the same day, Dec. 10, eighty Mitsubishis and fifty-two Zeros destroyed the United States naval base at Cavite, eight miles southwest of Manila killing or wounding at least five hundred men. The smoke could be seen all the way to Manila.

On the same day, the Japanese started bombing the capital city of Batangas. People started evacuating to the little barrios in the countryside. There was panic in the air.

Adelaide heard a roaring noise outside. She ran to her back porch. She looked up to the sky and in the distance she saw grey planes with red dots flying in V formation going in the direction of Batangas. She followed the direction of the planes. Looking toward Batangas, she could see miles of open fields. As she watched the planes passed over, she heard a faint rustling sound and then the noise of the roaring planes got louder and louder. Then another group of planes flying in perfect V formation appeared going in the same direction, never breaking the formation. She could see the red dot on their wings. She ran back inside and called her sisters. They all came outside and watched as the planes flew in the direction of Batangas.

There was a commotion in the street. The townspeople heard the loud noise too and they started coming out of their houses and looked upwards and talked excitedly. In a short while, they could hear loud explosions, then high billows of black smoke were rising from the distance. Adelaide followed where the black smoke was coming from. It looked like it was coming from Batangas. The Japanese were bombing Batangas, she thought. There was a series of explosions, then black smoke billowing up in the air. The black smoke started covering the blue sky. The explosions went on and on. Then Adelaide saw the Japanese planes make several low passes on the horizon, turning and twisting, and climbing and diving. She saw them coming out of the far distance and heading back north. Adelaide was watching the sky as the Japanese planes began to disappear from the horizon where they came from earlier.

After the initial bombing, the Japanese never came back as if they had finished the job there. Maybe because they found out the American soldiers were not there. The Japanese only bombed the gas stations and bridges in Batangas.

Fearing that the Japanese soldiers would come back, people from Batangas started evacuating to small barrios in Bauan. They moved with their small belongings to remote barrios away from the main road. After that bombing in Batangas, there was a big enlistment among young Filipino men. The army asked for volunteers to join the army. Some of them did. Some joined the Philippine guerilla group.

In a few days, the troops moved up north. Traffic was horrendous. The streets were alive with trucks, buses and jeeps bumper to bumper for miles and miles. The new recruits were being taken to the military camps near Manila. The army trucks full of recruits lumbered on a few feet at a time, stopping every so often as the trucks in front of them stopped and then waited till the trucks in front of them started moving again. It was a slow process. The townspeople watched as the army inched its way. Women, children and few old men cheered them on. There was a certain sense of patriotism and pride among those in the caravan and the civilians watching them.

Some old men who experienced war before looked sad. In their hearts, they knew this war would be different. The war just started and they sensed this war would drag on and on for a long time. Most of the young men in the caravan did not know what they were heading for. They were full of patriotic fervor, not thinking they could be killed or maimed or whatever. But young men didn't think that way. They were all looking gleefully as they rode through the dusty road and into the uncharted future.

# CHAPTER 8

Twice a year, Benjamin, his four brothers, and his two cousins would go to Mankayan to peddle their goods. They were traveling salesmen. They had a store next to their rented farmhouse but they also sold their merchandise in the nearby markets. They found this area very lucrative. Mountain Province attracted a lot of Filipinos who wanted to escape the oppressive heat of Manila and its suburbs. Lepanto Copper Mines just started operation in Mankayan a few years ago and a lot of Benjamin's customers worked for the Lepanto Copper Mines. Workers from the mining industry and the foreigners that stayed in this area were good customers.

Life for foreigners living in the Philippines and even those who worked for the mining industry was so different than the life they left behind in their native countries. Domestic help was so cheap that they could live like kings. They could have two maids, a seamstress, four gardeners, chauffeur, *lavantera* (laundry woman) and possibly her assistants, cook and her own assistants for next to nothing. Though the climate was very hot and there was no air conditioning except in movie houses, but with cheap labor, one could shower twice a day, change clothes and have their clothes and wet towels all washed, ironed when they returned from work.

Each time Benjamin went to Mankayan, they always stayed at the same farmhouse. The farmhouse was situated on a piece of land on a corner lot with various kinds of pine trees on the west side of the property and on the back. They had a store in front of the house on the corner with a scattering of coconut trees around it. The south

74

section facing the main thoroughfare had some tropical plants. The farmhouse was a two story wooden structure with a wide open first floor and a pyramidal thatched roof. All living quarters were on the second floor. At the top of the stairway was an entry hall. To the left facing the store was the sala or living room. Behind the living room were two bedrooms. In the living room between the two doors to the bedrooms was an area where a round table flanked two chairs. Facing the front wide window was a square table with two plantation chairs on each side. There was an *aparador*, a wardrobe cabinet in one corner. In the other corner was another table which was used as a writing desk and a chair with rattan seat and backing. The only access to the dining room and kitchen was through the entrance hall. Most homes had this typical layout.

From the stillness of the early morning mist that shrouded the mountains, Benjamin heard the cock crow. "Cock a doodle doo. Cock a doodle doo." He opened his eyes wearily. He began to stretch his arms and looked up. There was a slight breeze coming through the open window making a nice ripple movement on the mosquito netting. Up here in the mountains, the night air was cool and invigorating. He lifted the mosquito netting and got up quietly so as not to disturb anybody. It was still dark. He found his pair of slippers next to the banig, the straw mat he was sleeping on. He put on his slippers, went to the round table outside the bedroom door and groped for the matches. He lit the kerosene hurricane lamp, picked it up and headed toward the kitchen.

He passed through the entry hall into the kitchen. He started the fire in the stove. The stove was on a wooden platform with three connecting sections made of hollow blocks where you placed your pots over the fire. From the top of a canopy were hooks with wire loops to hang the kettle. He poured some water from the earthenware jug next to the sink into the kettle. He made coffee and then sat down waiting for the coffee to percolate. He grabbed his pencil and paper and started jotting down his plan for the day. When the coffee stopped percolating, he poured himself a cup. It was good. He felt energized. It just hit the spot. It rolled so smoothly in his mouth. It was strong but not bitter and had the best taste that he had ever experienced and he had tasted different brands of coffee in his travels.

"That Barako coffee from Batangas is sure to be the best," Benjamin said to himself. Hmmmm. He began to inhale its aroma. They always brought some from home to anywhere they were going. They could not find any other coffee as good as Barako in taste and aroma. The name Barako was an appropriate name for it. It meant strong like a bull.

The sun was just coming through from the horizon behind the mountain. The streams of light started pouring through the half-open window. It pierced through the windowpanes of iridescent capiz shell radiating a rainbow of colors.

"I hope today is a better day than yesterday," Benjamin sighed.

Benjamin was seated on the kitchen bench facing the window, staring at the fog and waiting anxiously for Mang Sylvestre to arrive. He was anxious and worried. He really didn't know how they were going to get home. They were too far north and their home was too far south. They could go through the mountains but that would be impossible and treacherous. He knew they had to hurry. There was not enough time. They had to move quickly for their own survival.

As Benjamin kept on looking at his notes for the umpteenth time, he decided they had to leave either today or tomorrow. Possibly today but no later than tomorrow. There was no other alternative. He was anxious on what Mang Sylvestre had to say. He did not wait long. He heard the hooves of the horse from afar and it sounded coming nearer and nearer. Immediately he got up, put on a light sweater and headed outside. Mang Sylvestre arrived outside in front of the store just as he was getting there.

"*Magandang Umaga, po,*" Benjamin said in greeting.

"*Magandang Umaga rin sa iyo.*" Good morning to you too, Mang Sylvestre answered.

"How are you this morning? Did you find out anything?" Benjamin asked.

"I'm fine. I'm just a little bit worried. The news is not looking good. Fort McKinley was hit Tuesday morning, Dec. 9. It could be that the Japanese are now on Philippine soil. They bombed Clark

Field two days ago. Nichols Field on the southeast of Manila was also bombed yesterday early in the morning."

"That does not look good at all."

"No, it doesn't," Mang Sylvestre continued, "There are other United States installations like the ones in Nielson, Iba, and Vigan that also got hit. Rosales, La Union and San Fernando were either bombed or strafed too. There was no escaping from them. Rumors had it that portions of Pasay and Makati were also hit. It's getting worse. I'm a bit concerned." There was a solemn look on his face.

Little did they know that a convoy of 15 Japanese ships escorted by the cruiser "Natori" from Taiwan had already landed in Aparri, Cagayan that morning in the early hours just before dawn. Cagayan Valley is in between the Cordillera Central and Sierra Madre mountains and just north of Mankayan. There were other landings in Vigan in northwest Luzon and in Legaspi in southeast Luzon. The Japanese were now encircling Luzon, two landings on the north and one on the south.

"That's really worrisome. My brothers decided we will be leaving hopefully today or tomorrow," Benjamin told Mang Sylvestre.

"I think that's a great idea. You never know what will happen. Hopefully I'll still see you tomorrow morning."

"Yes, most likely. But we definitely have to be leaving before it is too late."

"It might take the Japanese a while to reach the mountain from the beach. They might not even get here."

"We still want to go home."

"I do understand."

"We'll be winding down our affairs here today and be on our way by tomorrow. I'm sure of that."

"Adios. See you tomorrow morning."

Benjamin took his bag of bread and said, "*Salamat po*." Thank you.

Back in the farmhouse, everybody was up early. They were all eager to hear the latest news.

As soon as Benjamin returned to the farmhouse, he noticed everyone was up already, sitting and waiting in the kitchen with their cup of coffee.

"What's the latest?" Delfin was the first one to ask.

Benjamin told the group, "According to Mang Sylvestre, Clark Air Base was bombed two days ago and Nichols Field yesterday. He believed it is not good. We really have to go back home as soon as we can. There may not be any transportation so we may have to make other arrangements."

"Like what?" Elias asked.

"Yes, like what?" Felipe asked the same thing. He was scratching his head.

"Like walk home." Benjamin looked around and waited for reaction.

"No," Francisco muttered in horror.

"We can't walk that far. It will take us a whole month to go south," Manuel said. He gulped the last drop of his coffee and stood up to refill his cup. "That's impossible!" He muttered more to himself.

"What are we going to do?" Elias asked.

"I guess we may have to walk in case we cannot find any transportation," Delfin ventured to say.

"I can't see any other way," Benjamin said matter-of-factly.

Ramon was watching the group and saw they all looked panic-stricken. He said, "We will be leaving definitely tomorrow after breakfast. Benjamin and I will work on what route to take. We have to get out of here. We cannot delay. Finish what you have to do today. We will carry only the bare necessities for travel. Make sure you have with you at all times the St. Christopher medallion that mother gave us when we left home and don't forget the Holy Cross in your wallet. He is our talisman and he will keep us safe." His voice did not sound too sure of what he was saying.

"Do you think we'll be able to find transportation to go home?" Manuel asked with a worried look on his face.

"We don't know what lies ahead. As soon as we reached Baguio, we'll find out," Benjamin said.

They finished their breakfast in a solemn mood.

The day seemed too long. Benjamin was selling at the town market with Delfin. He reduced his prices to rock bottom. He sold everything he had and then helped his other brothers sell their wares. Delfin still had five blankets left when they decided to call it quits near the end of the day.

"What am I supposed to do with these?" Delfin asked Benjamin.

Benjamin replied, "Don't worry. It might come in handy on the way home."

"Are you sure?" Delfin asked, doubt etched all over his face.

"Yes. I'm sure. We can probably sell them in Manila when we get there," Benjamin said and patted Delfin on the shoulder to assure him, trying to sound as optimistic as he could. Inwardly, he had doubt that they would even make it to Manila.

While Benjamin was wondering if they would ever make it back to Batangas, Adelaide, some 465 kilometers from Mankayan was wondering if Benjamin was still alive or gotten shot or even killed by the Japanese. She was worried sick and could not sleep at night. She prayed that he was safe and would be able to return back to Batangas. She did not know how but she fervently hoped that he would return. She knew he would find a way to come home. She hoped she was right but she was scared. For the first time, she realized that she really cared for him. She hoped and prayed that he was still alive. "Dear Lord, protect him always."

Back in Mankayan, Benjamin helped Delfin pack all the unsold blankets and then they headed back to the farmhouse.

The road from the market to the farmhouse was crowded with people. It was mid afternoon. They decided to close early. There were times when they closed at six o'clock but today they wanted to go home early so they could get ready for the big trip tomorrow. They put the store in order and locked up. As Benjamin was locking up, his throat tightened up. He had a feeling this would be the last time he would be here. He was not so sure they would make it home. He said a silent prayer, made the sign of the cross and pulled the door shut.

By six o'clock that afternoon, they were all sitting for their last supper in Mankayan. They were all worried on what would happen next. They discussed what route they should take to minimize the dangers they were going to encounter on the way south.

Ramon said, "We should try to avoid the main road if possible. It will be tough getting out of the Mountain Provinces because of the treacherous road. Hopefully, we can get some transportation. If not, you know this area pretty well. I have this map and we can probably go through some of the valleys. Baguio might be a little rough because of the bombing at Camp John Hay. We should stay west of it and try not to get near the place."

"Can we hire a bus or a caretela? It would be a lot easier," Manuel asked.

"I doubt if there is any available," Elias voiced an opinion.

"Remember, there is a war going on. Nothing will be easy anymore. We'll be lucky if we even make it to Manila," Benjamin said to everyone's dismay.

"Don't say that," Manuel interrupted.

"I'm being serious. The Japanese are landing everywhere. We can be surrounded from every direction. The Philippines have beaches everywhere. General MacArthur cannot possibly guard all the beaches. I don't think he has enough men to do that. Even with all the Philippine Scouts joining his forces, it is an impossible task," Benjamin said.

"Benjamin is right. It will be a very dangerous journey. We don't know what lies ahead. But we shall not panic. There is strength in numbers. There are seven of us. If everybody cooperates, we will be able to make it," Ramon said.

"We should get to the bus depot as early as we can tomorrow," said Delfin.

"Yes, we have to wake up really early tomorrow and be ready after breakfast. We might have to walk to the nearest town because no transportation will be available here at that hour. Hopefully we can get some transport at the next town," Benjamin said.

"I'm sure we are not the only ones leaving in a hurry," Manuel said.

"What if we lose each other?" Felipe asked with a concerned look on his face.

Ramon answered, "One cardinal rule: We should stay together at all times. So no wandering around."

"And you, Francisco," looking directly at his brother with a stern face. Ramon knew his brother, Francisco who loved to play games all the time.

"What?" Francisco asked. He suspected what was coming.

"If you get out of our sight, you will be on your own. We cannot waste time looking for a lost person. This is a very serious matter, understand?"

"Yes," Francisco answered solemnly.

"Do I get everyone's agreement?" Ramon asked the group.

"Yes," was the resounding answer from everyone.

They finished their meal of *morcon* and p*ancit*. Morcon is a beef dish marinated in lemon juice and soy sauce, prepared with pork sausage, hard boiled eggs, carrots, bacon and pickle all rolled and tied with a string, dredged in flour then browned in hot cooking oil and then simmer in beef broth till the beef is tender. They also had pancit, a favorite noodle dish. It was a hearty meal for their last night in Mankayan, a Bon Voyage kind of celebration.

"That was delicious. Compliments to the cook," Ramon said.

"Wait till you see the dessert." Francisco got up and went to a table in the entrance hall. He came back to the kitchen with a package wrapped in banana leaves.

"So do you want the *kalamay,* (rice dessert) that I bought?" Francisco, the cook today asked. Without waiting for an answer, he opened the package. Kalamay is a sweet, chewy and nutty rice cake, golden brown in color, usually eaten as a dessert or a snack.

"Of course, we want some," Ramon said and got up to give Francisco a helping hand serving the kalamay.

"They look delicious." Delfin began eating.

Everybody ate their dessert with gusto as if that was the last food they would have. In essence, that was the only decent meal they were going to have for the next few days.

They packed few clothes to take with them tomorrow before going to bed. They went to bed earlier than usual and slept like the dead. They were mentally exhausted and needed the rest. They would be on the road all day and possibly most of the night starting tomorrow. They did not know the Japanese troops had already landed that day and were on their way inland.

# CHAPTER 9

On Thursday morning, Dec. 11, 1941, as General Homma's men made unopposed landings at three locations around Luzon – at Legaspi in southeast Luzon, at Aparri in northern Luzon and at Vigan in northwest Luzon, Benjamin and his group woke up very early and finished packing their bags in total silence in preparation for their long journey. They did not know that the Japanese were really closing in on both ends of the northern part of Luzon. They sat and waited for Mang Sylvestre in great anticipation. Everyone was full of anxiety and hoping the war had not reached the mountains. Little did they know that the Japanese were approaching inland from the beaches.

Mang Sylvestre was running a little late and everyone was getting nervous. Manuel was fidgeting and pacing the kitchen back and forth.

"What is holding him up?" Manuel asked.

"How would I know?" Benjamin answered.

Ramon tried to calm everybody. "Relax, he will be here soon," he said.

"I don't like it. He is usually on time. Now that we need him, he is late," said Manuel.

"Maybe because we woke up too early, it seems that he is late. Usually we have our bread here when we wake up," Felipe reasoned out.

"You're absolutely right." Ramon nodded in agreement.

"Why don't you have another cup of coffee while we wait?" Delfin, the cook today suggested.

"Good idea," Benjamin said and stood up aiming towards the stove. He was just getting back to the table when he heard the hooves of the horse.

"Benjamin, your friend is here. Hurry and get our breakfast. I am starving," Francisco said.

It was still dark outside and a little chill was in the air so Benjamin got his sweater, headed out the door and went out to see his friend.

"Sorry for being late. The last customer kept on talking. I could not get away without being rude." Mang Sylvestre apologized.

"It's OK," Benjamin replied. "Is there any new development?"

"The Japanese bombed Cavite." Cavite, the single most important naval station in the Philippines, lies on the south shore of Manila Bay.

"O my God! That is too close to where we are going."

"I know. That's another reason for you guys to get going. I hate to see you go but I'm sure you all want to go home."

Mang Sylvestre handed Benjamin his usual order and Benjamin paid him. He now felt the urgency to leave.

Benjamin told him, "We have decided to leave today before things get worse."

Mang Sylvestre looked sad and started filling two more bags with pandesal and boniti.

Mang Sylvestre got off the caretela and handed the extra two bags to Benjamin. He said, "Take these bags of bread as your going away present. There should be enough for you, your brothers and cousins to make it to Baguio. I hope you will be able to get some transportation there to get home."

"*Salamat po.*" Thank you, Benjamin said.

"I hope I'll see you again someday." He gave Benjamin a big hug. Then they shook hands and he blessed Benjamin. Benjamin was trying very hard to hold back his tears.

"*Adios!*" Godspeed, Mang Sylvestre said. There was a sense of a final goodbye in his voice.

He got back in his caretela, waved goodbye and then reined his horse. Benjamin stood transfixed watching Mang Sylvestre as he disappeared in sight around the bend. He had tears in his eyes. He would never forget his sad face. Benjamin knew Mang Sylvestre for several years now since Benjamin had been coming to this part of the country. Benjamin had been a generous customer to him. Benjamin thought of him as part of his family. With heavy heart Benjamin wiped the tears from his eyes and walked back slowly to the farmhouse.

Benjamin placed the bags of bread on the table. Delfin asked, "How come you have three bags of bread?"

"Two of them are presents from Mang Sylvestre. He wants us to bring them on our journey so we don't starve along the way."

"He is such a nice fellow," Delfin said.

"We will miss him tremendously. Hope we see him again when the war is over," Ramon said.

"You should see his face when we said goodbye. He looked so sad. I felt for him and I wished him well too." Benjamin turned around trying to hide the tears that he was holding back.

"We don't know what the future holds. We can only hope for the best," Elias said.

Everyone nodded their head and started eating in silence. Then Delfin got up from his chair and turned on the radio to hear the latest development.

The radio blurted out, *"The U.S. naval yard at Cavite and the township of Cavite were bombed by eighty Mitsubishis and fifty-two Zeros yesterday. Thousands were killed and hundreds were injured. Smoke, fire and flames were visible all the way to Manila along Dewey Boulevard. The wounded were being taken to Dewey Boulevard by boat across the bay to a triage by the yacht harbor before being transported to Philippine General Hospital on Taft Avenue."*

"No. It can't be," Francisco said.

"O my God!" Manuel exclaimed.

They looked at each other and saw grief and panic written all over their faces. As soon as they heard the news that Cavite, which is only 13 kilometers southwest of Manila was attacked, they began to hurry with their breakfast.

Ramon said, "So, what will happen next? Those damned Japanese are coming in full force. If you are about ready, we should be leaving any minute."

Benjamin said, "Let's go before it's too late."

They gulped the last drop of coffee from their cups. Delfin rinsed their cups, then went around the kitchen to make sure everything was all right. Ramon checked that everything was in order in the house, then they all gathered their belongings, made the sign of the cross, locked up and off they went.

They started the first leg of their journey south. It was a long way home. It was still dark and very early in the morning. They had a small flashlight to help them see the road. The sun had not come up yet. They followed a narrow road. The fog was dense and floating low and the air was chilly as they descended into the valley. It was eerily quiet on the road. There was nobody in sight except the seven of them. The only sound they heard was their own footsteps. Occasionally, they heard the hoot of the owls. They walked in silence, almost fearful to make any noise as if they would wake up the spirits and lead them astray.

Between the seven of them, the four older brothers, two cousins and Benjamin, they each had a bag which contained some bread and some clothing: underwear, shirts, pants, jacket and a mat to sleep on. Delfin got that extra five unsold blankets. They had plenty of cash tucked away, some inside their socks and some underneath their panama hat.

The temperature was cool, it was 16°C (61°F). They wore a light sweater with their hats on. They also needed the hats for later in case no transportation was available and they had to walk under the hot, bright sun through dirt roads and pathways. It was not bad when they started because they were walking through the valleys. They were used to walking because that was what they did all day. They were all peddling merchants. They were all in their twenties except for Ramon, their eldest brother who was thirty-one, all in good health and physically fit. As a matter of fact, Benjamin was the youngest in the group, short of a month before his 22nd birthday. Manuel was quite withdrawn. He was the second eldest and always very quiet. He felt his opinion was never counted for anything anyway so he just kept his mouth shut except for few comments which he ventured here and there. He was also the worrier. Ramon always made the decision since he was the eldest. Usually, he asked for Benjamin's opinions and advice. He thought Benjamin was more level headed than the other brothers in spite of his age. Francisco was the comic of the bunch. He was always telling jokes. Sometimes he would tell them crazy stories that he made up himself.

The fog was filling the streets with its thick, gray, rolling mists as they walked several kilometers before they reached the next town. They went to the bus depot. The bus depot was just opening up. There was no one in front of the building. It was still too early. Then Ramon saw a man open the counter. The man was shuffling paper inside the counter. Ramon waited a while. Then the man looked up and saw Ramon. Ramon went straight to him.

"Good Morning. You're early. What can I do for you?" The man asked Ramon.

Ramon took out his wallet and asked if he could buy some tickets to go to Baguio.

"I would like tickets for 7 to go to Baguio," Ramon told the man.

"I'm sorry, no bus is going to Baguio," the man said.

"Are there buses going south to another town?" Ramon asked. "We would like to take any bus going south," he added.

"No bus is running today. Bus service is suspended until further notice," the clerk told him.

Benjamin heard the conversation and joined in. "What do you mean no bus is running?"

"Sorry sir but that is the instruction I was told to give. You know, the war is going on now and there was bombing in Baguio and it is now in a state of chaos. Nobody in their right mind wants to go there. They are scared. They are all leaving Baguio. I can't blame them."

At that remark, Benjamin's heart sank. All he could think was how in the world could they go home if there were no buses to transport them. It seemed an impossible task. He looked at his companions and he saw the depressed look on their faces. They heard everything the clerk was saying and they were worried.

"I know you might think we are crazy. But you see, we want to go home. Our home is in Batangas. We belong with our family, not here." Benjamin tried to explain.

"I'm sorry sir. I can't help you," the clerk said.

Then Benjamin decided to try something else. He then asked, "Do you know anyone who might be willing to take us south to at least Tarlac? We'll pay him good money."

"Sorry sir but I do not know of anyone wanting to go anywhere beyond the city limit? It's very dangerous and nobody wants to get stranded. They are afraid they may not be able to get back," the clerk retorted.

"Even if we pay him good money?" Ramon added.

"Even if you pay him good money," the man at the counter repeated. "No sir. They are afraid."

"I do understand. Thank you anyway," Benjamin said in resignation.

Benjamin turned around and looked at his companions and asked, "What are we going to do now?" They all looked so downtrodden.

Ramon replied, "Let's just move on instead of wasting time looking for some kind of transportation. We might be lucky and find something along the way. Who knows?"

Having no other choice, the group picked up their belongings, turned around and headed out back to the road on foot.

December mornings in the mountains were mighty cold. With nowhere else to go, all the cold air in the mountains gathered at the bottom of the valley and numbed and froze the extremities of any traveler who might happen along. For a brief moment, though, it was also beautiful. As the first rays of the morning sun touch the high cliffs of the Mountain Province, the golden rays and the gentle light flooded the curves and folds of the hills below.

It was beginning to get light out. Dawn had finally arrived. They saw lots of out-of-towners who were in the same predicament as they were. These people also decided to leave town and head for home wherever it might be for fear that the war could escalate and they might be caught in the crossfire in a strange town. There was an exodus of people with their belongings, piling up on the street going in different directions. People were saying the Japanese were landing everywhere. They had not reached this far inland yet but they were getting closer. Still, things were pretty calm in this area.

The only area affected here in the Mountain Provinces was Camp John Hay which was in Baguio. There was a minor bombing there on December 8. Aside from that air assault, the Japanese had not penetrated the mountains. They were landing on the beaches. It would take them awhile to make it to the mountains.

And so their journey began through the mountains and valleys, always starting before dawn around 5 A.M. till their legs gave out at night around 9 P.M. They would sleep in the nearest municipal building. They would walk through villages with their thatched huts between the grand mountains of Cordillera Central in the Mountain Provinces. Most houses here were built of reeds and wood on tall stilts. The countryside around the villages was of such remarkable beauty, that one wanted to take it all in and remember it forever. With the breathtaking views from the top of the mountains all around them, it was almost a pleasant walk except for the ever nagging thought of danger looming ahead. They were passing along a winding road with a precipitous drop on the edge of the mountain. Deep ravines and cliffs are everywhere but the views from up on the mountains were magnificent. They mostly stayed on the inner side of the road. Walking down the mountain was a lot different than driving down. Nothing could compare with the beauty of the surroundings when you are taking in the scenery slowly, not like when you were in a bus when you viewed it, passed and disappeared instantly. While walking you saw the people up close and the carabaos moving up and down the hills. You appreciated the beauty of nature and it was so refreshing to your well-being.

Aside from the merchandise that Delfin had which slowed them down a bit, they did not have much weight to carry. There were only a few things in their bags. Benjamin, Ramon, Manuel, and Francisco had a satchel bag hooked to a bamboo pole that was slung on their shoulder. Delfin had his clothes in a satchel bag slung on one shoulder and his merchandise wrapped in a heavy blanket with four corners of the blanket tied in a bundle, papoose style and he carried this bundle on his other shoulder. He was using his bamboo pole as a walking stick. Elias and Felipe had their stuff also wrapped in a heavy blanket with four corners tied in a bundle, same as Delfin but hooked to a pole and slung on their shoulder. Each of them found their own way of carrying their stuff which was comfortable to them and to their liking. Also, the bamboo pole could be used as a walking stick if needed. They covered a lot of ground the first day.

They passed some rice terraces in some areas, though small they were still magnificent. There were rivers that supplied water to the rice paddies and vegetable farms. There were times when they were the only ones around climbing up and down the mountain. Delfin who loved to sing would sometime belt out an emotional ballad to break up the monotony. He had a nice deep baritone voice and it warmed their hearts and let them forgot the impending dangers that lie ahead. Delfin encouraged the group to join him and they would do a sing-a-long.

*"Negritos of the mountains*
*What kind of food do you eat?*
*What kind of food do you eat?*
*Negritos of the mountains.*

*"The people of the mountains*
*What kind of food do you eat?*
*What kind of food do you eat?*
*The people of the mountains."*

When the war broke on Dec. 8, all Filipino men 18 years of age were ordered to enlist. Batangas Transportation Company (BTCo) buses were appropriated to transport the Philippine soldiers to army bases. From the enlisting station in Batangas, the new recruits were transported for training through two different routes - one through Sambat, Bauan and one through San Jose.

Soon the troops started marching toward the north. At times, the troops went by Adelaide's house and down the dirt road and the dust they raised settled down around the yard and the house. The leaves of the trees and shrubs turned white with dust. Sometimes, Japanese planes would start coming in and could now be heard and seen coming in V-formation. Whenever the troops heard the roaring planes coming through, they hurriedly got off the buses and ran for cover. Once they stopped at Adelaide's house and ran for cover under Adelaide's house until the planes passed by. Those marching on foot, all ducked down under the trees by the roadside and some ran under the houses till the noise died down and then they continued their march.

While Benjamin was traveling down through Benguet province on his way home, the Japanese started bombing the gas depots in Batangas in the southern part of Luzon on Dec. 12 and the Batangas Transportation Company in Batangas known prominently in Batangas as BTCO. They were targeting some gas depots but most of the bombs were missing their target and were just hitting the street. People started to evacuate to Bauan. There was an exodus of people going into the farms close to Bauan. Adelaide's relatives in Batangas started arriving at her home in Sambat.

Since Adelaide's home was on high ground, Adelaide could watch the bombing from her back porch. She could see the Japanese planes coming in from the north in a V formation and she could see the explosion from her vantage point. She did not know about the perils of war and was so thrilled watching the scenery. She saw some awesome dogfights like she was watching a movie. When she found out what it was all about, she really got scared.

There were bombings for two days. Loud explosion could be heard coming from Batangas and then rumors spread that the Japanese had landed in Batangas Bay and moving inland. The Philippine scout rangers began to retreat and started marching toward Manila. Some of the townspeople started hiding mostly on the farms. Those who stayed behind built a dugout in their backyard where they could hide. Adelaide's brothers did the same and built a dugout in the backyard. It was a big hole and they put a roof on it made of planks of wood with leaves of several plants on top of it. Every time, there was an air raid, they ran and went into the dugout and waited until they heard everything was clear. On one of these raids, one of Adelaide's uncles who lived in a nearby town ran to their dugout but unhappily, a bomb dropped nearby and he and his family all got killed. After hearing that, Adelaide refused to go into the dugout for fear that she might get killed too. She thought of Benjamin and wondered if he was hiding in a dugout. He heard Baguio was bombed a few days ago and wondered if Benjamin was still alive or possibly got killed there. With communication cut off, she wondered if she would ever hear from him again.

Up north, Benjamin was on the second day of their journey. They reached Kabayan, an old vegetable farming town in Benguet province, in a wide valley surrounded by mountains and lakes. Kabayan was a friendly rural community located about 80 kilometers north of Baguio.

As they were gathered together for supper at one of the eateries in town, they realized that some of them had not really been to Kabayan although they had heard a lot of interesting stories about the town. They passed the town on their way to Mankayan but never stopped too long or stayed there. They sat at a table near the back of the eatery. Next to them was a table with two men deep in conversation. One of them was the owner of the eatery and much older than the other fellow. The owner saw them, stood up and greeted the group.

"How are you guys? What brought you here? You look like you are going somewhere. Are you?" The owner asked.

"Yes, we are. We are escaping from the Japanese. We are heading south but for lack of transportation, we are walking," Ramon said.

"Where are you walking to?"

"Batangas."

"Batangas?" The owner could not believe what he heard. "That's at the other end of Luzon."

"Yes sir. It's a distance."

"Hope you have good legs and bless you all. You need lots of nourishment." He went to the kitchen and brought some lechon and few beers and sat with the group. A waitress was right behind him with a big bowl of rice. She left the rice in the middle of the table and went back out.

"Thank you," Benjamin said.

"Eat, eat," The owner said.

As they began to pick on the lechon, Elias said suddenly, "I heard there are preserved bodies found in several caves in this town."

"There is a word for it. Do you know what they call them?" Felipe asked Ramon who was seated next to him.

"Nannies I think, not sure of it. Ask Delfin or maybe Benjamin," Ramon said.

"Benjamin, what do they call those preserved bodies buried in the caves?" Felipe asked Benjamin.

"Mummies," Benjamin said without batting an eyelash.

Isidro, the owner of the eatery looked at Benjamin and said, "He is right."

"Yes, that's it. Mummies, not Nannies," Ramon confirmed. Everyone laughed.

Isidro added, "Kabayan was renowned for its antiquated centuries-old mummies. Kabayan was recognized as the center of *Ibaloi* culture and out of several tribes in this area, the Ibaloi are the only people to practice mummification as a way of preserving their dead. They were made by members of the Ibaloi tribe hence called Ibaloi mummies or Kabayan mummies."

"Where are they located?" Elias asked looking very interested.

"They could be found in a network of mostly unprotected caves that were part of the Cordillera mountain range. They were either on the cliffside near the entrance to man-made caves or inside caves scattered around the villages."

Years later, these same caves containing the mummies will be designated as one of the 100 Most Endangered Sites in the world by Monument Watch, a non-profit organization dedicated to the preservation of important monuments and sites.

Isidro continued, "Well-preserved human mummies were initially found in Timbak cave, Bangao cave, Tenongchol cave, Naapay and Opdas. However, when the mummies were rediscovered in the early 1900s, many were stolen and later on even the 'smiling mummy' disappeared. It was known to have an intact set of teeth."

"How long have they been around?" Felipe asked curiously.

"They have existed for centuries even before the Spaniards came. Some believe that the mummies were created by the Ibaloi between 1200 and 1500 A.D. in the Benguet province of the Philippines and buried in caves. Others believe that the mummification practices date to 2000 B.C."

When the Spanish colonized the Philippines in the 1500s, they discouraged the making of mummies and the practice discontinued. Mummification is part of the Ibaloi tribe culture. They are a natural treasure and should be protected. Under Presidential Decree No. 374, the Kabayan Mummies were proclaimed "Philippine National Cultural Treasures" which mandates their protection. The National Museum of the Philippines is conducting a comprehensive survey and documentation of around 50 caves around Kabayan. Research and studies on the preservation and development of the mummy sites is also being undertaken by the conservators of the National Museum of the Philippines.

"Did everyone have to be mummified? Is that the right word?" Benjamin found this conversation intriguing and wanted to learn more about it.

"No. Not everyone was mummified. Mostly those in the higher social classes or tribal leaders were. You have to remember, mummification was not practiced anywhere else except in this region. Unlike the mummies of Ancient Egypt where they were wrapped in cloth, mummies here were naked with various tattoo marks still visible on their leathery skin and were in a fetal position. It appears that only tribal leaders were mummified, though this theory may change with more discoveries."

"Why is that? I mean why not everyone?" Elias wanted to know.

"It was a long ritual and the body could be sun-dried or smoked for 60 days or more. The wealthy people sometimes did it for as long as two years. The process could begin even when the person was not dead yet."

"O my Lord. That was crazy," Felipe said in horror.

"That was macabre!" Manuel joined in the conversation.

"When a person was about to die, he was given a salty drink," Isidro said.

"Then what?" Manuel asked.

"The mummification was begun, if possible, shortly before a person died," Isidro continued. "The person swallowed a very salty drink to start the process. Then, after death, the deceased was immediately washed and strapped in a sitting position to a wooden chair called *sangadil* or chair of death that was set over a glowing fire."

"That was horrible!" Delfin exclaimed.

"So that's why they were all in a seated position. If they were sitting on fire, they could be burned into ashes. Why were they not? I don't get it," Felipe asked.

Isidro answered, "The purpose was not to burn the body but to dry or drain the fluids by exposing it to external heat. Tobacco smoke was then blown into the person's mouth to dry the inside of the body and internal organs."

"That's disgusting," Manuel said. He got up. "I think I'm about to puke."

Isidro continued now that he noticed he had a captive audience. "Finally, the body was treated with indigenous herbs and oils. The drying/smoking process would have lasted many weeks and perhaps a number of months before the mummy was finished. Then the mummified body was placed in a capsule-shaped coffin carved from tree trunks and taken to a cave in high cliffs or in a niche from solid rock for burial." He paused.

"Then what?" Benjamin asked trying to figure things out.

Isidro swallowed, took a drink of water, then continued, "Complex rituals and animal sacrifices were practiced during curing and burial and the meat from the animal sacrifices passed to the entire assemblage. The officiating Benguet tribal priest called *mambunong* said the incantation to the creator, Kabunyian and to a folklore hero, Lumawig."

"All these rituals, are they really necessary?" Felipe asked.

"They have a very strong belief in these rituals. Look what happened when the mummified body of Apo Anno was stolen." The mummified body of Apo Anno, a tribal leader in the Benguet province, is a declared national treasure of the Philippines. The National Museum of the Philippines recently returned the mummified and intricately tattooed body of *Apo Anno* who died more than 500 years ago.

"Who is Apo Anno? What happened to him?" Ramon asked.

"Apo Anno was a descendant of a 12th century *Kankanaey* hunter who lived to a ripe old age of 250 years old."

"Wow! That's old." Delfin whistled.

Isidro continued, "Kankanaey is another tribe of Benguet and Apo Anno was the half mortal son of a goddess. His mummified body was dressed in his tribal chief attire before he was placed in a wooden coffin inside his burial cave. He was heavily tattooed, the mark of a hunter and warrior. He was covered with dried flesh, brownish color in a sitting position with arms held up to his face like a man praying to the heavens. There was an interesting legend about him."

"Go on." Delfin egged him on.

"Upon his death, his body was mummified by the Kankanaeys and buried beneath a rocky mountainside in Nabalicong, Benguet. There it rested in complete silence and solitude for 600 years until his mummified body had been stolen by a grave robber between 1918 and 1920. His mummified body's whereabouts remained unknown for several years. From the time it disappeared, tragedy struck."

Isidro paused. Francisco who was so quiet finally asked, "Did they ever find the mummified body at all? Maybe if they found the body, it would bring good luck."

"His mummified body briefly appeared in a carnival in Manila in 1922 and for some reason coincidentally or not, brought a heavy downpour in Manila. It wound up as part of a sideshow in a Manila circus and changed hands a number of times. Then, it disappeared again."

In 1984, a mummy appeared in an antique shop and a mambunong identified it to be Apo Anno. Eventually an antique collector donated it to the National Museum. After it was returned to the town in May 1999, it was given a reburial ritual and a grand feast that lasted for three days. At the end of the feast, a rainbow suddenly appeared in the sky as if to symbolize Apo Anno's triumphant return.)

"You said tragedy struck. What kind of tragedy?" Delfin was curious.

"From then on, the displeased spirit wreaked havoc. Heavy rains and landslides devastated the area. Some residents of the area believe that the region has been cursed by droughts, earthquakes, and famine since the mummy of Apo Anno was looted."

"That's incredible," Benjamin said.

"I wish we could visit some of the caves. If I had known about it before, I would have made a special trip here. Now, it is too late." Felipe sighed.

"I wish I'd known this before also. I would have made the trip too," Elias said.

"Yes, it is too late indeed," Ramon agreed.

Isidro stood up and everyone thanked him for the information. "So where to after today?" Isidro asked Ramon. Manuel just came back to the table.

"Tomorrow we're going straight toward Baguio and see if we can get a transport to Batangas. It's very worrisome."

"I hope you find some transportation. Next time you come up after the war if we all survive it, come and visit us and see the mummies."

"We will and thank you very much."

"Adios."

As they were leaving the eatery, Ramon said to no one in particular, "I wonder how far the Japanese are making inroads."

"If they are bombing left and right, they must have plenty of men fighting everywhere. We'll be in big trouble," Benjamin said matter-of-factly.

"I hope not," Delfin said.

"So do I," Ramon echoed his sentiment.

They stayed overnight at an elementary school in Kabayan. The next day, they started their journey just as the sun was rising over the mountain. With the fog so thick around them, there was a silvery pink glow to the sun rise. From Kabayan, Benjamin and his group followed a spectacular road to Baguio, about 82 kilometers long, crossing the Agno River along mountain edges with heavy vegetation. It was the most scenic areas of the Cordillera Mountains. As they descended the mountain into the Agno River Valley, there was the spectacular view of the Cordillera Mountain Ranges along the way.

From the distance they could see Mt. Pulog, the tallest mountain on Luzon, towering at 2,928 meters, (9,606 feet), located on the territorial boundary of the town. It is the second highest in the Philippines after Mt. Apo in Mindanao and considered the playground of the gods. To the south of the Cordillera Central in Nueva Vizcaya lies another mountain range, the Caraballo Mountains. Mt. Pulog was covered with pines at the mountain base and oaks at the higher altitude with an understory of ferns and moss. The fog that covered the mountains most of the time helped the moss to thrive there luxuriously. Alpines and bamboos dominated the summit and they thinned out at the peak giving Pulog its name meaning "bald".

The Cordilleras were inhabited by people collectively called the Igorots and for centuries had a different culture from the lowlanders. They had lived in much the same way as they did thousands of years ago. Though they lived in a cold region, they did not wear many clothes. Their only garment for men was usually a brief loincloth called G-string made of finely hand-woven cotton, decorated with colorful designs. The women wore nothing from the waist up with arms tattooed. The Igorots built the spectacular rice terraces at Banaue some 3,000 years ago. The rice terraces cover more than 260 square kilometers or about 22,000 kilometers of steep mountainsides and rise up to over 1500 meters. Carved from the steep hillsides, these rice terraces rise up like broad magnificent staircases to heaven.

Just before they reached Baguio located on the summit of Cordillera Central, they passed the farming suburb of La Trinidad in a valley which produced fruits and vegetables for the Philippine market. There were acres and acres of strawberry fields. *Bitsuelas*

(Baguio beans) could only be grown in that region since it thrived on cool weather.

La Trinidad was a big wealthy residential community. It is six kilometers north of Baguio and 100 meters lower. It lies in a fertile basin called the "salad bowl of the Philippines" whose temperate climate makes it the vegetable center of Luzon. Most of the farms were owned and operated by the Japanese. It was interesting to note that there were lots of Japanese laborers working in the vegetable farms in La Trinidad. Were they spies for the Japanese Imperial Army? One could only surmise they were.

It was now Dec. 15, 1941. The first four days were a little tough. They walked up through a winding road with panoramic views in all directions before they approached Baguio. In the distance they could see the oak forest. In the foreground everything was so green and pastoral. One could never be too sure when you walked through this winding road. Landslides could occur without any warning. They had to be very careful and alert at all times. Every 10 kilometers there was a gate and they had to stop. The road was so narrow they only allowed one car and a few pedestrians through at a time. The gatekeeper would call the next gate and if they have cars there, the other end stopped until the cars from the other gate passed and vice versa. That delayed the trip. As they were climbing up the mountain, the fog began to thin out. The view from the mountaintop was awesome. You could see the villages down below and the surrounding countryside was so verdant. They heard the birds singing early in their morning walk. The dew dripping from the branches of the trees glistened as it caught the morning light. They looked like thousands of pearly jewels dangling high up in the trees. Watching the beautiful scenery around them, you would never know they were in the midst of a war. There was so much beauty in nature around there, you began to wonder why they were leaving it. They must be crazy to go home at this time but home was where they belonged at this time of turmoil and it beckoned them to go back.

By this time, the Japanese forces were everywhere on Philippine soil. They were mostly near the coastline but they were marching inland. Benjamin and his group were still deep in the mountain region. They were going through scenic roads with extensive forests and mountain life all around them. The road curved among precipitous hillsides with intermittent wide open spaces where they rested for a few minutes and admired the surrounding high mountains. Oftentimes, they would walk under the canopy of trees to conserve their energy from the blazing sun. Lucky for them the air there was cool so they did not tire so easily.

# CHAPTER 10

On December 17, 1941, they reached Baguio from Mankayan walking for six days following the route they took slowly but with determination. Baguio is a lovely town nestled aloft a high plateau with old Spanish houses and parks with a profusion of flowers on a pine-clad mountain. Baguio is located in the southern part of the Province of Benguet with an area of 49 square kilometers and an elevation of 1,524 meters (4,920 feet) above sea level and approximately 160 miles (260 kilometers) from Manila. They still have a long way to go.

The province of Benguet (2,592 square kilometers) where Baguio was located was the gateway to the Cordilleras, the most spectacularly scenic area of the Philippines and had the well-preserved culture of the mountain people. There were a scattering of caves and caverns sheltering burial sites of Benguet mummies. Benguet was blessed with the wonderful beauty of nature – rugged but majestic mountain peaks dissected by numerous valleys, towering pines, cool mountain air, glorious flowers, great rivers, brooks and streams, breathtaking waterfalls and lakes, wonderful hot springs and rich and fertile land. Underneath this green and verdant landscape, the land is rich in mineral deposits. Mining is an industry that traces its roots to prehistoric times. The mountain people only panned and mined gold and copper that they needed and decided the gold was safer in the ground than in their huts.

They fiercely defended their territory and resisted all attempts at colonization or Christianization for 200 years. They were great craftpeople – weavers, woodcarvers, furniture makers and with the abundance of raw materials, they could practice their crafts skillfully and beautifully. The various tribes that lived in the mountains were beautiful and kind people that had great concern for its people to preserve their culture.

Baguio was called the summer capital of the Philippines because of its pleasantly cool weather, beautiful scenery with parks and gardens, where the President's summer mansion and Camp John Hay were located and the home of the Philippine Military Academy. The parks and gardens were laid out by one of the best American landscape architects, Daniel Hudson Burnham who also designed the original plan for Baguio City. Daniel Hudson Burnham (1846-1912) was one of Chicago's greatest architects and urban planner who also designed Dewey Boulevard (now Roxas Boulevard) in Manila. Baguio is also the home of the Igorots, the world renowned woodcarvers. Baguio was an important gold mining town and people there were mostly prosperous except the native *Aetas* and the *Igorot* tribes.

The Aetas, otherwise known as Pygmies, Negritos or Balugas and the Igorot tribes still maintained their primitive habits. They lived off the land and women wove strong colorful fabric. Their houses were made of grass and wood structures on tall stilts. They were the aboriginal inhabitants of the country with black complexion and stand only four-foot five to four-foot eight. They basically lived off the land. They had their own dialects, special type of housing and clothing. Men only wore G-string clothes and women wore skirts with no tops. Before the Spaniards ruled the country, they were notorious for being headhunters and warriors. They believed in spirits and practiced ancient rituals to honor their dead.

Baguio was home to the Philippine Military Academy, the elite military academy, affectionately known as the West Point of the Philippines. Camp John Hay, surrounded by tall pines, was a vacation spot for American officials and officers. It was bombed by the Japanese the same day as Pearl Harbor.

To the northeast of Camp John Hay was Wright Park where The Mansion, the summer home of the Philippines President was located. It was built for the U.S. Governors-General in 1908. Its main gate is a replica of the gate at Buckingham Palace.

When Benjamin and his group arrived in Baguio, the whole town was in a state of turmoil. Emergency personnel were everywhere. Army trucks were cruising in every direction. Several people were trying to leave the city. Everybody was on the alert for fear that another bombing might take place. Benjamin and his group stayed overnight at the outskirts of Baguio in a nondescript Rest House. Still, the view from the mountaintop was fantastic. Looking down from the mountain to the valley below was a breathtaking experience. Everything was lush and green.

After dinner and a cup of hot salabat (ginger tea), Benjamin felt less tense. He managed to go outside the Rest House and just wandered around the vicinity. He did not want to go too far from the Rest House. There was a curfew going on. The air was cool. He could smell the scent of pine wafting in the air around him. At this time of the year, temperature could average at 18.3°C (65°F). Luckily, he was still wearing his jacket so he felt comfortable. At the far end of the courtyard, he found a bench and sat down. All around him are thickets of trees with an understory of shrubs covered with blooms and fragrance of kalachuchi. Kalachuchi, (frangipani) is related to Oleander *Nerium oleander* and both possess an irritating, milky sap, rather similar to that of Euphorbia. It always reminded him of Adelaide because she had a big shrub which had grown into a huge kalachuchi tree next to her house.

Benjamin remembered asking her what plant that was and she answered, "It is called kalachuchi. Its flowers are very fragrant at night in order to lure the moths to pollinate them."

"How do they do that? I understand they have no nectar," Benjamin asked curiously.

"Someone told me the moths pollinate them by transferring pollen from flower to flower in their fruitless search for nectar."

"How interesting!"

"But you have to be careful when gathering the flowers."

"Why?"

"The flowers ooze some sap and it can irritate your eyes and skin."

"It is so pretty though and I bet some people do not even care about that."

Sitting here and seeing the frangipani and smelling its fragrance which was intoxicating gave Benjamin a sense of peace and serenity. There were several orchid plants ranging in color from white, yellow, pink and magenta that were blooming in abundance.

"How I wish Adelaide was here next to me. How ironic it is. Here I am in this nice and peaceful place but somewhere out there a deadly war was looming on the horizon," Benjamin mumbled to himself.

"Why can't we keep everything the way it is? The frailties of men! The need to conquer!! Is there a sense to it?" Benjamin asked himself.

The flickering light of the fireflies took him to the day when he first set foot in this town. He really fell in love with Baguio with all its pine trees and the profusion of flowers, and the whole Mountain Province at large. It was love at first sight at that time. Here he had spent a beautiful and wonderful time of his life. "Someday I would love to share it with the woman that I love. Oh, how I miss Adelaide. I wonder how she is doing."

Often times, he traveled further north to Bontoc and Banaue. Bontoc was a large residential city and most of the rice terraces in Bontoc were owned by Filipino lowlanders but worked by Japanese workers. Most of the houses in Bontoc were of stone and/or grass walls with cogon grass roofs. Pigs live under the owner's house. Bontoc was nestled deep within a valley at the junction where two rivers form the mighty Chico. Bontoc had an Igorot mayor there who went to work in his office in American style clothing, suit and tie but once he got home switched to his traditional outfit of G-strings. From Bontoc, Benjamin would travel to Banaue across Mt. Polis range in a most spectacular, dizzying cliff hugging route through verdant canyons. It was magnificent to look out the window of the bus.

Once he reached Banaue, there was no better place to stay than at the Banaue Hotel, the most expensive and only real hotel with private balconies overlooking the beautiful rice terraces. From his balcony on the fifth floor, the view was awe-inspiring. The vista of the rice terraces undulating for miles and miles toward the horizon was just incredibly breathtaking. It was said that if the Banaue rice terraces were placed end-to-end, they would stretch more than half way round the globe.

The Ifugao built the spectacular rice terraces long before the arrival of the Spaniards with painstaking manual labor. They dug down to the bedrock, carried in stones and constructed walls to make the terraces permanent. The walls and the way the irrigation system channeled the water from the upper terraces to the lower terraces was a wonderment of engineering prowess. The verdant mountains around you, dotted with a scattering of *nipa* huts with coconut palms around them, the terraces with the rice paddies in abundance was a sight to behold. With the cool wind blowing and the rice stalks swaying with the wind, the clouds an azure blue in the sky and a darkest gray in the horizon, it felt like paradise.

The temperature in this area was cool and in December, the temperature was cooler in this part of the country going down to 10°C (50°F) sometimes. There was cold air and the breeze emitted the perfume of this tropical paradise. The smell of jasmine and several species of orchids that were indigenous in this area were wafting through the air. Benjamin loved that fragrance. That scent would always be imbedded in his subconscious mind.

The people here, even the tribal group were nice and gentle people. He remembered one instance while he was selling at Burnham Park. He and his buddy decided to see a movie. They just left their merchandise in an area of the park where they were selling. Three hours later, they came back. Nothing was stolen. The merchandise was all intact. The honesty and moral of the people were phenomenal. He could never forget that. It would be a perfect place to raise a family.

Adelaide! As Benjamin stared at the soft light dancing in front of him, he let his mind wander and thought of Adelaide. The vision that immediately came was always the same one: it was always the same vision that was planted forever in his memory, the first time he met her personally. When she walked in the living room of her house with her long black hair braided and wrapped around her face, the deep set black eyes and the dimples on her face, as he surreptitiously glanced at her, he felt a lump in his throat. She was wearing a simple cotton dress but with the sun shining brightly, the silhouette of her young body was outlined in that simple dress. His heart leaped a bit and he knew at that instance, he was falling in love with her already. Then when she tried hard to lie to him when he asked her about his picture on the wall and how she blushed when she found out that it was he who was in that picture and then tried to salvage her pride and was about to bolt out of the room and he tried to grab her arm, he knew he wanted to marry her. Now, he hoped someday he could come back to this place. He would like to settle down here in this lovely place with Adelaide. He wondered if she would like to live here. He never really asked her. He didn't even know how she felt about him.

"Oh, how I long to be with her, just to talk to her. I hope she is safe," Benjamin said to himself. At this point, he didn't even know if he would ever see her again. He was so far away and this journey was so unpredictable. God knows what would happen along the way.

The next morning, Benjamin and his group got up a little later than usual. It must be the mountain air or they were just plain exhausted from climbing up the mountains for the last six days but they slept soundly last night. They felt rested and ready to move on again. They had a hearty and leisurely breakfast. They had scrambled eggs, sausages and bowl of fruits – papaya, pineapples, bananas and oranges. Nobody seemed to be in a hurry to leave. They wanted to linger and savor the beauty of this place. They got the feeling they might not see it again.

The news from the radio was now saying that mass evacuation was undergoing on in Manila. Some were retreating to Tagaytay, other people were heading to the south. All the trains were now packed with people trying to leave the city. Hundreds of thousand Manilenos have left Manila. They heard that the port districts of Manila were attacked on Dec. 13 and again yesterday. Benjamin and his six relatives didn't linger much longer. They wanted to stay awhile, but time was of the essence and decided to get going. Even in this paradise of a place, they could feel the tension and anxiety of the people. They knew life would never be the same again.

They headed to Baguio City Market. It was a big place with all kinds of goods for sale. Underneath the tin roof were open spaces with several sections that sell rice, corn, eggs, honey, homemade jam and kalamay. Other sections sell fish and meat. They also offered fresh produce, all kinds of fruits and vegetables from the nearby La Trinidad Valley. There were clothes, shoes, bags, ethnic fabrics, fresh tobacco and flowers. You could also find brassware, silver jewelry, all types of handcrafts, baskets, woodcarvings, textiles, blankets and the renowned Baguio brooms made from a grass called *boyboy*. Strawberries were also plentiful at this time of the year so Benjamin and his group indulged themselves and bought some for the road.

There were *karinderias*, food stalls where you could buy inexpensive cooked food at a *turo-turo*. Literally, turo-turo means point, point. You just decide from the food displayed and point at what you want. They bought some rice and *menudo* to take out. The vendor wrapped them up in banana leaves and then in newspapers. They carried them in paper bags to eat later for lunch on the road.

The Baguio City Market was bustling with activity. It was very crowded. The place was packed with customers getting some provisions. The tribal people wearing their traditional tribal costume made from strong colorful cotton fibers and barks could be seen everywhere. There were lots of talks about the war. People looked worried.

Benjamin and his group decided to buy some provisions just to make sure they had enough food on the way to Tarlac. They would be passing small towns and supplies might not be plentiful. They never knew if they would even have any. The big city was usually the best place to get them. Outside the market, there were few caritelas around. Usually there were plenty of cars but none today.

From the market, they made a detour to Burnham Park, named after an American architect who planned the city's layout. It was centrally located in the city with a man-made boating lake at the center of it, an orchidarium and several restaurants with terraces. It was so tempting to stay. They paused for a moment and savored the sights. They didn't know if they would be able to come back. Benjamin had happy memories at Burnham Park and could not help remembering it.

Then they went back to Session Road. Still more people were buzzing around. They were all going in different directions. There were so many people on the road walking, carrying bags and bundles. They followed Session Road bearing right to Governor Pack Road, avoiding the left road going to Camp John Hay where the recent bombing was. At the road junction, the road was packed with people going in all directions. They proceeded to the bus terminals hoping to find a bus that would take them south. It was a chaotic scene with people walking fast aiming for the bus depots. They inched their way, trying to get in line toward the counter. The bus terminal was a two-story building with the counter on the first floor. In front of the building were some *sari-sari* stores that sell newspapers and some provisions for travel. There were few buses standing in front of the building.

Ramon went to the sales counter and asked, "What time is the next bus going to Manila?"

"No buses were going south to Manila today," the clerk said.

"How about tomorrow?"

"None that I know of. All buses are reserved for the military and emergency personnel."

"What do you mean no buses?"

"Exactly as I said, sir. None of the buses are going to Manila."

"Not even one?"

"Not even one."

"Oh no."

"I'm sorry sir. We are at war you know."

"Yes, I know."

Ramon scratched his head and asked for something else, "Do you know of any other transportation going anywhere south, not necessarily to Manila?"

"I'm sorry sir. Nobody is going that way at all."

Ramon looked distraught, turned to his companions. They all felt very disappointed and discouraged. There were people behind him on line that also wanted to know if they could get any transportation. They were all in the same predicament. They were looking for some kind of transportation to get them home to their own provinces where they would be safer.

Ramon asked, "What do you think we should do?"

"I guess we have no choice. We have to walk," Benjamin ventured to say.

There was brief silence among the group.

"Do you know how long that will be?" Manuel asked.

Delfin raised his eyebrows and said, "Of course, we know. You're not the only smart man."

"Well, instead of figuring out what to do, why don't we just move on?" Francisco suggested.

"I have to agree. Let's just go," Delfin said.

"We might find somebody along the way who might be going our way. We can hitchhike," Benjamin said.

"So which way are we going?" Manuel asked.

Benjamin was about to say something when Ramon finally asked, "So is it the Naguilian Road or the Kennon Road? The Naguilian Road follows a scenic foot trail that goes westward to Bauang, La Union near the coastline. It is also less precipitous than Kennon Road."

Surrounding Baguio is a rugged and sloping terrain, dotted with hot springs and cut by rivers that drain into many valleys. There were two major roads that provide access to Baguio from the lowlands. One is Kennon Road which followed the course along a deep ravine of the Bued River and the other is Naguilian Road which followed the old trail from the town of Naguilian through Sablan.

There is also another access road, the Halsema Highway which connects Baguio with the Mountain Province and the rest of the provinces comprising the Cordillera Administrative Region but they were not near there at that time. Another highway recently built is Aspiras Highway formerly called Marcos Highway. All four major highways have been carved out of the slope of the mountains.

Sometime, on their trip up north to the Mountain Province, they would take the Naguilian Road. The Naguilian Road is a scenic highway that winds westward to La Union and was the best route to northern Ilocos. At the junction where the Naguilian Road meets the coastal road, they could catch a bus that would transport them to

Vigan, a historic Spanish city in Ilocos Sur with houses, plazas, horse drawn carriages on cobblestone streets which give the aura of colonial times or continue to Laoag, the provincial capital in Ilocos Norte.

The Kennon Road was the first road constructed by the Americans through which vehicles could access the Cordillera Mountains. It is one of the great legacies of the American Administration and marked the gateway for Americans, Europeans, Chinese, Japanese and lowlanders to the Benguet Province. It is a winding road that goes down south through the mountainside. Initially, the Americans built both ends of Kennon Road simultaneously from the top which is Baguio City and from the bottom which is in Rosario, La Union. Later, to make both ends of the roads meet, they had to make it a winding road through Bued River Canyon, affectionately referred to as the "Zigzag." The Kennon Road was opened for travel on January 29, 1905 and in 1909 Kafagway was renamed Baguio City. Originally called Benguet Road, it was later named in honor of its final builder, Colonel Lyman Walter Vere Kennon of the U.S. Army Corps of Engineers by virtue of Executive Order No. 9 in 1922. Coming from Manila or the provinces in the central plains of Luzon, it is the shortest route up to Baguio.

Without hesitating, Benjamin retorted, "I believe Kennon Road is more direct".

"We have less chance of encountering the Japanese in the mountains," Elias said.

"You're right, Elias. They are still landing on the beaches," Felipe nodded his head.

"We could just arrive in Bauang in time for the Japanese to meet us at the beach," Francisco said.

"Honestly, Francisco. Please stop joking around," Ramon said giving him a dirty look.

"But it's true," Manuel came to Francisco's defense.

"What do you think, Benjamin?" Ramon looked at Benjamin and asked for his opinion.

"Yes, I think Kennon Road is the best route."

Kennon Road is the most scenic road to Baguio. It is about 40 kilometers of a steep and winding road. There were small settlements along the road known as Camps 1 to 8 which were originally established by the original builders of Kennon Road. Its initial construction way back in 1903 was to cut across the mountains of Benguet. To carve out the road against river canyon walls, massive rocks had to be blasted with dynamite and in the process accidents could happen so that workers in the vicinity would be blown to pieces and scattered and disappeared in the lush jungle and rocky crevices below. Five hundred Japanese workers died while engaged in the project. By ratio, the toll of one Japanese life was sacrificed for every ninety meters of the road length. Aside from Filipino engineers and U.S. Army Engineers headed by Col. Lyman Kennon, one thousand five hundred Japanese immigrant workers contributed substantially to accomplish the difficult road project until its completion in 1905. All in all, a labor force consisting of Filipinos, Americans, Filipino-Chinese and Japanese nationals, Igorots and some foreign workers worked steadfastly to finish one of the most difficult and expensive civil engineering projects of its day.

With no better choice, the group then started walking toward the winding Kennon Road from Governor Pack Road aiming for the southern route. As Benjamin and his group were rounding the bend from Governor Pack Road into Kennon Road, they could not help thinking they would never see Baguio again. They were soon leaving Baguio proper.

As they continued their walk toward the outskirts of the city, they heard the siren going and did not know what to make of it.

"What do you think that siren is for?" Manuel asked.

"I don't know and I don't want to find out," Ramon said.

"We just want to get out of here and out of danger," Delfin said.

"Did you see the look of everyone walking?" Elias asked.

"Yes, It's really scary, come to think of it," Felipe said.

"Do you suppose the Japanese will win this war?" Ramon asked Benjamin.

"No, I have confidence in the Americans. They won't allow that to happen. Surely, MacArthur won't allow that."

At that point, they were just interested in how they would proceed to continue their long journey. The next few days would not be as strenuous as the last six days. They would be going downhill most of the time and it should be easier. However, they still had to be very careful not to slip and fall down the ravine. The bamboo pole on which they carried their bags should come in handy to steady them. As a matter of fact, Benjamin decided to hold his bag with one hand and used his pole as a walking stick. The rest of them thought that was a smart idea and did the same thing.

As they came down Kennon Road, a picturesque view of the mountains came into focus. There were lush vegetation and pine trees all around. A mountain river flows along a rocky canyon from dizzying heights, and following this course Kennon Road was cut above the river bed. Kennon was a toll road and the tollgate was located about 2.5 kilometers from the junction at Rosario, La Union down the mountain. The original road was a macadam telford-type road which in the ensuing years was replaced by an all-weather asphalt roadway.

After a few hours on the road, Delfin started singing,

*"Here we are coming down the mountain, here we come.*
*Here we are coming down the mountain, here we come,*
*Here we are coming down the mountain,*
*Here we are coming down the mountain,*
*Here we are coming down the mountain, here we come."*

It took about an hour from when they started at Kennon Road before they reached the vicinity of Camp 8. They kept on moving. When they reached Camp 7, it was beginning to get dark and the fog was setting in so they decided to stop and find a place to sleep there. They found a small rest house and so they bedded down for the night. They knew the next stretch will be horrendous and they do not want to get caught in the dark on those hairpin turns on the road.

The next morning, they were refreshed and were ready for the next part of their journey. A few miles down the road after Camp 7, the road bends to the right. You could see a few terraced lands along the way. As Benjamin and his group descended down the mountains, the view from the top of the mountain was awesome. Green and lush vegetation could be seen farther afield. Looking down the mountain, the view was spectacular. Benjamin thought he could just stay here and savor the beautiful scenery if not for the ensuing war looming around them.

Kennon Road's winding road is the steepest and sharpest road to Baguio but the view was so picturesque with wonderful waterfalls, springs, lakes and rivers along the way. The road was getting less crowded as they went down the hill. There were trees along both sides of the road and then they saw the river through the trees on the right side of the road. The river was clear and there were long stretches with pebbles running along the side of the river. Then they saw the water rushing down from the falls into the deep pool with water as blue as the sky. They passed bridges of heavy steel made by the Americans, farmhouses, saw-mills and huts near the mining town. The road went down to a valley, made a winding turn and up a small hill and down again and up and down in a dizzying zigzagging pattern till they reach Camp 6. The road descended steeply at some point they had to be very careful not to plunge and end in a deep ravine. They could look down the road and follow the river alongside the road and to the left of them, more mountain ranges were in sight, green and dark in the lower elevation and near the top, the clouds hovering near the summit.

Between Camp 7 and Camp 6, the road became very steep they had to be very careful. This was the steepest part of Kennon Road and was commonly known as "Zigzag Road." At every bend in the road, more breathtaking scenery unfolded. There were two sharp turns and it felt dizzying. Luckily they were going downhill. They could not possibly think how it must have felt going uphill. They had to walk slowly and hanged on to each other or to the poles that they were carrying. The road was not crowded except for people like them walking down the mountains. They had to stay near the inner part of the road because some of the road had a steep rocky cliffside on the other side of the mountain. At some areas, looking up the mountain from where you were walking, there was the rocky face of the mountain and looking down, there was a precipitous cliff with rocky edges and a jungle growth below on the other side.

As they descend along the zigzag bend near the steep Bued River Gorge, they past the Lion Head, a naturally shaped limestone boulder that looks like a lion near Camp 6. In 1972, the Lion's Club of Baguio City, a very active civic organization in Baguio, commissioned the larger Lion's Head sculpture to be carved from a natural limestone formation just a few meters away and dwarfed the original Lion's Head. The larger Lion's Head has a viewing deck and a souvenir store nearby.

Coming from the south, when you see the Lion's Head, it is a signal that you are entering Baguio City. The limestone must have been there for a million years. It did look like a lion's head sitting under the shade of a big tree with mosses and lichens growing next to it. There was a stone wall next to it as you were approaching from the lowland. People could not help admiring this boulder as if put there by the gods as a guard to repel enemies or to welcome visitors to Baguio.

The American engineer who built Kennon road named points of interest, a couple of falls along its way and visible from the road. Bridal Veil Falls is about six kilometers from the beginning of Kennon Road in Baguio and named after one of the most prominent waterfalls in the Yosemite Valley in California. The Bridal Veil Falls is a thin stream of cascading water alongside a huge boulder surrounded by lush vegetation and could be accessed by a pedestrian suspension bridge. Located a short distance from Kennon Road is Colorado Falls, a further two and a half kilometers plus a short walk upstream named after another spot at California Yosemite National Park. The stream of water is actually three giant falls that drop into a clear natural pool almost 10 feet at its deepest. They saw some bathers going for a dip. It was very tempting to join them. These picturesque natural wonders were as lovely and remarkable as they could get. The thunderous sound and hypnotic sight were so marvelous and soothing to a troubled soul.

From Camp 6 to Camp 3, the road was a bit tricky and treacherous with sharp turns and bends. Some areas were so desolate. There were no houses for miles on end. There were waterfalls and some of them right by Kennon Road from Camps 5 to 3. While there was lush greenery all around Kennon Road, one also saw some bald rock faces where some pine trees have disappeared. There were few skeletal trees that loomed up in front of them against the backdrop of the blue sky. There were a few scattered huts between Camp 5 and Camp 4. There were little clearings with houses in them, and once in a while they passed a sawmill. It was getting dark and as they were coming down the mountain, they could feel the temperature getting warm.

They made it to Camp 4 on the second night. They were totally exhausted. They found an elementary school and walked in and slept there. Sleep came easily this time. They were so drained mentally and exhausted physically.

Next day was another arduous trip with a long stretch of a desolate downward passage. For miles all you see is lush vegetation. There were few huts and another elementary school near Camp 3 then just the natural beauty of the surrounding with trees and streams and waterfalls with clear mountain spring water cascading from a sheer drop into a natural pool. There was a long stretch where there was nothing except the green vegetation. Then another scattering of a few huts in small villages and some small stores could be seen along the road near Camp 2 where you can buy an assortment of native handicraft, vegetables, brooms, and locally made delicacies. Twin Peaks also loomed ahead of them with hot Springs close by. The descent was now beginning to ease off a bit with the gradual decelerating decline.

Near Camp 1, they saw a great view of the Bued River to their right and waterfalls dropping near the road to the left. There was a suspension bridge nearby. There were small villages and rice paddies along the road. Before they reached the end of Kennon Road near Rosario, La Union, there was a toll gate.

Looking down from the mountains, they could see the country spread out below. In the horizon were the green mountains. They were strangely shaped. As they descended, the horizon kept changing. As the road zigzagged through the mountains, they saw the surrounding areas of the road thick with vegetation. There was a forest of oaks, and the sun came through the trees in patches. The road twisted and turned along a rise of land, and out ahead of them was a rolling green plain, with dark mountains beyond it and the clouds coming down above them. The green plain stretched off. The road showed through the trunks of trees that crossed the plain toward the south.

They made it out of Kennon Road. There were still no Japanese troops in sight. They were lucky.

# CHAPTER 11

From Baguio, it took Benjamin and his group three days to reach Rosario, in La Union just north of Pangasinan Province near the Lingayen Gulf. They were now getting close to the central plain which is known as the nation's "rice bowl". This area is one of the country's richest agricultural regions, with plantations of tobacco, sugar cane, mangoes, coffee, coconuts and of course rice.

They passed through several small towns, going through farming country with rocky hills that sloped down into the fields. The fields went up the hillsides and carabaos grazed on the fields. As they went downhill, they felt the wind and it was blowing the grain. The road was dusty, and the dust rose and hung in the air around them. They had to move quickly to the side of the road to pass a long string of carabaos, following one another, hauling a wagon loaded with freight. The wagon and the carabaos were covered with dust. Close behind was another string of carabaos and another wagon.

They reached Rosario and now a decision had to be made.

"Do you think we should go to Dagupan? We are very close to the main road to Dagupan," Ramon asked Benjamin.

"There are more buses in Dagupan. We can probably get a ride there," Manuel said.

Since earliest times, Dagupan had been a trading center in Pangasinan where hard bargaining among vendors was a common sight. The Pangasinenses are noted for their industry and their enterprise. *Buri* hat making, mat weaving, wooden shoe manufacturing, brick and pottery making and metalcraft are among the traditional industries that continue to thrive in Pangasinan.

Pangasinan abounds in handicrafts and is famous for bamboo and rattan artifacts. There are also handicrafts made of marsh grasses. Foreign traders, Ilocanos from the north and the Igorots tribes from the Cordillera Mountains came down through the Naguilian Trail to trade and some of them started settling there too. Several ethnic groups live in Pangasinan, enriching the cultural fabric of the province. About half the people of Pangasinan are native Pangasinenses, a distinct group found along the central coast and interior plains of the province, the rest of the province's people are descendants of Ilocano migrants who settled the eastern and western parts of Pangasinan.

Pangasinan means "land of salt" or "place where salt is made" derived from the word "asin" meaning salt in the native language. The term was derived from one of the main occupations of the first settlers who were engaged in the production of salt from sea water through the process of solar evaporation in the many well laid out salt beds of its coastal towns. Nearby is the Hundred Islands, not exactly 100 but a group of about 400 small volcanic islands, some still unexplored and uninhabited.

Pangasinan is a long, wide, verdant crescent bounded by the wild Zambales range to the southwest, to the east by the Cordilleras -- the formidable mountains that form the spine of the island of Luzon. To the south, Pangasinan extends to the rice-and-sugar farmlands of Tarlac, and north to the crowning glory of Lingayen Gulf and the South China Sea. This shoreline is a great arc of variegated character: from fantastically tall, craggy rock roughly shaped by the surf, to the mildest of white sand beaches. The coast is fringed by well-hidden coves, inlets, charming fishing villages. There are caves, forests and woodland, and then the islands.

Throughout history, Lingayen Gulf has played an important role in the settlement of its inhabitants. Aside from traders, Filipinos had experiences with pirates from China and Japan. In 1574, a Chinese trader named Lim Feng, (Lim Ah Hong in Fukienese) landed in Sual Bay with 64 war junks and over 3,000 followers and wanted to settle at the mouth of the Agno River. They were soon followed by the Spanish *conquistadores* led by Juan de Salcedo. Lingayen Gulf is a large inlet of the South China Sea from

Santiago Island (west) off Pangasinan to San Fernando's Poro Point (east) in La Union. It is 56 kilometers wide from the eastern end to South China Sea.

In a surprise attack, they burned Lim Ah Hong's ships and blocked their escape routes. Lim Ah Hong and his people fled to the mountains and built new ships there. They secretly dug a channel from the Agno River through the Bacnotan marshes to Lingayen Gulf and escaped to the sea on a dark night in 1575. The Limahong Channel is a courageous testimony to a group of brave and determined men of the Chinese pirate, Lim Ah Hong, to elude the pursuing forces of the Spanish conquistador, Juan de Salcedo. Some of his men remained and settled in the Lingayen and Dagupan areas and became the ancestors of Chinese *mestizo* (Spanish word for mixed blood) families. Even before 1590 when the Augustinian missionaries came, the natives had been trading with the Chinese and Japanese who traveled through the South China Sea.

"I'm getting tired walking," Elias said talking to Felipe.

"So am I." Felipe nodded.

"I can use a good meal," Francisco said.

Hearing all these complaints, Benjamin looked at Delfin who had not said a word.

"Delfin, what do you think?"

"I don't know. You guys make up your mind. I believe Dagupan is out of the question. The first thing the Japanese will do is go land at Lingayen Gulf. That place is a strategic landing point for anybody," Delfin said.

Dagupan was a transportation hub and a commercial city of bridges and waterways on the south shore of the Lingayen Gulf. Dagupan had a minor port and was the terminal point of the Philippine rail line, inaugurated in 1892. It was surrounded by lovely beaches with small fishing villages and fishing was a way of life. Fresh Philippine *bangus* (milkfish), the national fish were always plentiful, hence the city is known as the bangus capital of the Philippines. Nearby is Lingayen, an old sprawling town by the sea built by the Spaniards in one section with old churches and buildings in Spanish architecture all facing the town plaza. The newer section facing the water is more spacious and built by the Americans with early American architecture.

Benjamin said, "Delfin is right. Lingayen Gulf has been a natural landing place for an invading army bent on capturing Manila since they only have to cross 180 kilometers of flat terrain with good roads."

Ramon looked at Benjamin and said, "The only advantage of going to Dagupan is we'll have more chance to find transportation. But at this point, we might be in the same situation as in Baguio. All the transportation is probably taken by the military. It can be the same in Dagupan."

"I honestly believe Delfin is right," Benjamin repeated himself. "We could be facing the Japanese there. Better to avoid the shoreline. That is where the Japanese are landing everywhere. We have to move on before the Japs catch on. Don't even think of being tired. We all are. We have to keep on going to a safer ground. Maybe we'll find a decent place to stay overnight in Urdaneta."

They weighed their options and came to a conclusion. They were not going to Dagupan, but instead moving on south towards Urdaneta.

"We'll do better going straight south," Benjamin reassured everyone.

"Before we move on, can we find a place to eat here before we resume our journey? I'm hungry and tired," Francisco suggested.

Ramon nodded his head and said, "That's a great idea."

Not too far from the town, they found an eatery, a karinderia. The place was almost empty. There were few customers around. They decided to eat there instead of looking further. The owner of the eatery was an elderly lady and was so eager to please them.

"Come on boys. Welcome. Looks like you are evacuating, are you?" The lady owner asked.

"Yes, we are," Ramon said.

"Where are you aiming at? You all look tired."

"Well, we've been walking for days now since the war started. We're going to Batangas."

"Oh my. That's a long way off."

"It is."

"Well, follow me. You can have that table in the corner. It is big enough for all of you. What can I get you?"

"What do you recommend? We just want to have a quick meal and then we can go on."

"Of course. You can try the Maniboc bagoong, made obviously in the town of Maniboc. You can have it with your rice. The Maniboc bagoong is the best in the market, both locally and nationally. You can also have fried bangus."

"Sounds good. Yes, we can have those. If you have some pancit, we'll have that too."

"Okay guys. Relax and I'll be back soon." The lady left them, scampered to the kitchen and in no time, the dishes were placed on the table. True to her word, the Maniboc bagoong was very good.

As they were eating, Delfin who loved music started humming a tune. He got a pensive look on his face.

"I was just thinking."

"What?" Benjamin asked.

"I heard there were great festivals here and they usually featured some local dances. They were fantastic, I was told."

"What kind of dances?" Elias asked.

"Local dances - courtship dance called *Imunan, a tagam* which is a war dance and *kumakaret* which is a test of dexterity. They show the peoples' skills. These dances are part of the local culture and when accompanied by the music of *tulali* flute, it is just great. *Binasuan,* a colorful and lively dance from Bayambang in the Pangasinan province shows off the balancing skills of the dancers. The glasses that the dancers gracefully, yet carefully, maneuver are half-filled with rice wine. Binasuan, meaning "with the use of a drinking glass" in Pangasinan, is often performed as entertainment at weddings, birthdays, and fiestas."

Delfin stood up, took two glasses, put them on each hand and started swaying his hand back and forth. Everyone shook their head.

"That's not how you do it. The glass should be on top of your hand, not on your palm," Ramon said.

"But they're going to fall if I do that."

"Well, that's why the dancers are good. They balance them and also put one on their head. They do the same thing with *Binoyugan*." Binoyugan is a dance originally from the Ilokano region of Pangasinan. It features women balancing on their heads a *banga* or clay pot which they use to fetch water from the river or well, in which to cook rice. The dance culminates with the women laying stomach down on stage, and rolling from side to side, all while balancing the pot.

They started eating. The pancit was nice and hot. The bangus was fried crisply. Delfin took one bite and remembered, "There is another dance called *Oasiwas*. After a good catch, fishermen of Lingayen would celebrate by drinking wine and by dancing, swinging and circling a lighted lamp. The name "Oasiwas" in the Pangasinan dialect means "swinging." This unique and colorful dance calls for skill in balancing an oil lamp on the head while circling in each hand a lighted lamp wrapped in a porous cloth or fishnet. "

"They are skillfull people," Manuel said, finally joining in the conversation.

"Absolutely right. You should see the dance called *Sayaw ed Tapew na Bangko*. It is a dance native to the province of Pangasinan (especially in Lingayen), and demands skill from its performers who must dance on top of a bench roughly six inches wide.  It was breathtaking to watch."

"I bet it is," Ramon said.

They finished their simple meal, paid the bill and thanked the lady owner. They left for Urdaneta which was a bustling city, 69 kilometers from Baguio and 183 kilometers from Manila. It had a busy market where Benjamin and his group could replenish their supplies.

Here again, the locals have their own recipe of bagoong. Bagoong, a muddy colored, salty fish sauce made from microscopic shrimps or fish and then fermented was made there. Fresh fish is the secret in making a good quality bagoong. The fish are drained to eliminate extra vapor and laid out on receptacles to dry to a semi moist condition before salting the fish and adding their secret ingredient. Bagoong is a popular sauce for most fish based food and it is also used as a salt substitute. Bagoong is very rich in protein and a cheap protein source in the diet of Filipinos. The pleasant taste cannot be substituted by any different food preparation, though the fish smell is quite overpowering.

As Benjamin and his group were approaching the city, they saw planes swooping overhead. Every so often they had to duck down and hid under the bushes. They heard gunfire at a distance. U.S. soldiers in full combat uniform were everywhere. Benjamin and his group were getting very nervous by this time and afraid that they would not make it home. The sight of so many soldiers around was so disconcerting. The soldiers looked like they were getting ready for something big to happen. They had their packs and holding onto their rifles and waiting for their orders. The troops were everywhere. You heard them swearing. There were now multitudes of refugees getting out of harm's way too. The streets were crowded with people. It was rough going through the throng. Later that evening, they made it to Urdaneta. They stayed in one of the inns along the road.

The following day, they started early before dawn. They stopped to eat at one of the eateries along the way. They sat at one of the tables in the corner. A young Filipino girl was sitting at the next table flirting with an American soldier. Then she motioned to an elderly lady standing by the back door. The elderly lady joined them. The young girl said something to the elderly lady, turned to the soldier and whispered something. The soldier pulled her up and sat her next to him. The elderly lady sat across the table from them. Francisco was watching them intently. Then he saw the soldier put his hand on the table. He flipped his hand with the palm facing up. Then the elderly lady said something but Francisco could not hear her. Francisco was about to stand up and have his palm read but Benjamin restrained him.

With a stern look on his face, Benjamin said, "Sit down".

Francisco looked at Benjamin and sat back down. Then he remembered something suddenly and asked, "Do you know there are a lot of faith healers in this town?

"Yes, I heard that too," Delfin chimed in. "Pangasinan is considered the birthplace of spiritual healing in Luzon and Cebu

City is the center of faith healers in the Visayas. Why, I'll never know."

"In Urdaneta, there is an abundance of faith healers who live and work in the area, a mystery which nobody was able to explain," Benjamin said.

It is believed that the Philippines lies within a powerful "psychic center of influence", perhaps deriving from a conjectured link between the Philippines (and Pangasinan in particular) and the legendary lost Pacific continent of Mu or Lemuria, an Atlantis-like land said to have been the home of an ancient civilization with advance psychic powers.

"I know this place is loaded with them," Francisco said.

Ramon asked, "Do you really believe their power?"

"I bet it really works. Really works all the time. You really have to believe in it to make it work. To be a faith healer is a very rare gift from God," Francisco said.

Elias whose niece was now a full-fledged doctor said, "The Philippines has a tradition of folk medicine that was handed down from generation to generation and even after the establishment of top medical schools producing capable doctors and nurses, the faith healing still continues in remote islands and small barrios. I heard some even do operations with their bare hands and remove what ails their patients. Pretty scary."

"Honestly, will you go and use those quack doctors?" Ramon turned to Benjamin. "Benjamin, will you?"

"Let me put it this way. Our father does not believe in them and I tend not to believe in them too. I might use them in extreme cases when the doctor cannot do anything so I have nothing to lose. But I will consult the doctor first before I go see them."

"Manuel, how about you? What is your opinion?" Ramon asked.

"I'm not sure. I heard people got cured and they claimed the healing came from divine intervention, from God Himself directly, not the faith healer. Are they putting fear in us just to believe them? Hard to tell. I might see them just to prove to myself their miraculous power. How about you, Ramon?"

"Oh, I tend to believe them. If they do not work, why are there so many faith healers?"

"You could be right," Benjamin reluctantly agreed but deep down, he was not so sure.

There were some American soldiers patrolling the area and few of them stopped by. Francisco started talking to one of the G.I. Joes as they called them in the Philippines who were sitting at the next table. He found out that they were waiting for orders from the high command in Manila. It seemed that Gen. Douglas MacArthur could not make up his mind if they had to proceed and guard the beaches around the Lingayen Gulf. The G.I. Joes saw the extra blankets that Delfin was carrying, part of them were sticking out of the bundle.

"What are those in your bundle? Are they blankets?" One of the soldiers asked.

"They are indeed," Delfin said. Benjamin was looking at them. He remembered telling Delfin that the blanket might come in handy during their trip and he might be able to sell them somewhere.

"Are you selling them?"

"Yes."

"Can we see them?" Delfin opened his bundle. He pulled one out and showed them the blanket.

"Hey, they look magnificent. Where did it come from?"

"They were woven by hand in Mindanao of special silk in various earthen colors. The fringes all around make it look special," Delfin said. He pulled another one out. The soldier passed the first one to his buddies. Then he pulled another one and it was passed around too. Finally he decided to pull out the other two blankets and spread them on the table. The soldiers were delighted. They looked at one another.

"I like it, but I have no money," one of the soldiers said looking sad. He looked at his buddies.

"It's really beautiful. I wish we had money to buy them," said another.

Then one of them looked thoughtful and after a brief silence said, "If I exchange a can of corned beef for one of the blankets will you part with it?" He asked Delfin.

The other soldier said, "Will you? I want one too." Then the other three nodded and said the same thing.

"What do you say, my friend?" The older soldier asked.

Delfin looked at Ramon and Benjamin for approval. The GIs waited. Ramon and Benjamin excused themselves and went outside out of earshot. Delfin and the soldiers waited. After a few minutes, Ramon and Benjamin came back.

Delfin glanced at Benjamin. Benjamin nodded his head and said, "It sounds like a good idea. It's a deal."

The soldiers pulled out the can of corned beef from their backpacks and handed them to Delfin who in turn gave each soldier one of the blankets. They were so excited. They rolled the blankets and put them in their backpacks. They looked very happy to have them. Their faces were all brimming with smiles. They were very pleased to have a nice souvenir. Delfin in return could have something good and practical to take home.

After the transaction was done, Delfin said, "Enjoy those blankets and good luck to you guys. Hope you catch some Japanese. And thank you for coming to our rescue. You have our gratitude."

"Good luck to you too. Hope you have a safe journey wherever you are going," one of the G.I.'s said. They shook hands, said a quick goodbye and Benjamin and his group stood up and started to leave. They could not wait to get back on the road.

As they were leaving the eatery, a couple of ladies passed them decked with rosaries and crucifix pendants dangling from their necklaces. They looked at each other and as soon as the ladies passed, they whispered "Faith Healers."

They continued their trek going south again avoiding a much traveled route. They stayed on narrow dirt paths away from the main road.

As they got closer to Tarlac, they heard the first blast of gunfire. They stopped dead in their tracks and listened. They could hear it a long way coming toward them and then it was gone and going away south from where they were walking. They looked at each other. Then they heard more blasts and rapid firing.

"We better stay here for a while," Ramon said and looked around. He saw people coming out of their house and into the street. They were looking up at the sky and beyond the trees they saw black smoke bellowing up into the sky. People were now crowding the street and were pushing each other in front of them. Ramon looked at his group, signaled to follow him and squeezed through the crowd.

Manuel was right behind Ramon with the rest following and having difficulty going through the crowd. Francisco who was way behind finally was able to untangle himself from the crowd. Breathlessly, he asked, "What are we going to do now?" They saw a young man running down the street toward them.

"Hey, what's going on?" Benjamin shouted at him. "What is happening?"

The man continued running. Delfin chased him. "What's going on? We heard gunfire."

"There is a battle going on over there." He pointed towards the south. "I also saw planes flying with red circles on their wings. The Japs are here. The Japs are here," he was saying breathlessly.

The young man went on running down the street and suddenly they heard roaring and the roaring got louder and louder and then they saw planes up in the sky a little farther out from where they were standing. They saw the planes come down and up and down and up and away. They looked stunned and could not move.

After the noise died down, they saw the people all went back inside their houses. They saw a tree nearby near the road. They went toward the tree, stopped and contemplated on what to do next. They looked to Ramon for direction. Ramon was scratching his head. He looked worried.

"What are we going to do?" Manuel, the worrier asked Ramon.

"OK. This is what we are going to do. We have reached this far, we'll just keep on going," Ramon said matter-of-factly.

"But the Japs are here now."

"So what? They will be here for the duration," Benjamin said.

"Do we have a choice?" Delfin asked.

"I guess none," Francisco butted in.

"I'm afraid there is only one thing for us to do. Keep on moving. We're practically half way."

Elias and Felipe who had not said a word for a long time looked at each other. "We are nowhere near half way," Elias said.

"I agree," Felipe nodded.

"OK guys. Whatever but the main thing is we have come this far. We are not going back and we cannot hide here. We'll just take our chances. What do you think?" Ramon turned to Benjamin for approval.

"Yes, we have no choice. So let's stop stalling and move on." Benjamin picked up his pack and everyone did the same.

After that first explosion, it seemed everything went still. They did not hear anymore explosions but the air smelled different. They trudged along quietly.

On the evening of December 22, they made it to Paniqui, Tarlac on the way to the provincial capital of Tarlac. It was a good decision that they did not take the road to Lingayen. Delfin had the right instinct to avoid the area. They could be right in the face of danger. They were extremely lucky because that day, Dec. 22 at 2:00 A.M., General Masaharu Homma, Commander-in-chief of the Japanese forces in the Philippines, with his large fleet of warships and 43,000 soldiers landed on the palm-lined shores of the Lingayen Gulf, 120 miles north of Manila. There was heavy fighting but in the end, the American and Filipino troops were outnumbered and overpowered by the Japanese. Some of the Filipino scouts retreated to the mountains.

By this time, Benjamin and his group were already way ahead of the Japanese. But the Japanese were advancing toward Manila.

At 4:30 PM the same day, Dec. 22, Gen. Douglas MacArthur decided to declare Manila, an Open City in a futile attempt to save it. He ordered all supply depots and storage tanks razed. Manila was known as the Pearl of the Orient because of its majestic buildings and palm-lined boulevards. To be an open city, it meant it would not be defended and hopefully could be saved. In the meantime, stores were being looted of everything. Manila was in total chaos.

On December 23 Gen. MacArthur finally decided to implement War Plan Orange that called for withdrawal of his forces to the Bataan Peninsula where they would wait until help from America arrived. He didn't like the idea but he had no choice. He had to abandon Manila so thus began the withdrawal as lines of trucks and troops moved along the dust covered roads leading to Bataan.

General MacArthur together with President Manuel L. Quezon would later retreat on Christmas Eve to the rock fortress of Corregidor, an island at the entrance of Manila Bay where he would direct his troops. It was a moon-lit balmy evening but Manila was dark and quiet when MacArthur and Quezon sneaked out and headed for the safety compound of Corregidor. It was not a safe haven, they found out later on.

# CHAPTER 12

Benjamin and his group walked at a steady pace for another two days. As they were nearing Tarlac, they were hearing explosions close by. There were more explosions it seemed. Looking further out, they could see clouds of black smoke billowing up in the sky, then more explosions. Every so often, they would stop on their trek and waited till the explosion stopped. It just went on forever, it seemed. It could not possibly be too far because it sounded too loud. They were getting very nervous. They knew heavy fighting must be going on somewhere nearby. They could smell the gunpowder. They were hoping they would not encounter the enemy on the road. The road was very busy at certain sections but they had not seen any Japanese troops. They were mostly American soldiers and Filipino soldiers going the other way. At around 4 PM, they hastened their pace before it really got dark. They were determined to reach the provincial capital of Tarlac.

The name Tarlac derived from a tough weed called *tanlac* or *tarlac* growing in the wilderness north of San Fernando. Tarlac was founded in 1686 and in 1860, the Spaniards made Tarlac a constabulary zone to protect the settlers from the mountain tribes. However in 1896, Tarlac was one of the eight provinces that revolted against the Spaniards. In October of 1899, General Emilio Aguinaldo, the president of the revolutionary government transferred the seat of government to Tarlac. A year and four months later, the United States took over the province and established a civil government there.

When Benjamin and his group arrived in Tarlac, there had been heavy fighting there for at least two days. That explained the explosions they were hearing before. Over 700 American, Philippine and Japanese soldiers died in that battle.

They were looking for the municipal building where they usually stayed for the night when they heard the roar of army trucks and a band of Japanese soldiers approaching in their direction. There was no time to run away or hide from them. They knew the Japanese soldiers saw them. If they ran, chances were the Japanese would fire their guns. Better to stay calm. Still, there was that fear that they could get shot. Some of the Japanese soldiers got off the trucks and with their bayonet-tipped rifles brandishing away waved at Benjamin and his group and told them to stop.

"Stop." Benjamin heard them say.

Benjamin took a quick look at Ramon and Ramon nodded. They all stopped and stood frozen. The group thought that was the end of them. Still they tried to remain calm. They bowed to the Japanese soldiers who bowed back. One of the soldiers started talking in Japanese to his comrades and then turned to them. He looked at them up and down, one after another. The soldiers nodded their head. They talked to each other again in Japanese while Benjamin and his group waited. They could not make anything out of what they were saying but they were scared. They did not know what these soldiers were going to do. "Dear Lord, please help us." Benjamin was praying in silence.

Then one of the soldiers took a step and looked at them holding their packs.

"What's in those packs?" one of the Japanese soldiers asked. He spoke little English.

"Clothes," Ramon said automatically and bowed. Everyone bowed too. In his nervousness, he forgot about the corned beef that they exchanged with the American soldiers a few days ago. Within minutes after he said "Clothes", he remembered the corned beef suddenly. He felt sweat running down his shirt. He tried to remain calm.

The soldiers looked at them up and down again and decided they looked harmless. The content of the packs was forgotten.

One of the Japanese soldiers said in a very stern voice, "Drop down those packs and go over there." They looked where he was pointing. He was pointing to the farther side of the building with a clearing.

Slowly Ramon obediently dropped his pack and everyone followed his lead. They put down their belongings on the ground. "That was a close call," he thought. At least for now, the storm has past.

Then another soldier said, pointing to one side of the building. They turned to where he was pointing. "No, bring your things to that side of the building instead and hurry up." They looked at each other and nervously picked up all their stuff.

As they were taking their belongings to the other side of the building, Delfin whispered to Benjamin, "What are they going to do to us? They can't seem to make up their mind."

Benjamin answered, "I have no idea but I don't like it, whatever it is."

They looked worried and nervous. Ramon said to the six of them, "What can they do to us? We are civilians. We are not soldiers. Just do what they want us to do. Hopefully, they will not harm us."

"Get moving. Get moving. We do not have all day," another one of the Japanese soldiers barked.

"Follow me," the ringleader said. They did not know what to do. They looked at each other and without saying a word, started following the ringleader. They had no choice.

Benjamin started wondering what the soldiers were up to. Are these soldiers about to kill them? What would happen if they did? "God, please help us." He prayed again.

They got to the other side of the building and came upon a battlefield which was littered with corpses, wrecked trucks, guns, cartridges, maps and backpacks all strewn everywhere. Some of the bodies were on top of each other. The sight was unbelievable. The stench of the dead bodies in the tropical heat was awful. They wiggled their nose and covered their mouth. Some of the dead bodies were covered with flies and then the flies tried to land on their faces. They shooed them away quickly.

There were hundreds of men, in various conditions of carnage, young men in their late teens and early twenties all bloodied and lifeless. There were huge abdominal gashes, some with buried or protruded shrapnel. Some had severed arms. Others lost their legs. Some had disfigured faces and mutilated bodies. Some had their skull opened probably with bayonets or samurai swords. There were bullet holes and dried blood all over their bodies. Some of the dead had their eyes open and thousand of flies buzzed and maggots started swarming around the bodies. It was a gruesome sight.

"*Kura, Kura,*" the Japanese leader said pointing to the scattered dead bodies. "Pick them up and bring them over there to the front of the building."

They looked at each other and felt disgusted. They were incredulous. They could not believe what the Japanese soldier was saying. Their two cousins, Elias and Felipe, who had weak stomach threw up. One of the Japanese soldiers saw Elias and Felipe.

The Japanese soldier came over to them and with his bayonet stumping on the ground said, "Are you a man or a woman? Get up or you'll be one of them." pointing to the dead bodies. Elias and Felipe still nauseous tried to straighten up and moved slowly to the task at hand. Benjamin felt nauseated himself but he tried to control himself. Ramon held his stomach hard to keep from vomiting. Manuel, Francisco and Delfin looked at them trying hard not to vomit. They spat on the ground and tasted bile in their mouth.

One by one, with heavy heart and disgusted looks on their faces, they picked up the dead bodies of men, American, Filipinos and Japanese killed in the heavy fighting. They were so afraid to protest for fear of the consequences. They wanted to stay alive.

They started picking up the bodies and just dropped them in front of the building. Then one of the soldiers rushed back to the front of the building.

"Not that way. Like this." He pulled some dead bodies and then dropped them in a neat pile. Then he changed his mind. "Bring them instead to the back of the building and pile them up in a low".

Benjamin gave him a quizzical look.

"Like this," The soldier said. He walked from one side to the other side.

"You mean in a row." Benjamin bowed. The soldier bowed back.

The group tried hard not to laugh. Benjamin saw their mouth curved slowly in amusement. They were smiling. Benjamin caught them and gave them a dirty look. They quickly stopped smiling and pretended to not hear the conversation.

Then they dragged the dead bodies from the front of the building to the back of the building without saying a word. They lined the bodies from one end of the building to the other end. The stench of the dead bodies was so awful but they tried to ignore it. Their nose kept on twitching but they moved on. They finished the first row.

All the while, the Japanese soldiers were there watching them, leaning against a tree chatting, smoking and drinking. Someone had his cigarette hanging from his lower lip and looking over his shoulder while talking and watching them. Someone must have told a funny joke because you could hear their laughter. Then the leader of the soldiers slung his weapon on his shoulder and stood up straight and walked toward them.

Delfin saw him and flinched, whispered to Ramon, "What is he going to do now?"

"Just stay calm. Let me handle this," Ramon said.

The group had just finished the first row. As the commander approached them, Ramon bowed to him and asked, "What do we do with the rest?"

"Put them on top of one another."

"Like sandbags?" Ramon asked.

"Yes. Go."

Without uttering another word, they all went back to work. They just kept on piling the bodies without thinking. On and on, they flopped the dead bodies on top of the first row.

As Benjamin was helping pile all the dead bodies one on top of the other, he could not help thinking about the fate of these young men. How will their parents know that their sons are gone? Some of these soldiers are still young kids, a few years younger than him. The war is only just beginning. How many more men and women and possibly children will be lost in the following months? How many of these young men had their dreams shattered and lost in this battle?

How about their sweethearts that they left behind going to accept the fact that they will never get married and have that family and house that they dreamt of? How about those young wives who they left behind? Some probably even have children that were born after their husband went to war. The kids will never know their father. Suddenly he thought of Adelaide, then said a silent prayer to spare him and his brothers. He wanted to see Adelaide. He had to make it home and see her. He had to behave himself so the Japanese wouldn't harm them. He wanted to go home to see Adelaide. He wanted so much to stay alive.

They worked furiously for almost five hours without a break. At first it was hard to concentrate and the task was so gruesome, it was nauseating. After a while, they became automatons and they just piled the bodies without even thinking. As the night started to fall, they were beginning to get dizzy from hunger. They were so weary and exhausted when the Japanese soldiers told them to stop for the night.

Then out of the blue, which they could not figure out why, the Japanese fed them. They ate a meal of rice and some meat. It was not bad at all considering that they were at war with these people. Benjamin was thinking maybe this was their last supper. God only knew what would happen next. Then like another miracle in the night, the Japanese soldiers left. They were left alone in the municipal building. They looked at each other and could not figure out why they just left them there alone. But they were too tired to worry about it. The soldiers never thought of them running away since it was too dark at night already and they were exhausted from all the work. The soldiers were right but not completely right. It was late so they took out their sleeping mats and due to exhaustion, they all fell asleep in no time except Benjamin.

Benjamin lay awake, decided to go outside and sat on the front stoop of the municipal building. He listened to the faint rumbling of gunfire in the distance and the buzzing of the insects nearby that seemed to converge around him. Now and then, he slapped the mosquitoes haphazardly making a sharp crack at the buzzing sound. Benjamin was so tired that night but sleep was elusive. The sight of those young men kept on coming back. There were more in the field.

They did not finish piling them up. Maybe that's why the Japanese left them alone. He was sure they were thinking of them finishing them up the next day and God knows what would happen next.

The whole thing was really bothering him so much and he kept on thinking about the dead bodies. They were not just white American. People of every color, black, white, brown with blue, brown, green and black eyes. These young kids were here with a mission, fighting for a noble cause to defend the Philippines from the invaders. Benjamin could not get their faces out of his mind.

He sat there for a long time thinking he could get some fresh air. However, the air outside did not smell fresh. On ordinary evenings, you could smell the scent of exotic tropical plants and the evening would be loaded with fireflies dancing in the air but not tonight. It was acrid and smelt of death.

He looked up at the sky. The night sky was clear with the moon shining brightly and there was a sprinkling of thousands of stars. The stars were twinkling so bright and hanging so low. It looked like you could almost touch them. He just realized that tonight was Christmas Eve. It was hard to believe and yet here he was in the midst of a rotten place on Christmas Eve. It did not make sense whatsoever. He then realized maybe the Japanese had Christmas spirit after all and that was the reason why they did not harm them. They also went out to town for merrymaking perhaps. The Baby Jesus must be watching over them.

Then he thought of something else. If it was a different circumstance, they could have been home by this time. They should be getting ready for the coming of the Saviour, Jesus Christ. It should be nearing the time when they all went to church for midnight mass and then home to enjoy *Noche Buena*. "Oh, how I wish we were home now," he sighed.

His mind drifted to his hometown of his early childhood days during Christmastime. Tradition has it that Christmas celebration begins on December 16, nine days before Christmas Day and ends on January 6, the feast of the Three Kings. Great preparation was made before that date. Each day was busy. The house would be thoroughly cleaned, a tree with berries not necessarily a pine tree, would be brought in from the forest and the children would be busy making the Christmas decorations.

They would gather some colorful crepe paper, cut it in long strips and made an interlocking chain for a garland. They would drape it around the tree and hang on top of the windows. The crèche would be prominently displayed in the sala.

They made a *parol,* a Christmas lantern in the form of a five-pointed star. Sometimes it was inside a circle. It was made of bamboo strips and covered with cellophane in various hues. There usually was a light inside the star. These lanterns represent the star of Bethlehem, the guiding light that led the three wise men to the infant Jesus. They finished it up with a few adornments like hanging tail or tassels at the end of the two downward points of the star. Sometimes they also put tassels on the other two points on both sides of the parol, leaving the top point to put a string to hang it up. Sometimes they put some designs like rays emanating from the corners of the intersection of the starpoints.

They started making parols a couple of months before Christmas. When they were small, they made a small parol and then as they got older, the parol got bigger and more colorful and elaborate. Men cut strips of the bamboo, a plant with a hollow stem. Bamboo which was so pliable could be bent into various shapes. Strips of bamboo were shaped into five pointed star. In the center where it formed the five sided frame, they put a 4-6 inch brace to make it 3 dimensional. It was also the place where they put the light to create the illumination they wanted. Kids and adults enjoyed doing this tradition every year. Men cut the bamboo and the women cut the paper and glued them to the frame. By the time Benjamin was sixteen, they even had two big parols hanging by the front window. They had a very wide front window and they hung two bright colorful parols there during the Christmas season. The house looked festive and beautiful. Parols could be seen everywhere during the Christmas season. It was the main Christmas decoration at home, in stores and churches.

Every night during the Christmas season, they all went out caroling from house to house. It was a lovely way to socialize for the young people. Of course, young maidens could not go out unless they had a chaperone. With the accompaniment of guitar and banjo, they would be singing all the folk Christmas songs and the traditional Christmas carols. It was always a welcome entertainment for the town.

Starting on December 16, they would wake up very early in the morning and would go to *simbang gabi*, the predawn mass. The air was usually cool and they walked to church in the nice cool air in semi-darkness. After mass, they enjoyed seeing their relatives, friends and neighbors in front of the church by the food stalls, buying hot *bibingka* (pancake), *puto bongbong* (cylindrical rice cake like a pirouette) and kalamay (rice cake), and eating them on their way home. The predawn mass was celebrated every morning from December 16 to December 24. Then on the midnight of Christmas Eve, everybody went to church to celebrate the birth of Christ. They always had a lovely treat for that day. All kids received new clothes and a new pair of shoes. After church, they were excited to get home and got treated with a delicious Noche Buena, a post-midnight gathering with table laden with delicious traditional Noche Buena fare of lechon, pancit, chicken relleno, embutido, bibingka, kalamay and other delicacies. Then they were allowed to open their presents. Usually it was a doll for girls and a car or truck for boys. Nothing big or fancy but kids were happy to get them.

On Christmas Day, they went back to church in the morning and afterwards went visiting their godparents and grandparents. It was traditional that they visited them on Christmas Day. It was expected of godchildren to visit their godparents and they in turn got presents from the godparents, usually in the form of cash. Even if the godparents were in another town, the parents made every effort to take the godchild to see the godparents.

A big flash of light burst across the sky. It jolted Benjamin's senses. "I must have been sitting here for more than an hour. I better go inside and get some sleep if I have to wake up early tomorrow?" he said to himself.

Then the images of war started again and he thought to himself. "The war just started. How many people will die before this conflict is over? Is it safe for us to be in this building? What if the Japanese kill us next? What if the Japanese come back tonight? How are we going to escape if the Japanese take us prisoners?" These questions kept nagging in his head. The thought gave him goose bumps.

He went back inside and lay down on his mat. It took him a while but he finally drifted to sleep. He was determined to get up early tomorrow before something horrible happened. Apparently everybody was thinking the same thing because they all got up very early the next day before the Japanese soldiers came back. The Japanese soldiers left last night after they had dinner and were not back yet. Hopefully they would not be back for a while.

They gathered their stuff and walked out quietly. It was still dark but they wanted to get out of there and far away before the Japanese came back and found out they were gone. They walked as fast as they could to get away from the place.

As they were leaving the city hall building, it occurred to Benjamin that the way they piled those bodies was meant for something. The Japanese soldiers were going to use those bodies as a shield and shoot from behind them. Benjamin was horrified at the thought. Maybe they should have rearranged the bodies but there was no time. Suppose the Japanese soldiers came back. Better to get out of here and fast.

They walked faster this time. Adrenaline was pumping. Their hearts were beating faster. They were practically running to be as far away from the place as possible. They were afraid to look back. They felt the Japanese eyes were bearing down on them and that the Japanese soldiers might want them back either for slave labor or to be killed. The war was escalating and they would not want to be taken prisoners.

From Tarlac they tried to avoid the main road for fear they might encounter some more Japanese soldiers again. They decided to follow the railroad track and walked along side of it but far away for fear of being noticed. If they followed this route, they knew this would lead them to Tutuban Railway Station in Manila.

By daybreak, they had logged already a good number of kilometers. Delfin started singing

*"Silent night, holy night*
*All is calm, all is bright*
*Round yon Virgin Mother and Child*
*Holy Infant so tender and mild*
*Sleep in heavenly peace*
*Sleep in heavenly peace.*

*"Silent night, holy night!*
*Shepherds quake at the sight*
*Glories stream from heaven afar*
*Heavenly hosts sing Alleluia!*
*Christ, the Saviour is born*
*Christ, the Saviour is born.*

*"Silent night, holy night*
*Son of God, love's pure light*
*Radiant beams from Thy holy face*
*With the dawn of redeeming grace*
*Jesus, Lord, at Thy birth*
*Jesus, Lord, at Thy birth."*

Everybody joined in. When they finished the song, they greeted each other *"Maligayang Pasko"*. Merry Christmas. Maybe the Baby Jesus was with them throughout this journey since so far they had been very lucky. Last night was a close call. Could it be because of Christmas that the Japanese did not harm them? They kept on wondering about it. Who knows? They just had to count their blessings. They just kept on singing carols as they walked along to keep their minds off what they saw yesterday. But in spite of that grotesque scene of yesterday, they still managed to get into the Christmas mood. Just singing those carols made them feel better and close to home.

They passed small barrios and they saw the manifestation of Christmas. Every little bahay kubo, nipa hut had a small parol. The kids were still being kids, playing on the street. Most of the adults were busy cleaning the house and going about the business of their daily life. It was nice to see that the Christmas spirit was still with every Filipino in spite of the uncertainties of the time.

While Christmas and Easter are purely Christian festivals, the enterprising Filipinos are always quick to make any festivals reflect their own baroque spirit. Christmas, which officially begins nine days before Christmas Eve (actually it can begin as early as September 1st) and ends with the Feast of the Three Kings, is the longest Yuletide celebration in the world. The symbol of Christmas in the Philippines is not the Christmas tree, but the parol that probably had its origins in the Mexican's *piñata*. While parols come in all sizes, in Pampanga, the electric parols in later years stand 20 to 30 feet high, giving off a blaze of kaleidoscopic color and light that fills the evening sky.

As they were getting close to Angeles, they decided to head for the town. Maybe they could get a ride there to Manila. Instead they saw all transportation - buses, trucks, calesas, taxis, limousines, army trucks were loaded with Filipino and American soldiers all heading up north. Some of the troops were on foot, still walking north. They had this determined look on their faces. There was so much chaos on the street. Everybody seemed to be going in the same direction and in a hurry. They were getting away from the Japanese which they suspected would be in full force pretty soon.

Here Benjamin and his group were going south and the rest of the people were going in the opposite direction. It made them very nervous. They could not get any transportation to go south. They had no choice but to continue their trek on foot. They tried to look for a store where they could buy some supplies. After searching for a few minutes, somebody pointed out there was one store that was open. They hurriedly went there and bought some provisions in case they got stuck somewhere.

News was circulating that more raids were directed to the port districts of Manila on Dec. 20 and Dec. 21 and yesterday Dec. 24 which left the places badly damaged. They heard that long columns of the 26th Cavalry, the last horse unit of the U.S. army were now marching to Lingayen Gulf. The Philippine Constabulary had commissioned all buses and trucks to Lingayen Gulf where the troops and refugees were being evacuated. All the army vehicles were passing through the University of Santo Tomas to be serviced and refueled before heading to Lingayen Gulf.

The University of Santo Tomas which is the oldest university in the Philippines and the second oldest university outside Europe was founded by the Spaniard in 1611. It had a great roster of prominent alumni, including Manuel L. Quezon, the president of the Commonwealth and Dr. Jose Rizal, the national hero. The place was now being used as a service station for the army.

After they bought their provision, they decided to head back on the road toward the railroad tracks. It was weird thinking that they were walking against the tide. Everybody was heading north and they were heading south toward the conflict. They still had no idea how they would cross Manila which apparently was now in a war zone. As they were going south towards Manila, 10,000 Japanese soldiers had landed at Lamon Bay and were now advancing north towards Manila.

# CHAPTER 13

They were now getting extremely worried that they might not make it. Every day it seemed it was getting more dangerous as the journey progressed. The war was finally escalating which gave them more motivation to get home as soon as they could. They were practically half way but they were getting very tired and exhausted. They moved at a slow pace. They were physically worn out but determined to keep on going.

On the way to Angeles, they heard gunfire and explosions in the distance. They could see bright orange flames backed by huge black walls of smoke. They were nowhere near any battlefield so they believed they were still pretty safe. It looked like all their surroundings were on fire. They stayed alert at all times.

They heard the latest news that another large Japanese force had landed on the 24th of December at Atimonan in Lamon Bay on the southeastern shore of Luzon about 60 kilometers from Manila and were headed towards Manila. They wondered how they were going to pass through Manila. They could be in the line of fire. They had to find a way to go through Manila without getting killed.

With the mass landings of Japanese forces at Lingayen Gulf and another one in Lamon Bay and advancing in both directions, MacArthur's forces faced complete destruction. In a futile attempt to save Manila from destruction from possible air or ground attacks, Gen. Mac Arthur declared Manila an open city the day after Christmas. He thought this should help preserve the city like they did in Paris, Rome and Brussels because the military would not be there so the enemies had no reason to bomb or attack it. MacArthur ordered his men to retreat to Bataan and fight a jungle war there where they had the advantage of knowing the terrain. Everyone was in a hurry to get out of Manila. Due to lack of military transportation, the military commissioned all commercial transports to help in the evacuation proceedings. Drivers were instructed to wait 10 minutes in between departure to try to dispel the convoy idea. They stopped for shelter when they heard planes flying overhead.

On Christmas Day, the Japanese arrived in Manila. They hit mostly warehouses and ships on the waterfront. Flight after flight of Japanese planes kept bombing and strafing most of the day. They were only hitting their targets per their orders and ignoring the people evacuating. The fighter pilots were not interested in the people. All they were interested in were the military installations and supply depots.

Two days after Christmas, Benjamin and his group passed Angeles, about 80 kilometers (50 miles) north of Manila, near Clark Air Base, a U.S. army post formerly called Fort Stotsenburg established in 1902. It was renamed Clark Air Base after Major Harold Clark, an airman who was killed in a crash. Clark Air Base then became the headquarters of the 13th United States Air Force, the largest U.S. military installation outside the United States encompassing over 550 sq. kilometers. Even before MacArthur declared Manila an open city, the army was being evacuated to Bataan. When Benjamin and his group arrived at Angeles, the place was in a state of chaos. The American troops were everywhere. The road was now congested with all the soldiers and army trucks. There was bumper to bumper of traffic.

Fighter planes were buzzing overhead. They could hear loud explosions in the distance. Sirens shrilled so intensely. They felt their eardrums were about to burst. They heard more explosions which sent them diving for cover. The ground shook and shudders at each explosion. The Japanese have arrived in Manila and the bombings were intensified.

Japanese zeros would come from nowhere chasing the American's P-40s and a "dogfight", an aerial battle between the Japanese pilots and the American pilots would ensue. The pilots would do all these dangerous maneuvers, diving, twisting, swooping, and turning their planes trying to outmaneuver the other pilot while firing their machine guns and flying at a speed up to 300 miles per hour at an altitude ranging from few feet above the ground level to high up in the sky.

The Japanese Zeros were much better planes than the American P-40s. They were light and could climb faster. The Zeros turned and twisted with their guns aimed at the American pilots. The P-40s could climb to a higher altitude and shoot and climbed away. When a Zero got hit, the pilot bailed out without a parachute and his plane spiraled downward bursting in a huge explosion. People started running for cover. It felt like the explosion was so close by but it was not. Flames erupted from the burning fuselage with shards of metal and debris flying everywhere. It was fascinating to watch this aerial battle but Benjamin knew it was very dangerous.

Headlines in the papers and on the radio said Gen. MacArthur had declared "Manila es ciudad abierta." Manila is an open city. It was the very reason why Gen. MacArthur withdrew his 80,000 men to Bataan to avoid the destruction of Manila and fight a jungle war with the Japanese in Bataan. Since the bombing of Pearl Harbor, the radio had been giving a daily account of what was going on and predicting the victory of the U.S. army.

Once Benjamin and his group found out what was happening, they decided to go back to the railroad tracks from Angeles and followed the track to Manila. They would be safe on their route even if they had no place to hide in a rice field. They would be far enough from where the Japanese planes were dropping bombs and when they flew back they had no more bombs to spare so they considered themselves very lucky. They ventured to the nearest town only near dusk so they could stop for the night. At night, some of them would collapse on their mat. They were totally exhausted.

What they saw in the aftermath of the battle in Tarlac was too gruesome but they tried to forget it during the day. Their mind was too busy trying to stay alive from all the dangers around but at night, it all came back in their dream. The images in Tarlac kept on coming back. In Tarlac, they could not really talk there while they were working. The Japanese soldiers were watching them like a hawk.

They were afraid to even look at the Japanese soldiers for fear that those bayonets the soldiers were holding would aim towards them. Without any expression on their faces, they just kept on working, picking up the bodies and moving them into the pile.

They remembered hearing the clicking of the guns every now and then and the tapping of the bayonets on the ground. A few of the soldiers had a sword hanging in their scabbard. Once in a while, the soldiers would take the sword out and swished the sword through the air. It made a frightening sound. Benjamin and his brothers looked at each other and their blood froze. They could not imagine their life ending there. Their parents would never know what happened to them. Ramon said a silent prayer for all of them. They could not even ask the soldiers if they could take a breather. For a back-breaking five hours of work with their life dangling in the precipice of death, they wondered if God would intercede. But a voice within them said "Keep the faith!" and that sustained them through the whole ordeal.

When the commander ordered them to stop for the night, they were all relieved but when they had their meal, they thought that was their "Last Supper". When the soldiers finally left them, they said a prayer of thanks to God and to St. Christopher for watching over them on their journey. They didn't sleep well that night as everybody admitted. They were very alert and feared for their life. They did not know what they would have done if the Japanese soldiers came back that night. They were very lucky.

Now, here at Angeles, they wondered why their luck was still holding. They believed God and his angels were still watching over them. But for how long? Fatigue was slowly overcoming them. Only their sheer determination was sustaining them. They had been walking continuously for 16 days now. They were tired and exhausted. A few hours of sleep at night did not help. The explosions and fear for their safety at night and even during the day were just too much. But they had to stay focused. They had to make it home. They had to. They kept on saying to themselves. They had to be alert and careful at all times. They had to make it home. They wanted to go home. That ardent desire to make it home kept them going. They slept at night with that thought in their mind and were eager to start their trek again the next day.

They would make it home. They knew they would. God would help them.

# CHAPTER 14

The provincial capital of San Fernando in Pampanga was established in 1775 and named after King Ferdinand III of Spain. It is located 16 kilometers south of Clark Field in Angeles City and 67 kilometers north of Manila. As Ramon and his younger brothers and cousins arrived near the San Fernando Junction, there was a horrendous traffic jam. People were coming from different directions, some from the north and some from the south. They were about to cross the twin-spanned Calumpit Bridge. Calumpit Bridge crosses the Pampanga River and its surrounding marshes. One span had a two-lane road and the other had the railroad tracks. To go to Bataan Peninsula, one had to pass over Calumpit Bridge.

When Ramon and his group reached Calumpit Bridge, the only steel-thrust type of bridge in the country designed to accommodate six-by-six trucks, they saw military tanks and six by six trucks full of American soldiers still on their way up north. Calumpit Bridge was just south of San Fernando Junction, where the highway from the north to Manila joined the highway from the south leading to Bataan.

People and military men were fleeing in civilian buses, taxis, calesas, military trucks, oxcarts and anything with wheels which were also carrying refugees going over Calumpit Bridge on their way to Bataan. Few civilians on foot were following the military on their march to Bataan. To speed up the evacuation, the military appropriated all commercial motor vehicles. Day and night, they moved ammunition, equipment, medical supplies and all kinds of goods together with all the evacuees from Manila to Bataan. The faces of the multitudes betrayed their emotion, scared of what would happen to their lives. In the sky farther out, the Japanese pilots continued to bomb military targets and portions of Manila. They were ignoring the long streams of military and civilians marching to Bataan and were completely concentrating their attack on the military targets. Their priority was the capture of Manila and that's what the Japanese were concentrating all their efforts.

Just as Ramon followed by his brothers and cousins were trying to squeeze through the multitude of people and transportation going in the opposite direction, one of the soldiers saw them walking the opposite way. There was an exodus of refugees being guided to move faster going north. The refugees carried their small belongings. They carried their children on their backs and in their arms.

"Hey, where are you going?" A soldier called out. "You are going the wrong way." Ramon and his group were directed to follow the throng. Ramon ignored the order and kept on going the opposite way.

"Turn around. You." The soldier pointed to Ramon.

Ramon glanced and kept going. The soldier blocked his way.

"Do you want to get killed? You are going towards the enemy." One of the American soldiers started yelling.

"No," Ramon answered and signaled to his brothers to follow him. The soldier was still blocking his way.

"Don't you get smart with me. Go on with the group," he commanded.

"Please sir. We can't, sir. We want to go home." Benjamin came to Ramon's rescue.

"It's not safe. We are evacuating everyone to Bataan."

"We still want to go home. We have walked this far from Baguio and we will continue till we reach home," Ramon said. He looked at his group and they all nodded.

"Did you say Baguio?" The soldier asked incredulously.

"Yes sir. We've been walking since the war started," Benjamin said.

"That is way up north. Where is home?" The soldier was incredulous. He could not believe what he was hearing.

"Batangas," Ramon and Benjamin said in unison.

"It's too dangerous. Do you want to get killed? The Japanese are on their way. You'll encounter them on the road. You'll be trudging on dangerous territory." The soldier was still trying to dissuade them.

"No, we don't want to get killed and that's the reason we are going home. We have faith. We'll try to avoid the main road. We'll be on the alert. We'll follow the railroad tracks. We have to go home. We'll be safe there with our families," Benjamin said.

Some of the people in the crowd started shaking their head. Some looked our way but no one spoke. They probably thought they were crazy. Benjamin turned to Ramon and the rest of the group.

"What do you think, guys? Shall we join them or keep on going south?"

"We'll go south," Ramon answered without hesitation. Everyone nodded in agreement.

Benjamin turned to the soldier and said, "There you are, sir. We will take our chance. At least when we get home, we know our area. We know where to hide."

"Still there is the danger along the way."

"We are totally aware of it, sir. Thank you for your concern."

"Are you really sure you want to do this?"

"We are, sir. So please let us do it our way."

"OK. But don't think I didn't warn you."

"We know, sir. Thank you again."

"OK. But you go at your own risk. Be careful. God be with you." He waved them goodbye. At that, they quickly turned toward the opposite direction. Everyone was going the other way.

Ramon gathered his brothers and cousins and they began to cross the Calumpit Bridge. They heard people murmuring something but they could not care less. They were eager to get out and be on their way.

It was difficult because the throng was going in the opposite direction as they were heading south. After pushing their way through, they finally crossed the bridge and went through a dirt path towards the railroad track. Then they were back on their trek once again, heading southeast towards Manila.

Ramon was apprehensive as to whether they did the right thing. A voice inside him was telling him they were right. Their path was practically empty since most of the throng was on the main road. They did not waver in their faith. They followed the railroad track path all the way to Manila. They kept on walking. At times, they felt like quitting but Ramon and Benjamin prodded everyone in the group to keep on going. When their feet could not carry them anymore, they found shelter under trees nearby and rested for a few minutes, ate something and then kept on walking.

For two days and two nights, the American soldiers ferried guns, ammunition, troops and fleeing civilians to the other side of the bridge. In their haste, they forgot to take with them tons of food, clothing and military supplies. A million pounds of rice were left in some storage areas.

Early December 31, the South Luzon Force crossed the bridge. By afternoon, General Homma finally realized what was going on and decided to follow them. In the meantime, MacArthur commandeered the tanks to cross over the bridge. By 1 AM on New Year's Day, 1942, the American tanks from the 192$^{nd}$ and 194$^{th}$ Tank Battalions started crossing the Calumpit Bridge through the darkness. When all the U.S. troops were safely settled on the other side of the bridge with the last infantrymen making it by 5 am, they waited.

The Japanese forces were soon advancing on the southside of the Calumpit Bridge trying to follow the exodus of American soldiers and refugees escaping to Bataan. At about 6:15 AM, twin four-ton dynamite charges blew up the Calumpit Bridge right in front of the advancing Japanese troops. A billowing mass of mortar and steel exploded in the faces of charging Japanese troops. Both spans dropped into the deep currents of the Pampanga River. The Engineering Battalion of the United States demolished the Calumpit Bridge to stop the Japanese forces in their pursuit of the American troops.

MacArthur together with his troops and civilians were safe for now. Benjamin and his group were way too far from Calumpit Bridge and were also safe now. By early morning, they were already entering the city of Manila, feeling safe that they did not join the exodus to Bataan. Something was telling them, they made the right choice.

# CHAPTER 15

Benjamin and his group reached Tutuban Railway Station near Divisoria in Manila at early dawn around 6 A.M. on New Year's Day. After 22 days of walking, they reached Divisoria about the same time General Wainwright ordered the Calumpit Bridge to be blown after all his troops had passed.

As they were approaching Manila, they could smell the stinking smell from the burning oil depot. They were wondering what happened. Have the Japanese arrived in Manila? They wanted to know. At Tutuban Railway Station, they tried to find out what was happening.

It was a bright morning and Divisoria was rather quiet from what it used to be. It used to be too frenzied there. Before the Japanese invasion, Divisoria was the biggest bargain emporium there was. Divisoria was famous for its indoor wholesale market, providing shoppers with a plethora of cheap items sold at various stalls. Its offerings include all kinds of merchandise: clothing, jewelry, and furnishings, textiles of various colors and weaves, handicrafts of all sorts were everywhere. Anything you needed for the house, you could get it at Divisoria at rock bottom prices.

It was still early. Not a lot of people were there yet. They decided to have breakfast at one of the eateries that was open. The shopkeeper ushered them to a table and they ordered bibingka and some coffee.

Ramon started talking to the shopkeeper, "What is happening? Did the Japanese blow the oil depot? It stank very badly and we could smell it from a far distance before we even got here."

She was looking at them up and down, wriggled her nose and before she could answer them, she could not help asking, "By the way, where did you all come from?" The shopkeeper asked suddenly.

They looked at each other and saw how they looked. They looked terrible, bedraggled, haggard and unkempt and knew right away why she was asking the question.

"I'm sorry for the way we look. We've been on the road for three weeks now. I mean, we've been walking since the war started all the way from Baguio. As you can see, we are totally exhausted and we still have a way to go."

"Baguio!" She exclaimed. "Did you say Baguio? What were you doing in Baguio?" She asked.

"We have a business there," Ramon said.

"O my God! You better eat good to keep your strength. Where is your destination, if I may ask?"

"We are going to Batangas where our home is."

She started scratching her head. "Better hurry up. I think the Japanese are on the way here. Some left already trying to chase MacArthur. But there is still a scattering of Japanese here and there. Be very careful when you leave here," she cautioned them.

"Thank you for the advice."

Benjamin remembered Ramon's prior question. He then asked the shopkeeper, "Did the Japanese burn the oil depots?"

"No, the Americans did." Everyone was astounded to find that out. They didn't think the Americans would do such a thing.

"Why?"

"From what I heard, the order came from MacArthur. Apparently he ordered all supply depots and oil storage tanks be razed."

Elias and Felipe who had been very quiet for sometime shook their heads. Delfin ventured to ask, "Why would he do such a thing?"

"Everyone was wondering the same thing. But come to think of it. MacArthur was afraid the Japanese could get hold of these supplies and oil for their use. MacArthur and his men could only take so much to Bataan so the strategy was to blow up the oil storage tanks in Pandacan. They did those four days ago."

"I guess MacArthur got the right idea. That was smart of him. Except it really stinks," Ramon said.

"That was just part of it. For a couple of days after they started blowing the place, the fireballs from Pandacan could be seen from a distance of several kilometers. The city stank with the foul-smelling smoke also coming from the blown-out giant fuel tanks along the Pasig River. Streams of burning oil flowed down the river, setting fire to many of the piers and buildings along the riverbanks. It was scary, like the whole city was going to go up in flame."

"That sounds scary all right," Benjamin said.

The shopkeeper kept on talking. "Food distribution warehouses were opened and food was distributed to Filipinos and Americans on hand. The authorities did not want the food also getting into the hands of the invading Japanese. The Filipinos took everything out of the warehouse then they turned to small shops next and looted them too. It was total chaos. It was disheartening to see Filipinos behaving badly."

"I guess you cannot blame them. They wanted to make sure they have enough to eat later on. They were afraid of what will happen next," Manuel finally said something.

"We better move on." Ramon motioned to Benjamin to pay the bill so they could leave.

Benjamin took some money from his wallet and they gathered their stuff, thanked the shopkeeper and left.

For Benjamin and his group, it was nice to see Manila again in spite of it being under siege. Amidst the parol, they could see the evidence of the raging war. Storefronts were boarded up. Some of the buildings were burned. They could still smell the stench from the burned oil storage. There was so much looting everywhere especially in the wealthy section of the city. Manila was destroyed. It was a surreal sight. It was not the same city as he knew it.

In spite of the fact that Manila was officially declared an open city, the Japanese started bombing the city. There was so much destruction. They learned that Intramuros was bombed on the 27th together with the Church of Santo Domingo and the convents of Santa Rosa College and Santa Catalina College nearby. Escolta, the most fashionable street in Manila, was also hit.

Spanish colonists had founded the city of Manila in 1571. In the battle of Manila Bay, Admiral Dewey destroyed the Spanish fleet on May 1, 1898 and the city itself capitulated on August 31, 1898 and so the American administration began. By the time the Second World War started, Manila proper had a population of over half a million people and with its surrounding suburbs, greater Manila included more than a million inhabitants. Located south of the Pasig River was Intramuros, a centuries-old Spanish walled city. The twenty-foot high walls stretched for two and a half miles. In places they reached twenty-five feet in height and had a thickness of up to forty feet at the bottom. From 1935 to 1941, MacArthur resided in a penthouse atop the Manila Hotel, off the southwest corner of Intramuros.

Intramuros' medieval appearance has been modified by the vigorous measures which have been taken under the American administration to improve the harbor, streets, sanitation, and water supply. Effectively utilizing the Intramuros District together with the city's strongly reinforced concrete buildings of prewar construction, the Japanese would bring in heavy-caliber guns from damaged and sunken ships in the harbor.

From Tutuban, they walked east on Azcarraga Street till they reached Quezon Boulevard and then turned south to Quiapo. Quiapo named after the water lily, *klyapo*, was at the center of Manila where everybody seemed to congregate at Plaza Miranda, next to Quiapo Church, the shrine of the Black Nazarene. Inside this Mexican baroque church was a hand carved life-size statue of the Black Nazarene, a Meso-American Christ kneeling with the heavy cross on his shoulder. It was said to be made by the Indians in Mexico and transported to the Philippines by the Spaniards during the 17th century. Filipinos believed in its miraculous powers and there were special mass and novenas every Friday with a feast day on January 9. One of the most famous devotional processions is the Feast of the Black Nazarene in Quiapo, Manila. Thousands of men (it was an all-male fiesta) worked their way to the *carroza* carrying a life-size image of the kneeling Christ to touch their handkerchief to the statue. The handkerchief which actually touches the icon was said to have healing powers.

Before the war, outside the church one could see all kinds of merchants, fortune tellers, medicine men in makeshift tents hawking their products and services. The medicine men had all kinds of herbs for the cure of various ailments. For people who wanted to try their luck on lottery, there were merchants selling lottery tickets too. It was the liveliest place to be in. Now, very few merchants were there.

Benjamin and his group walked up toward the church and went inside. The place had not changed. It was dim and dark, dank and dreary inside. The pillars went up high and there were people praying, and it smelt of incense, and there were some wonderful big windows. People were still coming and going in different directions inside the church. They saw some women walking on their knees in fervent prayer. People were lined up to see the Black Nazarene. One could see them taking their handkerchief, rubbing it on the statue, rubbing the handkerchief on their forehead and their children's forehead then rubbing the statue again and putting the handkerchief inside their shirt near their chest.

Benjamin found an empty pew near the front. All seven of them lit a candle each and went to the empty pew. They knelt and started to pray and prayed for everyone they knew and that they would be able to get home safely. They knelt in silent prayer for a few minutes and then went out in the hot sun on the steps of the church and moved on.

They went through Carriedo, then crossed the Santa Cruz bridge. They saw Intramuros with the St. Agustin Church with its Doric and Corinthian columns, the only structure to remain intact from the bombings a few days ago. They passed the grandiose General Post Office Building, the monolithic City Hall and on to Taft Avenue where they could see the Legislative Building, the Finance Building, the Agricultural Building located on the south side of the Pasig River, a couple of hundred yards southeast of Intramuros on Burgos St. and a little over hundred yards from City Hall. Taft Avenue was comparatively empty. Few people were walking. There was no transportation around. The military had appropriated most transportation to evacuate everyone. Only a few people remained in Manila.

They crossed the trolley tracks, down the main boulevard. They passed the Ermita district, a quiet, genteel area bounded by Dewey Boulevard to the west, Taft Avenue to the east, San Luis St. to the north and Herran St. to the south and then proceeded to the outskirts of Manila and headed south towards Paranaque and Las Pinas. They passed Sternberg Gen. Hospital, a few miles from Cavite. Hibiscus, acacia, palms, orchids and other tropical plants practically hid the two-story building. A screened porch hugged the front of the first and second stories. The windows were made of capiz shell windowpanes that emit soft light into the interior. They noticed that the American flag was not hoisted to the pole above the central entrance to Sternberg Gen. Hospital. They felt sad. It used to be flying gently in the breeze there all the time.

Benjamin remembered the days when he came to Manila in happier times when he would sit by the shore on Manila Bay and watched the sunset. It was the most beautiful sight he had ever seen in his life except maybe the Banaue Rice Terraces. During the day he would walk up and down Taft Avenue with its wide promenade and those ornate lampposts in the median of the street. Filipinos and the Americans in their white suits with their ladies in their finest gowns holding their parasols walked up and down the avenue. It seemed like yesterday.

Now the sight all over Manila was so different. Rubble from burning buildings were scattered throughout the city. American soldiers had abandoned the city. They were now fighting the war up north in Lingayen Gulf. There were some scattering of Japanese Army men with the rifle slung over their shoulders and bayonets on hand. People with their worried faces were walking faster to get where they wanted to go for fear that they might be stopped and God knows what would happen to them.

The Japanese troops started arriving in the southern outskirts of Manila on the evening of January 2 coming from Lamon Bay, about 95 kilometers (60 miles) southeast of Manila. They arrived in Manila in the predawn hours passing through Dewey Boulevard shouting "Banzai!" Tanks and trucks rolled by with Japanese troops greeted by Japanese civilians waving Japanese flags along the boulevard.

The Philipiines was still under the leadership of Manuel L. Quezon as President and Sergio Osmena as Vice President though they were running the government at Malinta Tunnel in Corregidor. They moved there on Christmas Eve. During the turmoil, both Quezon and Osmena were evacuated to Gen. MacArthur's headquarters in the rock fortress of Corregidor. By January 2, Manila had fallen and the American and Philippine troops had retreated to the Bataan Peninsula.

In Manila, the Japanese took over the running of the city on January 3. They came with all kinds of propaganda to entice the Filipinos to change their western ways. They moved into public buildings, hotels, university and school buildings. Government offices, banks, newspapers and other establishments came under Japanese control. Japanese officers, armed with the new occupation pesos, bought up souvenirs wherever they found an open store. Meanwhile, they started rounding up American and British expatriates and sending them either to the University of Santo Thomas which was now used as a prison or to Bilibid, a regular prison building outside Manila.

Benjamin and his group narrowly missed the arrival of the Japanese in the city by a couple of days. Their luck was still holding out but for how long. They still had about 100 kilometers to go. They were now at the outskirts of the city traversing the quiet road away from the main highway. They passed Pasay, Paranaque, and into Las Pinas, the home of the world's only bamboo organ whose pipes were 832 bamboo and 122 metal. It was built in 1821 and was housed at San Jose Church in Las Pinas.

They would soon be in the province of Laguna, getting closer to home. For another three and a half days they trekked from Manila and finally reached Calamba. Calamba was always a stopping point on a journey to and from Manila. Buses stopped here all the time to refuel or for passengers to take a break from their long trip. Vendors usually hawked through the window of the buses goodies like *espasol,* a candy type of snack and *balut,* a delicacy of unhatched hard boiled partly-incubated duck eggs surrounded by a thin, brownish liquid eaten feathers and all. Calamba is also famous as the hometown of a famous son, Jose Rizal who is their national hero. He sacrificed his life to get the Filipinos their independence from the Spaniards in 1896.

Benjamin and his group did not want to stop, not even for the night. They knew they were so close to home. They were very anxious to get to their destination. They felt like flying to get home faster.

From Calamba, they kept on walking day and night, only stopping for few hours in some secluded areas to catch some sleep and then kept on going. They could almost taste home. The road was very busy. There were too many sentries along the way. Japanese soldiers were everywhere. The Japanese were now occupying the Philippines.

By January 5, 1942, all of MacArthur's soldiers had marched to the wilderness of Bataan. They were tired and hungry and were expecting warplanes and reinforcements that Washington, DC had promised but never arrived. A radio station in Corregidor broadcast a message from President Roosevelt from Washington, DC to the American and Philippine soldiers fighting the Japanese:

*"The resources of the United States have been dedicated by their people to the utter and complete defeat of the Japanese warlords. I give to the people of the Philippines my solemn pledge that their freedom will be redeemed and their independence established and protected. The entire resources, in men and material, of the United States stand behind that pledge. The United States Navy is following an intensive and well-planned campaign which will result in positive assistance to the defense of the Philippines Islands."*

Roosevelt knew there was no help going to the Philippines and yet he made these remarks. MacArthur waited and waited for supplies and reinforcements but nothing came.

While MacArthur and his men were fighting the Japanese at Lingayen Gulf, Benjamin and his group were fighting fatigue and worry trying to reach home. They did not know how they would get through. Only their faith was strong enough to keep them going. It would still be few more days and these were the most hazardous parts of the journey. The Japanese were everywhere now. The Japanese were not only fighting in the sky but had finally arrived inland.

# CHAPTER 16

After walking for 27 days they finally reached Lipa City in the province of Batangas, at around 3:30 in the morning, Jan. 6, 1942, tired but in good spirits because they were almost home. At least they were now in their home province. Luck was with them because they finally saw a calesa.

Ramon being the eldest, thought he was more influential and asked the cuchero if he can take them to Alitagtag.

"*Magandang umago po*. Good morning sir. Are you taking customers?"

"*Oopo*." Yes sir. The cuchero said, "Where do you want to go?"

"Alitagtag *po*." Alitagtag sir.

"Alitagtag?" The cuchero stared at them in disbelief. "At this hour? No, I can't," he said.

"I thought you just said you were taking customers."

"Yes, but not to Alitagtag. That's too far."

"Please do it for us. I'm asking you a big favor," Benjamin said pleadingly.

Delfin joined Benjamin trying to convince the cuchero to say yes. "You see, we have been walking since they dropped the bomb at Clark Air Base. We had walked all the way from the Mountain Provinces farther north of Baguio for the last 27 days. We are almost home but we don't think we can make it through Cuenca. The road was too steep and winding through the mountains. We're very exhausted. Please help us."

"We'll be very grateful. We just want to be with our family," Felipe joined in.

"Please, really can you help us?" Elias added pleadingly.

"It will be worth your while," Manuel said.

"Please help us," Benjamin said and opened his wallet and pulled some bills.

The cuchero looked at them and thought hard. They looked like a pathetic bunch and felt sorry for them. They looked so worn out. He decided maybe he should really take them all home.

"OK. You talked me into it. Everyone. Hop in." Everybody jumped into the calesa.

As they got seated, Benjamin said gratefully, "Thank you so much. We are truly grateful. God bless you."

"Thanks. Thanks. Thanks." Everyone seemed to be saying all at once.

"You're very welcome." He started questioning them. "You said you walked from Baguio. How did you happen to walk that far?"

Ramon answered, "We travel to Baguio twice a year and stay there for a long time. We sell dry goods there to the miners. We got caught there when the war started. We could have stayed but decided to go home. We don't know how long the war is going to be. We felt it would be safer here than there."

"You are smart. We don't know how things will turn out. The war can go on forever. Did you encounter any Japanese along the way?

"Once. It was a close call. I thought they would kill us. It was on Christmas Eve. I don't know if it has something to do with Christmas but all they wanted us to do was help them pile the dead bodies from a battle in Tarlac. It was gruesome. I don't want to see that kind of things again."

"That must be scary."

"It was. But then they fed us and left us alone for the night. We decided to leave early the next day before they came back. I get goose bumps thinking about what could have happened if they came back and we were still around."

"I guess your guardian angels were still watching over you."

"I believe so."

The calesa lumbered on. Ramon sitting on the back with his brothers and his cousins started to doze off. He was so tired. Benjamin was riding next to the cuchero in front. He was trying to keep awake and alert. How weary he was, he thought. Bits and pieces of things that he saw the last three weeks kept flashing in his head. He could not seem to shake it.

The ride was going smoothly until they reached Banay-Banay. The calesa began to slow down.

"What's going on?" Ramon woke up bleary eyed.

"We are going through the sentry," the cuchero said.

"What?"

"They must have posted it recently. I didn't know that at all."

"What are you going to do?"

"We have to stop. I don't want to get shot any more than you do."

They stopped at the sentry. A Japanese soldier who knew a little English started asking them questions.

"Where are you going?" He asked sternly. Benjamin who was sitting in front with the cuchero was the first one to be asked.

Benjamin bowed his head and said, "Batangas sir, to our home."

"Who are they?" He was pointing to the six guys in the back seats of the calesa.

"They are my brothers and cousins."

"Get down," the soldier commanded.

Benjamin got off the calesa. He was very nervous. He bowed to the soldier.

"*Bahala na.*" Come what may. He muttered silently and glanced at his brothers. Ramon looked worried.

"What is in those bags?" The Japanese soldier asked.

"Just a few clothes, sir." Benjamin answered and bowed again then kept his eyes focused on the bag without blinking. He tried to hide his nervousness. He began to perspire. Thank God it was still dark. The soldier didn't notice his nervousness.

"Open the bag," the soldier commanded. Benjamin did as he was told to do. He had a hard time keeping his hand from trembling. The soldier looked all over the bag like an inspector at the airport. All he could see were a few clothes.

"Open the other bags." Benjamin took another bag and did what he was told to do. Then another one. Then one more. He opened the bags slowly, one after another. He had opened four bags so far. They went through the same routine. The Japanese soldier nodded. He paused. Benjamin was waiting. It seemed an eternity. Then the Japanese soldier turned around and went to talk to his companion. Benjamin waited without saying a word.

All this time, Benjamin was saying a silent prayer because he knew Delfin had the five cans of corned beef from the American soldiers and hopefully the soldier would not get to that. The Japanese soldier came back, motioned to the driver and said. "Pass."

Benjamin bowed again, breathed a sigh of relief and smiled inwardly and thanked his guardian angel for that. Then he bowed again, thanked the Japanese soldiers quietly and then climbed back into the calesa. He thought they would never pass inspection. He honestly believed the soldier would never let them through if the soldier saw those American cans of corned beef. They could be detained and it could be the end of them. They could have been taken prisoners or even gotten killed.

They got to Alitagtag at around 8 AM. The sun was already up. The whole town was so desolate. Nobody seemed to be around. It was so disheartening to see the town totally abandoned. The town was a ghost town. It was eerily quiet. Not a soul was on the road.

Ramon and his brothers rushed into their house but his family was nowhere in sight. "Hello, anybody home?" No one answered. They went out in the backyard but nobody was around there either. Even the neighbors were gone. They were getting very worried. His cousins did the same thing. It seemed all the people had left town.

Their two cousins went to seek their families and Benjamin and his brothers went searching for theirs. They decided to go to the school first. They met some people they knew and asked if they had seen their parents. Nobody knew where they were hiding. They went from building to building and searched and asked anyone. Their parents were not there.

Benjamin decided to try the church next. They saw the sakristan and asked him. He had not seen their parents either. The sakristan told them to try the rectory. Maybe the pastor had an idea or someone has seen them. They went to the rectory but still nothing.

Benjamin's heart sank. Where could they be? They must be somewhere. Benjamin and his brothers decided to go back to the house, hoping their family might be back home now. Nothing. They were starting to get frantic. They were expecting the worst now.

Ramon gathered his brothers in the kitchen. He tried to calm them down and planned what to do next. "We cannot stay here in the house. Staying on the main road is dangerous. I'm sure the Japanese will be patrolling the area soon."

"Where can we go?" Benjamin asked. Then he remembered the farm. He knew his parents owned some properties about a kilometer from the house in the rice fields.

Benjamin suggested, "Let's search at the farm. They could be hiding there. There was a place at the farm where they could hide."

They found out later that everybody went into hiding when the Japanese arrived. Some went to the school building and took refuge there with the American soldiers. Some went hiding in the church thinking that they would respect and spare the house of worship. Some like my family went underground so to speak.

"Ramon, the trench!" Benjamin told Ramon excitedly.

"What about the trench?" Ramon asked.

"They could be there. It is a perfect place to hide. Let's go and check it out." There was a trench at the farm where there used to be a stream flowing through his parent's property at one point in the past but had been dry for a long time.

They picked up all their things and all went out and practically ran toward the farm. They all remembered during their childhood days that there was a trench there between two big mango trees. They used to play hide and seek there when they were young and then enjoy climbing trees and eating all those delicious mangoes, *guava* and *duhat,* a Filipino version of blueberry.

"I bet you they are there." Delfin was so sure of it.

"I hope so," Ramon said and made a sign of the cross. "If they are not there, we can all stay there and use it as a hiding place. We'll use it as a base and then look for them," he volunteered the information. Everybody was agreeable.

As they got near the place, they heard voices. They crawled on the ground trying not to make any noise and approached quietly.

They heard their father's voice. They peeked through the bushes. The whole family was snuggled in that tight spot. Francisco, the clown got up quickly and ran full blast. Everybody at the trench was startled. They thought the Japanese had found their hiding place. They saw Francisco. Her mother gasped, put her hand on her mouth. She thought she was about to faint. Enrique caught her. They recovered fast. The whole family was very happy to see them.

"O my God!" Everyone exclaimed.

"You're home. You're alive." Barbara came forward and embraced each of them and started crying. She kept on crossing herself, glad that they were safe.

"Yes, we made it home," Ramon said.

Barbara could not stop crying. Even Enrique had tears in his eyes to see the boys back home. They looked thin and haggard but happy nonetheless to be home safe.

"We were very worried. All we could think was that there was no way you would make it back. There was no transportation available," Enrique said.

Enrique and Barbara were just finishing their meager breakfast of rice and some dried fish when they arrived. Their mother picked some banana leaves and placed them over a tin plate and put some rice and fish on it and gave everyone something to eat. "Here, eat this. You must be starving."

Delfin and Manuel were the first ones to take the plates. They started eating ravenously while Ramon tried to relate the story of how they walked all the way from Mankayan, how they encountered the Japanese along the way. Ramon saw tears in his father's eyes. Their father knew how far that was because he used to go with them.

Benjamin looked around. He saw they just had the bare necessities, few clothes, some bed linen, *banig* (bed mat made from straws), some plates and coconut cups, *palyok* (earthen pot to cook) and *banga* (a jug) to get some water from the lake. The lake is about a kilometer trek through the forest and they got their water supply there from a fresh water stream near the lake. They had some rice and dried fish to divvy among themselves.

Their mother said, "Sometimes we just eat rice with some salt to get by."

Delfin took his pack and pulled out the five big cans of corned beef. "I got these things for us."

"Corned beef!" His mother exclaimed. "Where did they come from?"

"From the American soldiers. I bartered them for five blankets that we did not sell in Baguio."

"The Japanese soldier did not confiscate them? Ramon said you went through the Japanese sentry." His father was wondering how they managed to smuggle them.

"We went through the sentry all right. Benjamin was grilled by the Japanese soldier and we were very nervous. They went through four bags but never got to mine. They let us through. We were extremely lucky."

"O my God!" His mother crossed herself again. "You could've been killed."

"We could have but the Holy Cross protected us. We always kept the Holy Cross with us. We have a strong faith and felt we would make it home although at times, we did not know how."

"These should keep us from starving when the dried fish runs out. It is like manna from heaven," his mother said now holding a can of corned beef.

The whole family was so happy to see them alive. They lost a lot of weight walking and looked haggard and tired but their spirits were up. Their family never thought they would make it home safe. They were so far away and there was no communication whatsoever. They were so lucky that nothing happened on their journey. Their mother reminded them that as long as they had St. Christopher and the Holy Cross with them, they would be safe. The Holy Cross was not really a cross. It was a little piece of wood that they always carried with them as a talisman everywhere they went. Their mother told them it was part of the Holy Cross that was the patron saint of their town. She was so religious and she probably kept on praying that her sons be spared the horrors of war. She said their homecoming was the best Christmas present they could ask from the three kings whose feast day was the day they came home.

On the same day they reached Alitagtag on Jan. 6, at the earliest hours of the day, the bridge at Layac where the last groups of U.S. troops crossed to reach Corregidor was blown up to stop the invading Japanese from reaching Corregidor.

They thanked their lucky stars for giving them the courage and strength to move on when they were on the road, otherwise they would not have made it. They could have been stranded in Corregidor or worse yet died in the hands of the savage Japanese troops.

# PART III

# CHAPTER 17

Benjamin woke up with a start. He was disoriented. He tried to get his bearing. For a while he could not remember where he was. He thought he was still on the road somewhere in Central Plains on his way home. He rubbed his eyes and tried to focus. The sun was peeking through the bamboo trees surrounding the trench casting shadows here and there. It was a glorious morning. The air was cool and pleasant and the birds were chirping merrily. Then he realized he was home now. Home in the sense he was now with his family, not in his house but close to the people he cared for deeply and home was Alitagtag.

Alitagtag was a small municipality in the province of Batangas. It was located south of Cuenca and west of San Jose and north of Bauan and Batangas and east of Taal. Alitagtag at that time was subdivided into 9 barrios: Dalipit, Dominador, Pinagkurusan, Balagbag, Poblacion, Kanluran, Muzon, Tadlac, and Munlawin. Alitagtag, a "sister town" of Bauan, an old mission founded as a *visita* of Taal in 1590 and was administered by the Augustinians from 1596 until the end of the 19th century.

Five years after the establishment of the mission of Bauan, a cross made of *anubing*, a local hardwood was found on a promontory above the rice fields in Alitagtag. They called the place Binukalan meaning 'where something sprouted" which was a very literal description of where the cross was found. It was close to where Benjamin was entrenched right now. It was believed that the cross had protected the people of Alitagtag from disaster.

According to a document found in 1790 at Bauan Cathedral Archives, the cross was made few years after the foundation of

Bauan Mission from a strong post of a demolished house and placed in Alitagtag to drive away bad spirits. The cross was 2.5 meters in height with a 1 meter crosspiece. It had a golden sun embossed with a human face with radiating rays where the arms intersected and was believed that water gushed from one of its arms.

At some point, the head of the *barangay* wanted to move the Holy Cross of Alitagtag to a safer place to escape the violent eruptions of Taal Volcano nearby. Neighboring villages attempted to pull it out from the original site at Binukalan but the Holy Cross wouldn't budge until the parish priest from Bauan church attempted it and it came out easily. They claimed it was because Alitagtag was thought of as a sister barrio of Bauan and was the rightful choice to be its caretaker.

The long trip must have taken a heavy toll on Benjamin's body. He was totally exhausted - physically from walking so many kilometers for the last 27 days and mentally from strain and worry on whether they would make it home or get killed by the Japanese on their way. His whole body ached but he slept so soundly in spite of the uncomfortable position he was in. The trench was so snug, narrow but long. With so many of them there, there was not much room to move. They looked like sardines packed tightly in a can. He remembered sitting upright against the wall of the trench and sometime during the night must have dozed off instantly. His bones ached and he felt stiff. He looked around and saw his other four brothers who were with him on the journey were still asleep. Delfin was snoring loudly. He began to yawn and tried to get up. His feet felt stiff and numb. He tried to rub them to get the circulation going. He did not realize how tired he was.

The sun was beginning to shed its bright rays and was peeking through the slits among the bamboo grove surrounding the trench. It started to get warm. He reached for his comb and combed his hair a little bit. He tried to maneuver getting out from between his sleeping siblings without waking them up. Finally, he crawled up the wall and got out of the trench. He looked around. Besides his four brothers who were still asleep, no one was nearby. He stretched his arm up and down, then just sat on the edge of the trench, trying to absorb his surroundings. He looked around and found the surroundings very pleasant and peaceful. To his right were rows of fruit trees - *sinigwelas, duhat,* several banana trees, breadfruit trees, coconut trees and a couple of mango trees. In front of him were open fields that soon would be planted with corn and rice.

In the far distance, the topography was more rugged with rolling hills and a ravine going down to Taal Lake with the constantly active Taal volcano. Taal Volcano is a complex volcanic system composed of a small volcanic island (Volcano Island), located within a 20 x 30 km. lake-filled complex *caldera.* A caldera is a large, usually circular depression at the summit of a volcano formed when magma erupted from a shallow underground magma reservoir. The removal of large volumes of magma may result in loss of structural support for the overlying rock, thereby leading to collapse of the ground and formation of a large depression. Calderas are different from craters, which are smaller, circular depressions created primarily by explosive excavation of rock during eruptions.

To the right of the cornfields on top of a hill is the Binukalan where it was believed that the Holy Cross was found near a well. A far distance beyond Binukalan is a huge mountain called Mt. Makulot in Cuenca. Cuenca was established as a town around 1875, and as an independent parish in 1879. There was a church built before 1879 together with a convent which was enlarged later and then a cemetery was built in 1887 nearby. In the late 19th century, cocoa was cultivated here in Cuenca.

After a few minutes, he stood up, inhaled, filling his lungs with fresh air which felt so good and exhilarating. He wondered where everyone was. His legs were still stiff and he tried to shake them several times to limber them up. Then he started looking for the rest of the family. He looked to the right but there was no one around. He decided to walk toward the left section of the property where there was more vegetation near a big mango tree. There he found them all sitting on a banig spread on the ground and eating their meager breakfast under the cover of the nearby mango tree. Next to the banig was a makeshift stove made of pieces of rocks where they cooked their meal and boiled their coffee. They used pieces of banana leaves on top of a plate for eating so they did not have to

**175**

wash the plate and a coconut shell as a drinking cup. They used their hands to feed themselves. A bamboo shaped like a big spoon served as a kitchen utensil. An earthen pot called palyok was used to cook rice and a tin can to boil coffee. They were having plain rice with a sprinkling of a little salt and black barako coffee.

"Good morning," Benjamin said as he approached his parents.

"Good Morning. Did you have enough sleep?" His father asked.

"Oh yes, I did not realize how tired I was."

"Here, have something to eat. It's not much but we have to save the big meal for supper. There is not much food around," his mother said looking sad.

"I know. I hope the war does not last long."

"We are hoping the same thing. God only knows how long," Enrique said.

Benjamin sat down at one end of the banig next to his mother and joined his parents for breakfast. He picked up pieces of banana leaves, placed them on a plate and took a portion of rice and poured a little salt on it and began eating.

"You looked very tired and exhausted yesterday. We were very worried about you and your brothers. We never thought we would see you again. How you managed to get here was short of a miracle. I still can't believe it." His mother patted Benjamin's hand.

Benjamin looked his mother in the eye and could see her concern. "I'm still wondering about it myself. What strength did we have to make it through. I can't believe we walked that far. We were determined to go home and very happy to make it home alive. There were some scary instances where we thought we would be taken prisoners by the Japanese but we had faith and that sustained us through the whole ordeal."

He paused, ate some more, then trying to change the subject he asked his mother, "So when did you move here?"

"On Dec. 12, there was some bombing in Batangas. We were told to evacuate then. We figured it would be safe for us here."

"You are absolutely right. The Japanese are now on the street. I don't know if they would venture out in the rice fields."

"Most of the people of Alitagtag are all scattered in gullies and ditches around here. Some moved further near the lake. There is a spring well there so water is not a problem but we like it here. We just fetch some water there when we are about to run out." Enrique said, then asked Benjamin, "So why are you up so early? I thought you'd sleep most of the day after that long journey."

"Now that I am finally home, I have to go to Bauan today and see Adelaide. I just want to let her know that I am still alive and made it back home. I will leave as soon as I can get ready and will be back before dark. I will be home for supper."

"Can it wait another day? You just got home yesterday." Barbara glanced at her husband for support.

"I really have to see her. I won't stay long."

"Be careful, son. The Japanese soldiers are now patrolling the road," his father said.

"I know. I'm not stupid. I will take the path through the rice fields. The Japanese soldiers do not go that route. They stay on the main road. Nobody will see me out there. After that long trip we did, this should be a breeze. I had a good night rest last night and that swim in the lake yesterday did me good. I feel refreshed."

"Of course," his father agreed.

Benjamin ate his breakfast with gusto in spite of it being plain rice and a little salt. He felt safe now that he was home which gave him some appetite. There was a bottle of bagoong on the mat so he put some on his plate.

"Hmmmm. This is better than the one we had in Urdaneta. Where did you get this bagoong?" Benjamin asked his mother.

"Your father was in Balayan before the war broke and he brought some. I have some bottles saved."

"Oh yeah. I heard Balayan has the best tasting anchovies." All of a sudden he felt very hungry.

His father joined in the conversation. "I was in Balayan and stopped at one of the *sari-sari* stores that operated along the road. It was a very hot day and I stopped for some ice-cold *halo-halo* snack. Halo-halo is an ice shake with sweet beans and preserved fruits served with ice, milk and ice cream. The sari-sari store sells all kinds of everyday goods in small packets or bottles. I saw packets of salt, sugar, coffee, and candies. There were soft drinks, canned goods and ice-cold San Miguel Beers and some liquors like lambanog. What caught my attention were the bottles of bagoong. I know that Balayan was well known for their delicious bagoong so I decided to buy a couple of small bottles. They said they were homemade. Each one tasted a little different from the other because everyone had a special secret recipe of the anchovy sauce that was supposedly handed down from generation to generation."

"So did you ask them how it was made?" Benjamin wanted to know.

"First of all, this one is called Bagoong Balayan to differentiate it from those made in Urdaneta up north. There are two varieties of anchovy used in Bagoong Balayan. The special bagoong is made from *dilis,* while the ordinary bagoong are made from *galunggong.* Bagoong Balayan is a saline product made by partial fermentation. Fish and salt are mixed together and stored in a container called *tapayan* (a large earthen jar). Intermittent mixing is important to maintain an even absorption of salt. It is stored for several months, at least 4 months of fermentation. It is brownish in color and taste like cheese with a fishy scent."

"It is really good. Maybe we can sell them here," Benjamin said with the thought of making money as usual in spite of the ongoing war.

Bagoong is the most popular sauce in this area. It is an excellent dip for mango especially for the unripe green mango. It is used to flavor food by sautéing it with garlic in cooking oil though some people do not like the smell of it. It permeates the house.

"So what do you think of my idea?" Benjamin could not shake the idea off his head. "We can make good money. People love the product already. It is a matter of procuring the product. Maybe after the war is over, I'll check it out more thoroughly. I can go to Balayan and check it out. Too bad, we have this war. We cannot go too far, what with the Japanese everywhere."

He finished his coffee, got up, stretched and yawned. Just then he saw his siblings marching in from the trench. Francisco was being playful again. He was swaying his hands by his side.

With a big grin on his face, he said, *"Magandang Umaga Po.* Good morning. How is everyone today? Are we catching some Japs today?"

His father started shaking his head. His other brothers were behind him walking solemnly and still looking tired and haggard. They all sat on the banig, grabbed some banana leaves and helped themselves to some rice and coffee.

Benjamin turned around to leave and Ramon, his eldest brother asked, "Hey, what are you up to? Where do you think you are going?"

"I have a mission to accomplish today. I'll be home for supper."

Francisco asked, "What? Are you going after the Japanese who stopped us on the road?"

"No, I'm going to see Adelaide. Just to let her know I'm still alive,"

Delfin could not help himself and whistled, "Oh My! That's what I call love. Are you sure she cares? She probably thinks you've been killed at the bombing in Baguio."

"That is why I have to see her. To let her know I'm home and out of danger."

"You are totally crazy."

Ramon nudged Delfin to stop teasing his brother. "Delfin, stop it now."

Then Ramon turned to Benjamin and said, "Just be careful. We made it home alive. We do not want to see something happen to you now that we are safely home."

"I know. I'll be careful."

"*Adios*!" Godspeed!

Benjamin glanced at his mother, smiled, waved his hand and went back to the trench. He changed his clothes, grabbed his panama hat, and headed toward the dirt path leading to the main road.

# CHAPTER 18

Since taking the main road might be dangerous, Benjamin decided to cut through the rice farms. He left the trench around 7 in the morning. From where his parents were hiding, he traversed a narrow path bisected by rice fields. The dirt path was uneven, rising up and down on a narrow slope and sometimes lush vegetation was in his way. He passed farmland where he saw some carabaos grazing. They were strong domesticated water buffalo. Farms that were not cultivated had thick covering of tough *cogon* grass swaying in the wind. He tried to be careful not to get too close to them because of its razor sharp edges. Luckily he knew this path very well. Since he used to come here all the time when he was home, he knew this area in and out. He navigated thru thick vegetation and made it to the main road. He walked slowly, hid under some bushes and listened. The road was eerily quiet. There was no sound except the singing of the birds. He peeked through the bushes, did not see anyone. He ran across the road towards his house.

He stopped by his house, went inside quietly and looked around to see if anybody was around. He was very alert just in case some Japanese soldiers were around. However, not even one person could be seen. There were no Japanese soldiers either. He went back behind his house, passed through some bamboo groves and headed southeast through a narrow path. There was open field for several yards. He kept his steady pace following a dirt path through rice fields, looking back and around every so often and listening for any sound.

The sun was getting bright and the temperature was now rising. The sun was beating warmly on him now. He had his panama hat on. He could see the crows flying from tree to tree like nothing was happening in the world. There were some carabaos grazing in the meadows. There was a slight breeze which made the *cogon* grass sway with the wind. It seemed like a nice day to be strolling in the field with someone dear to your heart.

He passed the two mango trees on top of a rise which was a local landmark. This spot was known locally as *Mag-asawang Mangga* meaning Mango Couple. Farmers usually stopped there and rested under its canopy. It was so cool and breezy underneath the mango trees. He was tempted to stay and rest awhile. However, he decided otherwise. He thought of Adelaide. He felt a lump in his throat. He wanted to see her now and the sooner he got to her place, the better it would be. He was wondering if she missed him. How would she react when he appeared at her door? She probably thought he was dead. He had not written her for a month. He hoped she was okay. She probably was. He was the one who had difficulty coming home. He was the one who was in danger. Sure, she and her family must be okay. He did not think the Japanese would bomb their place. But who knew.

So in spite of the sun beating down on him, he kept on pushing on. He desperately wanted to see her soon. He walked through rice fields and corn fields for miles. He passed a tiny village with half a dozen *nipa* huts. It was extremely quiet. Nobody was in sight. He wondered where everyone was.

He kept on walking. Then he heard the hooves of a horse. He stopped in his track. His heart started pounding heavily.

"Who can it be? I hope it is not a Japanese," he was talking to himself.

He saw a patch of *cogon* grass. He walked there and hid behind it. He was getting very nervous. He lay very still. He did not know what to do. He should really just stay home. He was really crazy to leave his parents' hiding place. What if it is a Japanese soldier? That would be the end of him.

Benjamin began to pray.

*"Our Father, who art in heaven.*
*Hallowed be Thy name.*
*Thy kingdom come,*
*Thy will be done on earth as it is in heaven.*
*Give us this day our daily bread.*
*And forgive us our trespasses*
*As we forgive those who trespassed against us*
*And lead us not into temptation*
*But deliver us from evil.*
*Amen."*

Benjamin asked for the Blessed Mother's help too.

*"Hail Mary, full of grace.*
*The Lord is with thee*
*Blessed are you amongst women*
*And blessed is the fruit of thy womb, Jesus.*
*Holy Mary, mother of God,*
*Pray for us sinners now and at the hour of our death,*
*Amen."*

"Nobody knows this area. Who can it be? The Japanese cannot possibly know this place," he was talking to himself. "Maybe I should have listened to my parents and stayed home for a while. Dear God, please help me. I don't want to die now that I made it home. Please, dear God. I implore for your help and mercy."

The sound was getting closer. He started peeking through the grasses. The man on the horseback spotted him and got closer. He froze. He knew that would be his end. If this man was an enemy, he would be questioned. What if the man thought he was a spy?

As the man on the horse approached him, Benjamin kept his panama hat on, closed his eyes and pretended he was napping. *"Bahala na,"* then he crossed himself.

The man on horseback said, "Hello, are you all right? Can I help you?"

Benjamin heard him and opened his eyes. The voice seemed friendly. The voice asked again, "Are you okay? Do you need help?"

Now, he recognized the voice. He sounded like one of his old buddies. It had to be him. He knew the man.

Benjamin took off his hat and stood up from where he was laying down. He squinted and tried to look at the man. The man on horseback recognized him at once. The man was an old acquaintance who sometimes came to town to buy some supplies for his entire village. He was a tall, lanky fellow, very dark skin with a mustache and wearing an eye patch. He looked like somebody you would see in a Western movie. He looked more like a pirate.

The man dismounted from his horse, tipped his hat and extended his left hand in greeting. First Benjamin was startled to see the left hand, then realized in an instant that this man had a severed right hand due to some accident while he was stealing some parachutes from the army. The parachutes were wrapped around a bomb and the bomb exploded. His name was Pedro. He always kept his right hand in his pocket. Kids were always fascinated by this man who never showed his right hand. They wanted to see what it looked like but Pedro never took his right hand off his pocket ever.

Pedro said in greeting, "*Kumusta*?" How are you?

Benjamin replied, "*Kumusta. Mabuti naman.*" How are you? I'm fine.

"Did I scare you? I'm sorry."

"Yes, you scared me to death. I thought you were one of those Japanese soldiers."

"No. You will not find them here."

"Why not?"

"They don't venture off the main road. They don't know this area"

"Are you sure?"

"Positive. They are afraid of the guerilla."

"Good to know."

"I have not seen you for a long time. I understand you were in Baguio. You look like you lost a lot of weight. When did you come back?"

"Yesterday early morning."

"How? The Japanese are everywhere. There is no transportation around. Every cars and buses are being appropriated by the army. How did you manage? What happened?" Pedro was asking all these questions in rapid succession.

"I was caught in Baguio when the war started last month. We had a tough time coming home. We were glad we left when we did. We could not get any transportation so my brothers and my cousins walked from the Mountain Province to home."

"*Sus, Maria!*" Jesus, Mary! Pedro whistled. "Really?"

"We walked every day, since the war started and just got here yesterday. It was almost a month. At times we thought we would never make it. We saw some horrible events along the way. The journey was so exhausting to say the least but we made it. There were some close calls."

"Boy, you were very brave to do that. Most people would probably stay where they were and waited. But who knows when the war will be over."

"We debated whether to stay or not but we figured the best thing to do was try to go home if at all possible. We were very lucky to make it without one being killed."

"You are lucky indeed. You're alive and that's all that matters. Why don't you come to the house and we can have a drink or two like we used to?" Pedro invited him to his hut which was not that far from where they were.

"Isn't it too early for a drink?"

"No. I have tuba or lambanog hiding somewhere."

Tuba or palm wine is made from coconut trees and is produced in a natural process. It is chemical free and is best drunk on the first day. It tastes a bit sour with just a hint of alcohol. Lambanog is another beverage made from coconut but stronger in taste when distilled. It is commonly described as coconut wine or coconut vodka. Lambanog is an alcoholic beverage known for its potency and high alcohol content about 80 to 90 proof.

The lambanog making process is inexpensive and coconut trees are abundant in Quezon Province, about 143 kilometers southeast of Manila where most of the lambanog is made. The lambanog making process has been a tradition passed down through generations of coconut plantation farmers. Because the process of distilling lambanog from tuba is a relatively inexpensive process, it is known as a poor man's drink and has been a part of Filipino tradition for centuries. Farmers often wind down by drinking lambanog after a long day's work.

The process involves collecting the sap from the unopened flower of the coconut tree. To extract tuba, you have to climb a coconut tree every afternoon. Then, the tuba gatherer called *mangagarit* has to prune the coconut flower. The space left by the flower is replaced by a tube made of bamboo so the coconut sap will drip liquid drops in a bamboo tube called *tukil* which collects the juice from its cut end. The process is similar to rubber tree tapping. The process looks simple but it is not. It is a bit hazardous. A worker will climb up the tree about 30 feet high having a bamboo and sickle and getting the sap from 35 coconut trees that are connected to each other by two long bamboo trunks.

Foliage is tied at the bamboo tube to prevent other particles from adulterating it from other substances like rainwater. The next morning, the mangagarit returns to collect the sap from these bamboo tubes. The tuba gatherer must also climb the tree every 12 hours to remove the extra slice from the stem. If you don't do it regularly, the wound will be cured, and liquid sap will stop flowing. The sap that was collected was put in a big plastic drum and then when it was full it was transferred to a cooking pan and heated. The sap is then cooked and fermented to become tuba. The tuba is then distilled to make lambanog. A coconut tree normally produces a gallon of tuba per day.

Benjamin looked at his watch and said, "Maybe next time. I'm on my way to see Adelaide. I want to tell her I'm still alive."

Pedro looked at him and said, "As I understand she lives in Sambat. Do you know how far that place is for you to be walking, especially on this rough terrain?"

"I know."

Then Pedro remembered that Benjamin had just finished this long journey. He started laughing.

"What is so funny?"

"What was I thinking? This must be nothing compared to what you have been through."

Benjamin smiled.

Still, Pedro felt he wanted to help his friend. A light bulb flashed in his head. "Wait a minute. I have a great idea. Why don't I take you to Sambat on my horse? I have nothing else to do right now. It will save you some time. Hop on."

"Are you sure you want to do that?" Benjamin was really hoping Pedro was serious and not just being polite. Benjamin still tired from walking decided maybe he should take his friend's offer. He figured it would take him almost three hours to go to Sambat on foot. This way, he could be there faster and save his energy for his trip back. He could probably leave Sambat at 2 o'clock in the afternoon after a nice visit with Adelaide and still be home before dark. That surely was a splendid idea. He won't be as tired as he thought he would be.

"So, what do you think? Come on. What's a friend for but to help his friend? Let's go. We can be there in no time."

Benjamin mounted the horse behind Pedro and the horse galloped through fields and forests until they reached a clearing near the town of Sambat. Pedro reined in the horse, allowed the horse to trot to cool him down. A dirt path loomed ahead.

"You can drop me here."

Pedro stopped and Benjamin dismounted at the nearest field less than a quarter mile from the road.

"Thank you very much. That was a big help." Benjamin extended his right hand and Pedro took it with his left hand. Then Pedro went his merry way. Benjamin took a glance at his friend, turned around, adjusted his hat and headed toward the main road.

As he approached the main road, Benjamin stopped. He stood and watched Adelaide's house from the other side of the road. The place looked the same. He was right. They were safe here and there was nobody around. The road was very quiet. He looked left and right before he crossed the street. He climbed the ladder quietly, crossed the walkway and up the stairs. He tooked a deep breath. He was very nervous. He heard voices from inside the house.

He knocked at the door and waited. Then he heard footsteps.

Inside, Adelaide heard the knock at the door. Adelaide put down the embroidery ring that she was working on, looked at her mother and said, "Who could that be? Are we expecting someone?"

Her mother, Regina said, "No one that I know of but go and check who it is?"

Adelaide dusted her skirt and got up. Passing a mirror on the hallway, she looked at herself. There was a strand of hair dangling on her face so she pushed it back. She walked to the door, opened it slowly and almost fainted. She gasped, put her hands over her mouth and could not speak. She thought she was seeing a ghost. She blinked her eyes once and then again. Benjamin was standing by the door, thin and haggard and looking exhausted. She rubbed her eyes, not believing what she was seeing. She wanted to say something but no words came out of her mouth. She remained transfixed where she stood.

"It's me," Benjamin said.

"O my God," is all Adelaide could say.

Then she added, "It's you."

"Yes, it's me. You're not seeing a ghost. Are you going to let me in?"

"Of course."

After she steadied herself, Adelaide stepped aside and let Benjamin walked by. She followed him into the living room without saying a word. She thought her knees would buckle. She was still trembling. She still could not believe what she was seeing. She kept on thinking, "Is it real? It is. I'm not dreaming. Benjamin is alive and he is here."

She looked up and still could not believe it that he was here in person. If this is a dream, she does not want to wake up. But there he was, standing there in front of her with a bright smile on his face.

Benjamin placed his panama hat on the nearest table and finally broke the silence.

"How are you Adelaide? How is everything here?"

"I'm fine. We're fine." She rubbed her eyes still not believing.

Benjamin smiled and stifled a laugh.

"Who is it?" Adelaide heard someone from the back of the house say.

She finally pointed to a chair. "Why don't you sit down and I can get something for you to eat and drink. You look like you can use some." She left him in the living room and went to the kitchen.

"Guess who was there at the door. You won't believe it." Adelaide told her mother and sisters.

"Who?" They all asked.

"Benjamin." Adelaide replied.

"What? My God. He is back?"

"Yes."

Her mother and her sisters got all excited. Her mother went to the living room followed by her sisters. Regina wanted to welcome Benjamin on his sudden arrival. She was jubilantly happy to see him. After some welcoming greetings, Regina told the girls, "Go help Adelaide with the merienda."

Isabel, one of the sisters, went back to the kitchen where Adelaide was boiling some salabat (a hot beverage made with ginger root).

"Can I help you? I can bring the salabat when it is ready. Why don't you bring the merienda now. Go back and talk to your friend."

"Thank you." She picked up the plate with the *suman tamales* and a spoon and grabbed a napkin on the way back to the living room. Suman tamales is made from powdered rice flour, coconut milk, ground peanuts, chicken, pork and boiled eggs. It is wrapped in banana leaves in a rectangular form and steamed. It has a strong, sharp taste, spicy and a little bit salty.

Regina turned to Benjamin. "I want you to stay for lunch. I'll join you all for lunch. See you later." She left and went to the back room.

Adelaide came back with the plate of merienda. Since Benjamin was now a regular visitor, the family let him talk to Adelaide alone in the living room although one of the sisters was not too far away in the adjoining room. In a few minutes, Isabel brought in the salabat.

Benjamin talked animatedly about his journey. She was eager to hear his story, how he was able to make it home. Benjamin told her about his adventure on the way down from Baguio, how they encountered some Japanese along the way, how they bartered some goods from the American soldiers, the devastation in Manila when they got there, the close encounter at the checkpoint with the Japanese and reaching home to find nobody was there. They seemed to talk for hours.

Pretty soon it was noon and time for lunch. Regina asked Isabel to fetch Benjamin and Adelaide to the dining room and they all joined in. The dining room table was covered with a white table cloth with fine embroidery and matching napkins all made by hand by the girls in the family. The family has been in business making fine embroidery linens and baby clothes for U.S. companies in Manila and they saved the most exquisite ones for their own house.

Benjamin sat at one end of the table with Adelaide on his right. He seemed to be enjoying the company and the atmosphere of his visit. They had *bulalo* which is beef bone marrow and shank boiled with malunggay leaves and some rice.

Benjamin took a sip of the broth and said, "The last time I had bulalo was when I was in Mankayan. However, this is better tasting than what I had back there."

"It tastes better here because beef in Batangas was considered the best in the Philippines," Regina said.

Regina made it a point to have something special for dessert since it was a special occasion. She asked Isabel to make some tablea tsokolate for a drink after dessert instead of coffee. Special occasion called for a special drink, she told herself of which Adelaide was very grateful. It looked like Benjamin needed it anyway from the way he looked. He looked like he lost some weight and tired. His hair was longer than usual. He had not had a haircut for almost a month. Regina thought tablea tsokolate would revive his physical appearance. Tablea tsokolate is distinctly different from other hot chocolate. Tablea means tablet and tsokolate means chocolate in Spanish. Why it was called tablea was beyond her. She always knew them to be round balls. They were considered Batangas delicacies. The hot drink was very thick and served in a demitasse cup and made from cacao beans. Maybe in the olden days, it was flat or even square. Leave it to those Spaniards who ruled the country for almost 400 years.

When the tsokolate was ready, Isabel pulled out six demitasse cup and saucers and six dessert plates from the kitchen cupboard and poured the steaming hot tsokolate into the demitasse cups. Then she took some kalamay and put it in a plate. She sat them on the dining table with spoons and forks.

Benjamin looked at the meal in front of him and made a remark about the tsokolate.

"My, My. That looks delicious. What is the occasion?" He acted surprised seeing the tsokolate. He knew it was only served for special occasion.

"It's for your homecoming. You're very lucky to make it back. I can't believe you escaped the Japanese. We really thought you might have been killed in Baguio," Regina said matter-of-factly.

Benjamin almost choked in tears. He finally said, "We escaped all the bombings in Baguio and along the way but there was an instance almost close to home when we reached the checkpoint that it got pretty scary. We were very close to getting caught with some supplies from the G.I.s. We were very lucky indeed."

Benjamin took a sip of his tsokolate and asked, "Where did you get the cacao beans?"

Regina answered, "Oh that! We have a couple of cacao trees in the backyard next to a coconut grove there. It must be growing there since my grandparents were living here. That tree must be more than 30 ft. tall and its fruits are more than a foot long. The fruits are brownish yellow to reddish purple and contain plenty of cacao seeds. These are the cacao beans which we dried and made into tablea tsokolate or cacao chocolate. My father who was a *Cabeza de Barangay* used to serve them at breakfast or merienda especially on special occasion when town officials came to the house. It was so thick in consistency and I remember serving it in these small cups and it just became a tradition in our home."

Benjamin said, "It's delicious and this kalamay goes very well with it."

All of a sudden, Isabel got up. "You must taste this dessert. This one is my specialty. I just made some this morning." She pulled out a small bowl from the cupboard, scooped some white stuff from a pot sitting on the stove and handed it to Benjamin. He took one look at the cup and exclaimed, "*Pinindot*! You are all terrific! How on earth are you managing well at this time?"

Pinindot or *ginataang bilo-bilo* is a tepid dessert soup made of coconut milk and sweet rice balls served in cups or bowls. Stuffed with taro root, sweet potato, jackfruit and purple yam, it is a white colored soup, a little bit sweet and creamy.

"Well," Regina replied. "Since our house is up on the hill and farther back, nobody can really see us. I believe the Japanese are mostly in town anyway. Whenever they come to his area, they seldom look up. They just walk on the street. The shrubs in front of the house shade us from scrutiny. Also, we take out the bamboo steps upfront once in a while so probably the Japanese soldiers don't even notice that some people live up here. I believe we're pretty safe."

"Thank God for that," Adelaide agreed with the sentiment.

While Benjamin ate his dessert ravenously, Adelaide could not help thinking how her family acted as if he were already a part of the family. That was a good sign and she was happy about that. Her mother especially from the way she was treating him obviously liked him very much. Her sisters she was sure felt the same way. Well, she thought, he was really a very likeable fellow. There was no doubt about it. However, she still did not know about her brothers. Benjamin had not met any of them. Will there be a problem? There might be. Benjamin seemed more at ease with the ladies but as she understood, he had a way with men too. So she should not worry.

After a hearty meal, Benjamin and Adelaide returned to the sala and caught up with more news. The hours seem to be going fast and then it was time to leave. He had a long way to walk so he better be on his way. There was limited bus transportation and even if there was, it was subject to inspection and investigation. Things had really changed. At night, there was now a curfew so at sundown, everyone went to their hiding place. Nobody moved. There was a blackout everywhere.

He picked up his hat from the table and asked Adelaide to fetch her mother so he could say goodbye.

"I don't know when I'll be back but I'll come as soon as I can. Thanks for the delicious lunch," he told them as he said goodbye. Adelaide shook his hand and Regina gave him her blessing. He tipped his hat and off he went downstairs and down the bamboo steps to the road. He looked left and right and not seeing anyone, he crossed the road and followed a path leading him back to Alitagtag.

The sun was still beating its golden rays across the field. He kept on walking. He felt he was getting warmer and tired. He spotted a mango tree and decided to rest a while. He sat underneath the tree and soon his mind drifted to the day in the summer of 1939 when he spotted Adelaide's picture in a magazine about a Flores de Mayo and Santacruzan at a nearby town. It's been more than two years and he still considered himself lucky to have seen her picture and had kept it. He was glad to have met her.

# CHAPTER 19

As early as January 1942, life in Batangas started to be very difficult. There was a shortage of food and there was the constant warning of air raids. People were asked to turn off their light at night because the Japanese could mistake it for an American base and they could drop bombs on them. At Adelaide's home, they had to light a lamp and put it on a liter can and placed under a table and close the window.

During one of those raids, a bomb fell close to Adelaide's uncle's house which was only a kilometer away from her home. As soon as people heard the roar of planes, they started running for cover in their dugouts. Everyone had a dugout in their backyard. However, the dugout was not a guarantee you would be safe. Adelaide's uncle and his family were hiding in their dugout when a bomb dropped too close to their dugout and everyone in the family got killed.

The fighting continued. The news from the front kept on coming in bits and pieces. Recently, they heard that President Roosevelt was not sending the food and supplies that Gen. Mac Arthur was expecting. The fighting American and Filipino men of Bataan desperately needed food and supplies and were poorly armed. The troops were suffering from malnutrition and diseases and were so demoralized that they called MacArthur "Dugout Doug" and composed a verse that epitomized their flight.

*"We're the battling bastards of Bataan,*
*No mamma, no papa, no Uncle Sam;*
*No aunts, no uncles, no nephews, no nieces;*

*No rifles, no planes, no artillery pieces;*
*And nobody gives a damn."*

They also heard about the fall of Bataan on April 9. After the Fall of Bataan, the Japanese started moving inland. The Japanese started moving to Bauan. When the people from Bauan heard that they were coming, some went into hiding. Others stayed put.

Then on May 6, 1942 after the Japanese crossed the narrow channel to Corregidor, the last American resistance in the Philippines ended with the surrender of the island of Corregidor. General Wainwright, fearing that the Japanese might kill not just the soldiers but the nurses that were treating them ordered his men to surrender. After a major attack, 78,000 American and Filipino troops under the command of General Wainwright as commander on Bataan surrendered to the Japanese. It was the largest surrender of an American army in its history. Consequently, they suffered brutal inhuman treatment and atrocities from the Japanese during the "Bataan Death March" where about 750 Americans and as many as 5,000 Filipinos died. It was so unfortunate that they surrendered to the Japanese who viewed that surrender as an act of cowardice and dishonor and the prisoners especially whites should be treated like animals for the cowardly act of surrender.

The Japanese only expected 25,000 prisoners but instead found out the number to be three times that much and did not know how to handle them. Some were taken by truck to Camp O'Donnell, but some were forced to walk much of the way under the blazing hot sun. The Bataan Death March was the most horrific atrocity by the Japanese soldiers.

The Japanese now occupied the country. When the Japanese occupation started, the Japanese seemed to be friendly to the Filipino people. They tried to win the loyalty of the Filipinos. But under the Japanese rule, freedom was severely curtailed and labor was often forced. The only news they got was from the rumors going around the town. They had no radio to turn on. All radios were confiscated by the Japanese when they conquered the land. Japan had plans of making the Philippines its territory but the Filipino people distrusted their intention. Some 250,000 Filipinos joined the guerilla movement against the Japanese. In Washington, DC, a Philippine government-in-exile was formed under the leadership of President Manuel L. Quezon.

During the Japanese occupation, Benjamin still went to see Adelaide. One time, he stayed too long and it was getting dark. Feeling it was too dangerous to travel at night, Adelaide's cousin invited him to sleep over. It would look improper if he stayed at Adelaide's house so Benjamin accepted the offer from her cousin. Little did he know that the cousin had a sister the same age as Adelaide. Zenia, the cousin's sister, was flirting with Benjamin during breakfast after she realized Benjamin slept over at her house.

The following morning, Zenia even went to see Adelaide and told her that Benjamin was so nice to her and they got along very well.

"I think he likes me. Would it be nice if he likes me better than you? I'm sure he's tired of you playing hard to get." Adelaide felt pain in her chest like she was punched. She tried to ignore it, not to let her cousin knew how she felt.

"Well, you can have him. I don't care," she said.

"Ok then. I'll be glad to have him. Since you don't care, it is fair game. Don't tell me I didn't warn you." Then she left Adelaide.

After Zenia left, Adelaide started pacing, then sat down wearily. She felt pain and jealous. She could not understand why Benjamin would turn his attention to her cousin. Oh, it could not be true. Why would he prefer her cousin? She's not even pretty. He could not fall in love with her. She's a mousy little pest, she snickered. I know Benjamin loves me but does he really? God knows how many girls he goes out with while in Baguio. Now she felt worried. For the first time, she realized she was really in love with him and wanted him for herself.

Benjamin came to visit the following week. Instead of being gracious to him, she asked him why he came. Benjamin was bewildered with the question. On top of that, she could not help being cold to him.

"Adelaide, what is wrong? You're acting weird today. Did I do anything wrong for you to behave differently?"

"Did you? What a question?"

"I don't understand." He scratched his head and started thinking. He still could not find a reason why.

"I asked you why you are here. You should be at Zenia's house."

There was a grin on Benjamin's face. "So that's why you are acting the way you are."

"Why are you smiling?"

"You are jealous."

"I'm not. She said you liked her better than me."

"Do I really? I didn't know that. She must have the wrong man."

"She did not."

"Adelaide, listen to me. There is no other woman I love better than you. Please believe me. I wouldn't be coming here all these time if that's not true. But I'm glad to know you're jealous."

"I'm not jealous," Adelaide insisted.

"Okay, okay. Now, are you still mad at me?"

"All right. I guess not."

"Good."


When the war broke out, Regina got stuck with so much inventory of embroidery materials on hand. There were 18 sacks of embroidery materials left. Regina decided to return some of them to the local suppliers. Later she found out that more dealers were selling them either in Manila or in Batangas in the black market. Some of the people who went into hiding took their inventory with them. Some merchants wanted these products, searched for them and bought and sold those goods. Business was booming.

In Bauan, there were only a few Japanese in town. Most of them were in Manila. They did not move in till later and then conditions got worse. By this time, Regina had accumulated a good amount of money. She gave money to peasants in exchange for grain after the harvest which she in turn sold at Marta's store. Slowly, she was able to buy more tracts of land and each kid was given land when they got married. Regina made sure all her children had a good start in their married life.

As the war went on, the Filipinos started getting cautious. They did not believe the Japanese would give them their independence three years earlier than the Americans. Deep in their heart, they believed Gen MacArthur would return and liberate them. However, in spite of incessant fighting, nightclubs and bar flourished. Clientele were ruthless businessmen doing business selling war materials to the Japanese. As the war intensified, the Japanese atrocities in the Philippines got worse. There was an increase in Japanese brutality.

As you enter the town of Bauan from the main highway, you can see the big Post Office building on your left. It was a one story building, ochre in color with great architecture built by the Americans during the early part of the American era. Across the post office were rows of old houses built during the Spanish regime. As you turn right to go to the center of town, the whole street was dotted with homes of Spanish architecture. At the end of the road as you turn left was the imposing Bauan Cathedral. Next to it to the right was the old convent which stretched the whole length of the property. The Japanese captured the Bauan Cathedral and the convent next to it. They were using the convent to store their supplies. They dug a tunnel from the back of the church all the way to the bridge by the next town.

Across the Bauan Cathedral is the Town Plaza. Going straight ahead on the road are rows of business establishment of all sorts. Prominent among them is the Bauan Restaurant noted for its delicious pancit canton. A few blocks from the Cathedral to your left were the busiest parts of town. It was where the Town Market was located in the center of town, a block away from the main thoroughfare.

The Town Market was fully staffed during the weekend. During the week, some areas where there were enclosed stalls were open all week. The areas that had open space under an encompassing roof were generally open on weekends only with few exceptions. There was the wide open covered building with no walls designated for the meat and poultry section. There were freshly skinned chickens, freshly butchered pigs and cows with their meat hanging from a hook set up to hold them with the scale on one end that could be seen in several rows. The meat and vegetables sections were located in this open space. Outside in the open field was open to vendors of dry goods which encompassed clothes, linens, household goods. Sometimes, desserts of all kinds were also sold in this area after they ran out of space in the covered area.

On this particular weekend, the market was buzzing with activities. On the street next to the Town Market, the street was congested with all kinds of traffic. Calesas were all lined up close to the iron fence. People were milling around up and down the street. There was so much hustle and bustle at the market and the surrounding areas. Outside on the open fields, merchants were all lined up with their wares. There were rows and rows of merchants selling clothes and household stuff. Another section was for fresh produce and home cooked snacks and all kinds of rice cakes. People were milling around bargaining for their food and provisions.

The commotion was interrupted by the sound of heavy footsteps. Somebody whispered to Cayetano. "They are here."

Cayetano asked, "Who?"

"The Japanese ....." The informant did not finish his sentence.

They heard them now. *"Kura...Kura...."* Everybody bowed their heads. Nobody dared to speak. Nobody dared to look up either. The Japanese soldiers, about two dozen of them were going from row to row looking for young able men and pretty young women. Their bayonets were pointing at the merchants ready to charge if anybody made a bad move.

"You," he pointed to Cayetano. "How old are you?"

Cayetano looked up and shook his head. The soldier looked at his Filipino comrade, a *Makapili,* wearing a hooded mask and told him to ask the young fellow how old he was.

Makapili is a short term for *Makabayan Katipunan Ng Mga Pilipino* or Alliance of Philippine Patriots. It was a militant group formed in the Philippines during World War II to give military help to the Japanese. After the war, they were accused of their involvement in Japanese brutality and faced trials for treason.

*"Ilang taon can ba?"* How old are you? The Makapili asked.

*"Labing tatlo po."* Thirteen sir. Cayetano lied. With the sad look on his face, he added, "I'm helping my mother support us. She's a widow with nine kids."

The Makapili looked him in the eye and knew he lied about his age. "Is he your brother?" glancing at the small boy next to him.

"Yes sir." The Makapili felt sorry for the kid. He turned to the Japanese soldier and said, "He is too young for the army." The soldier did not argue with the Makapili and just moved on to the next row.

Cayetano was so relieved when the soldiers left and moved on. Since the day was not too profitable because the crowd was not as big as the weekend crowd, he decided to pack his wares early and head home. Besides he had specific instruction from his mother that he had to be home early and not get caught in the dark. His mother did not trust the Japanese. One would never know what the Japanese would do to you. Anyway, he had enough money to buy some rice and dried fish to take home. After he packed his wares, he dropped at the General Store to buy the supplies that his mother wanted him to bring home.

Cayetano and his younger brother, Nicolas who came to help him carried all the leftover goods and started walking home. They could not take the calesa because it would cost them money and money was so important to the family. They were strong boys and they could walk two kilometers to home. Nicolas was carrying the provision and Cayetano was carrying the sack of unsold goods. About half kilometer into the walk as they were turning the bend, they heard noises and footsteps. Sounding the alarm, they hid behind some shrubs, and afraid even to breathe for fear that whoever was coming their way might hear them. The moments seemed like eternity. Then the footsteps sounded like they were moving away and then silence. They were about to get out of their hiding place when they heard a rustle at the nearby bushes on the neighbor's yard. Then they heard the sound of water dripping. They realized that one of the soldiers was relieving himself. Nicolas was about to burst out laughing when Cayetano hurriedly cupped Nicolas' mouth to suppress his laughter. They waited a while and when Cayetano thought the soldiers had left, they tiptoed in the opposite direction and then started walking faster. They got home in a hurry.

There was one incident before Adelaide got married which probably contributed to her decision of getting married soon. One day, only Adelaide, Cayetano and Nicolas were home with their mother. The older kids were all out at the market. Cayetano heard heavy footsteps coming near their house. His mother told him to take Nicolas and run outside in the field and hide there.

Adelaide hid behind the bedroom door with all the mats and pillows around her. Her mother pretended she was busy doing embroidery. She heard the knocking at the door.

"Open up." Regina heard the soldiers.

Regina opened the door and one of the Japanese soldiers asked for the men in the house. She said, "I am a widow. My husband died years ago."

"Where are your boys?"

"They are at the market," she replied.

"Any girls around? Daraga?" The soldier meant dalaga. Dalaga is a Philippine word for unmarried young lady, a virgin and Japanese soldiers were known to take them and rape them.

"None, she is working with her brothers at the market." The Japanese soldiers had a penchant for Filipino virgins. Finding no young girls around, they left. They went to the next house, and the next.

When Regina sensed that the Japanese were already gone, she called Adelaide to get out of her hiding place. She was so shaken. That night, she could not sleep. She decided if Benjamin asked her to marry him, she would say yes. She could not take this any longer. She was totally scared of those Japanese for her safety. Her brothers could not defend her in front of those bayonets. Why take a chance? Benjamin loved her and she loved him, so why keep on prolonging her decision. "Stop playing hard to get, and put some sense into your head," she reprimanded herself.

But at the same token, Benjamin had not asked her to marry him. Benjamin was getting too worried about Adelaide but had not gotten the nerve to ask her to marry him. However, he was afraid somebody would be interested in her which was a good assumption. He lived too far away and she being so pretty, he was not surprised if somebody asked her to marry her before he did. Little did Benjamin know, Adelaide had five other suitors besides Benjamin. One was a teacher from the next town. Another one was an engineer from Batangas, the provincial capital.

There was also a salt distributor who people nicknamed "*asindero*", (*asin* means salt) compared to an *haciendero* who owned a big hacienda. The "asindero" was very persistent. After distributing his salt on his route which ran from Bauan to Lemery, back to Alitagtag then up to some barrios east of Alitagtag, he would circle back to Sambat and often would drop by Adelaide's house before returning to his hometown in Batangas near Batangas Bay. On one of those visits, he asked Adelaide to marry him. They had only met for three weeks. Adelaide thought it was too fast. She said, "No".

One day, Adelaide bumped into the mother of the "asindero" at the market. She found out why he was in a hurry. He was about to join the army at that time and wanted to marry before he went to war. "You should have married my son," the lady said.

"It was too soon and I did not know him at all. Besides, I don't know a thing about married life." Adelaide reasoned out.

"If you married him, I could have a footprint," the woman added.

Adelaide got confused and asked, "What do you mean by footprint?"

"He died in the army a few months ago. I could've had a grandchild." Adelaide suddenly realized what the lady was talking about. She felt indignant but after she recovered, Adelaide conveyed her sympathy graciously.

"I'm sorry to hear that he passed away. He was so young." Then she said, "Excuse me but I have to go back to my sales booth. My sister is all alone there. I have to help her out. I'm so sorry about your son." She walked to her sales booth and breathed a sigh of relief to be away from the woman. She thought to herself that she was glad she did not marry the "asindero". Otherwise she would be a widow now. What a horrible thing. Besides, she loved Benjamin, not anyone else.

By Christmas of 1942, as the war was going on, Benjamin decided that it was just too risky to be going back and forth to Bauan. He would be 23 years old and had a good business going. He had been playing the field for quite some time now and it was time to get settled. There were 7 ladies in town vying for his attention. He compared everyone and he thought long and hard and decided he had found the right girl and should do something about it. He was determined next time he saw Adelaide, he would ask her to marry him.

Since her birthday was coming soon, he would ask her on her birthday. He knew she cared about him but he had not asked her about her feeling. Every time he visited her, her sisters seemed always to be around and he could not really talk privately. Maybe they could stroll in the yard and then he could ask her then and there.

He got to her house but there were so many people. She was having a party and all the relatives were there. He had no choice but join the fun. He could not talk to her privately so he decided he had to postpone his mission somehow. During the whole Christmas season, every time he came to see her, the house seemed to be loaded with relatives. He kept on saying to himself, "How am I going to ask her to marry me with all those people around?"

There was an instance when he was able to get a word with her without anybody hearing it. He said, "I'll come Saturday, next week. Will you be home?"

"Of course," Adelaide said.

Saturday came. Benjamin came but she was not home. Intentionally, she called her cousin who lived across the street if she wanted to go to town. Her cousin said yes. They lingered in the market and Adelaide was hoping Benjamin would be gone by the time they got home. She was wrong. Benjamin dismissed the cuchero and waited till she returned.

Adelaide was surprised that he was still there when she got home. Benjamin handed Adelaide the bouquet of Everlasting. "Here is something for you."

"They look beautiful." She put her nose on the bouquet and tried to smell the flower. It had a faint sweet fragrance. "I love it. Thanks."

Benjamin smiled, "You're welcome." They sat down and talked for a while. At the end of the evening, Benjamin asked her to marry him. Adelaide said, "I have to think about it."

By the time he left her home, he missed the last bus. He ended sleeping at Adelaide's cousin house again. In the meantime, Adelaide's cousin, Zenia was getting cozy with him.

The next day, Zenia invited Adelaide to go to the beach with the family and said Benjamin would join them. Adelaide said, "No, I don't want to go."

"Why not? It should be a lot of fun."

"I'm not interested. If Benjamin is coming, I don't want to go. If you want him, you can have him."

Benjamin found out that Adelaide was not going so he backed out. No matter what Adelaide did to fend him off, Benjamin was determined to pursue her.

Then something happened unexpectedly. Delfin, one of Benjamin's brothers got very sick. All of a sudden, he didn't feel right. He went to bed and his condition started to deteriorate everyday. His fever was running high and the doctor was called in. He had typhoid fever. The doctor diagnosed his condition dismally. He struggled hard for days but his condition worsened. He was near death. All the family was worried about his condition. Benjamin who was very close to his brother got very worried. He knew that they were losing him. Benjamin decided that he should ask Adelaide to come and visit his brother. Delfin and Adelaide were the two people dear to him and if he was going to lose his brother, he wanted Delfin to know Adelaide. So he wrote a note and sent it to Adelaide and begged her to come to see his dying brother. She could bring a chaperone if she had to but begged her to come. He was not sure how she would take it but it was worth a try. He sent a calesa to fetch her. Regina, her mother and her sister, Esmeralda went with Adelaide.

When they got to Alitagtag, there were so many people at the house. She found out later that the relatives had been checking, scrutinizing all Benjamin's girlfriends. Enrique, Benjamin's father, was very solicitous of Adelaide and her mother and sister. He even asked a fortune teller what he thought of Adelaide. Once it was established that Adelaide was the best amongst the 7 ladies, Enrique wanted to make sure Benjamin had the same feeling.

Enrique even asked Adelaide, "Please consider marrying my son. He is a fine fellow."

"But I do not know any housework," Adelaide ventured saying.

"I wouldn't worry about that if I were you. We'll get you a maid."

Adelaide smiled and said, "I'll think about it."

A few days later, Delfin died. Benjamin sent a carriage again to bring Adelaide and her mother back to Benjamin's house. The wake was at Benjamin's house, in the sala as was the custom. Delfin's body lay in a simple coffin in the middle of the room. Chairs and benches, some brought in by neighbors were arranged in neat rows around the coffin but closer to the wall. More chairs were lined up on the entry hall. There was just enough space for people to walk through to view the body.

As the carriage arrived with Adelaide and her mother in tow, people started to wonder what it all meant.

"I think Benjamin is serious about Adelaide," one neighbor ventured to say.

"I think so myself. Why would he send a carriage for them if he were not?" Another bantered.

"Well, she is very beautiful and very gracious."

"Nobody is like her in this town."

"What about Felicia?"

"No, you can't compare her with Felicia."

"There is something about Adelaide that's special."

"I heard she comes from a well-connected family."

"Her grandfather is a cabeza, is that so?"

"Yes, something like that. However, her mother is a widow and brought up all her children by herself."

"She must be some lady."

As Benjamin and his father, Enrique, ushered in Adelaide and her mother, Regina, into the house, there was a hushed silence. Everyone stopped talking and watched them as they approached the coffin. In deference to the dead, both mother and daughter were wearing black. Regina was in a black terno (gown) and Adelaide in an ankle length black dress. They went straight to view the body. Regina and Adelaide made the sign of the cross, bowed their head in silent prayer. Everyone was watching them. After a few minutes, they made another sign of the cross. They turned around and offered condolences to Barbara, Benjamin's mother. Then Benjamin pointed to the empty chairs next to Barbara and they all sat down in silence. Regina sat between Barbara and Adelaide with Benjamin on Adelaide's left. Enrique sat on the other side next to Barbara.

The silence was interrupted when a priest came and led them in saying the rosary. In between *Our Father* and *Hail Mary*, you could hear Barbara weeping. Enrique put his left arms around her to comfort his wife. Adelaide glanced at Benjamin and their eyes locked. Adelaide felt an urge to touch Benjamin hands but restrained. Benjamin gave her a faint smile and deep down they understood each one's feeling. She knew Benjamin was very close to his brothers but more so with Delfin who was the nearest his age. Delfin was two years older and also the liveliest of the bunch. Now he would really miss Delfin.

After the prayer service, some of the visitors started piling up to view the body. Some of the aunts were wailing and making a big scene. The little nieces and nephews were gathered and being held by their parents and carried across the coffin to keep the spirit from coming back to see the kids. Some of the kids did not want to get near the coffin. The adults were having a hard time with the youngest one. He was crying and scared.

"I don't want to go there. Why do I have to go?"

"He'll come back and see you," one of the adults was saying.

The child cried louder. The mother came to the child and tried to appease him.

"Be good now and say goodbye to your uncle Delfin."

"Is he really coming back if I don't say goodbye?"

"Yes, he would."

Reluctantly, the boy stopped crying and meekly held his mother hands and let her take him on one side of the coffin. One of the men raised him up across the coffin and the men on the other side grabbed him. Everyone cheered.

"See, there is nothing to it," his mother said as the child was put down.

"Now, is he going to visit me, is that true?"

"No, he'll now go to heaven. Good boy."

The visitors were now served merienda and afterwards, Regina and Adelaide took their leave and left in the same carriage that took them there. Enrique and Barbara graciously thanked them. It now looked like the two families were getting along very well. So it was established that the two young lovers would marry soon.

# CHAPTER 20

One day, Benjamin came to visit Adelaide and told the cuchero to come back for him in two hours. As soon as the calesa pulled over, Benjamin saw Adelaide looking out the window. Adelaide was waiting for him. He went up the steps and she greeted him cordially. None of the million relatives of hers were there.

He asked, "Can we walk outside?"

She asked, "Why?"

"I want to talk to you without them around, meaning your sisters."

"But," she faltered.

"I know. They can still see us from the window." She sensed that he understood that it would not be proper to be seen outside without a chaperone.

They went outside. He felt she was uneasy being alone with him. She was so afraid neighbors would see them and gossip would go around. Luckily as they came down the stairway, nobody was around. Her house being on a bluff, nobody from the street could see them what with the garden in front of the house blocking the view from the road. The neighbors from either side of the house could not really see them because of the tall shrubs around the perimeter of the property. So they walked to the back and went underneath a *tamarind* tree.

"Why do we have to be alone?" Adelaide asked.

"I have been thinking a lot lately. We have been writing for so long and I have been courting you for more than two years." Benjamin could not continue. He waited for her reaction. She remained silent.

"Adelaide, you must know how I feel about you otherwise I wouldn't be coming here as often as I do. Tell me something. Do I have a chance?" Benjamin asked.

"Chance about what? I don't know what you are talking about." She was being coy.

"Do I have to spell it out? I love you Adelaide and I want to marry you. Please say yes." Adelaide turned her back and was now facing the tree.

"Adelaide, I don't want to hurry you up. Just say I can hope for something."

"Benjamin, I'm still young and I don't know anything about housekeeping."

"If that's your only problem, I will get you a maid as soon as we get married."

"I don't know. I have to think about it. Besides I don't know how I can tell my brothers. I think they want me to marry somebody from around here."

"I will be patient but think about it. I promise you you'll have a nice life. I do love you very much." They went back inside the house. They had merienda and her sisters joined them. This time, they had suman tamales and barako coffee. He noticed Adelaide was a little quiet at the table.

In exactly two hours, his calesa came back for him. He bid goodbye and as Adelaide was showing him to the door, he gave her a pleading look. He knew she understood. She smiled and Benjamin's heart leaped with joy.

His face must have shown it because the cuchero asked him why he was so happy.

"Ha? What are you talking about?" Benjamin asked.

"You look like you won the sweepstakes."

"Oh, not yet. I'm getting there," and immediately changed the subject.

With the Japanese occupation, citizens were forced into manual labor to plant cotton. They went from house to house to gather young men and young women to work the fields. Regina had two of the boys work in the cotton fields occasionally. Adelaide sometimes accompanied her sisters during the harvest time and helped harvest the cotton.

Then one day, they noticed the Japanese attitude had drastically changed. They started abusing the people. Everyone became suspicious. Japanese soldiers started eyeing the young pretty Philippine girls. Since all of the girls had married except Adelaide, Regina tried to protect Adelaide from the roving eyes of the Japanese.

One day, looking out the window, Regina saw another group of Japanese soldiers coming. Regina told Adelaide to keep quiet. Regina hurriedly wrapped Adelaide around a straw mat behind the bedroom door. Regina shove boxes and some pillows all around her, left the door opened and put some boxes to keep the door open while Adelaide hid behind the door.

One group of five Japanese soldiers with their bayonets slung on their shoulders climbed the bamboo steps leading to Adelaide's house. They marched up the stairway and knocked at the door. Regina holding her embroidery ring pretending she was busy doing embroidery, quietly opened the door and bowed. The soldiers bowed back.

"May I help you?" Regina politely asked them.

"Where is your husband?"

"I don't have a husband. I'm a widow. He died fifteen years ago."

"How about your sons?"

"They are out in the market."

"When do they come home?"

"I have no idea. When the market closes I presume."

"How about daraga?"

"None. No daraga here, no daraga. She went to cotton field."

While the leader was asking questions, one of the soldiers walked to the bedroom which has an adjoining door to the hallway and the living room. The door was open. He went through the open door to the bedroom without checking behind it. Adelaide could hardly breathe. She kept still. The soldier entered the living room.

Seeing no one, he went to the kitchen and checked there and went to the back stairway.

"Let's go. There is nobody here except the old lady," he yelled to his comrades. The leader and his four comrades bowed. Regina bowed back and they went downstairs in a hurry and went down the bamboo steps to the street.

Regina tried to steady herself. She could not open her mouth. Her heart was pounding fast. She was rooted to her spot. Finally, she peeped through a small slit at the window. She waited a few moments. When she thought they had gone, she went to the bedroom door and rescued Adelaide. She was falling asleep waiting for her mom to tell her the coast was clear.

Several months passed and the Japanese were now known to be getting young girls and raping them. Benjamin was getting nervous about Adelaide. She was too pretty for the Japanese not to notice. One Japanese soldier noticed her already and started talking to her at the market. Adelaide got very nervous about that.

"Maybe I should get married. Next time, Benjamin asks me, I think I will say yes."

By Valentine's Day of 1943, Benjamin asked her again to marry him. This time, she said yes. But she was still afraid of her brothers.

"Maybe we can elope. Then they won't have any say in the matter." Benjamin saw her eyes light up.

"How are we going to do that?" Adelaide asked.

"I will hire a calesa to pick you up in front of the bus stop at the market. He will take you to Alitagtag. I know a prominent judge who can marry us quick. Then my father will see your mother after we get married and settle with the family and ask for forgiveness. Are you willing to do that?" Benjamin waited nervously for her reply.

She hesitated, then said, "Yes, I will. I love you so and I'm so afraid of those Japanese soldiers. So when are we going to do this?"

"I'll come next week and tell you the details once I talked to the cuchero and the judge. I love you," Benjamin said.

By the following week, the situation got complicated. Felicia who Benjamin escorted at one time realized that he was interested with this girl in Bauan. Felicia wanted him and was pushing herself on Benjamin. He was trying to avoid her but since she lived close by, it was rather difficult not to see her. She always came to his house. She had the impression that Benjamin was interested in her. As a matter of fact, she was telling all her friends that Benjamin was about to ask her to marry him. Benjamin was in a big quandary now. Here he was asking the girl of his dream to elope with him and here right in his midst was another girl ready to become his wife without being asked. If Felicia kept this up, he might have no choice but to marry Felicia to avoid a scandal. But his heart belonged to somebody else. He had to make a decision quick.

Sunday came and Benjamin went to see Adelaide. He was a little apprehensive but he had to convince her that they had to get married right away.

Benjamin asked her, "Can we elope tomorrow at noon?"

"What? Why so sudden?" Adelaide asked.

"Adelaide, please say yes. With the war going on, I'm just afraid something will happen to you. I want you to be my wife and take care of you." Benjamin pleaded.

Adelaide was in a quandary and could not figure out how they were going to do it.

"If you can find an excuse to go to the market tomorrow, I can meet you there at the bus stop." Benjamin suggested.

She was a little nervous but said, "OK. What time?"

"Say around noon," Benjamin replied.

The next day was a glorious day. The sun was shining brightly and Adelaide was in a good mood but a little apprehensive. She kept on thinking if she was doing the right thing. What will her brothers do when they find out? The thought scared the hell out of her. But then her heart prevailed over her head. She tried to stay calm and acted normally.

At around 10 o'clock, Adelaide was trying to figure out how to go to town without any objection from her mother. She knew that her mother would not let her go alone but she would figure out something so she told her mother, "I need some thread for my embroidery and I have to go to town." Then she added, "Maybe I can buy some vegetables too for the house while I am there." She knew that was a better possibility of her mother letting her go to town.

Just as she expected it, her mother said without even thinking, "OK." Adelaide thought that was easy. But then her mother added, "Take Esmeralda with you and keep a sharp eye out for the Japanese."

Now, how was she going to do what she wanted to do if her sister was with her. Just then a thought entered her head. Maybe she would take her sister aside and into her confidence. She knew her sister liked Benjamin. She sure would cooperate with her. What if she did not want to? She would just take her chance.

As Adelaide and Esmeralda walked to town, Adelaide asked her sister if she could keep a secret. Her sister got very intrigued and asked, "What secret? Of course, I can keep a secret."

Adelaide said, "I am going to elope with Benjamin today and I want you not to tell our brothers who would not agree with my choice. They want me to marry somebody from here but I love Benjamin. You do not have to tell Mother either."

"Do you know what you are doing?"

"Yes, I do."

"Do you know how dangerous that is?"

"I know. But Benjamin is afraid for my safety and so am I. He is afraid of the Japanese getting their hands on me."

"I can understand that. OK then. Oh, this is so romantic."

They reached the market at around eleven thirty in the morning. At one of the stalls near the bus stop, Adelaide bid her sister goodbye and Esmeralda hugged Adelaide and wished her good luck. By the time Adelaide got to the bus stop, the cuchero was there. She hopped into the calesa and without looking back, she got seated and the cuchero started to drive off. She saw from the corner of her eyes that her sister was watching her from the stall where Adelaide left her. Adelaide's heart was pounding very hard.

The cuchero took a left turn at the end of the street and proceeded straight away instead of turning right at the first street going to Sambat. Adelaide knew they were taking a different route. They passed the big post office building at the next intersection and a few blocks away, the cuchero pulled over. Adelaide saw Benjamin who seemed to appear from nowhere. He got into the calesa and they drove off.

Benjamin sat next to her in the back seat. He nodded to Adelaide and she smiled back. He asked in whisper, "Nervous?"

She just nodded.

"Happy?"

She nodded again and leaned her head on his shoulder. He squeezed her hand. They rode in complete silence. The cuchero was humming a love song all the way to the judge's house.

They alighted from the calesa. The judge and his wife met them at the gate of their enormous house. The judge motioned them to go to his office on the second floor. There waiting were two of Benjamin's brothers.

The ceremony was solemn and very simple. When the judge pronounced them man and wife, Benjamin turned to Adelaide and for the first time in their courtship kissed her. First he kissed her lightly and then passionately. He almost forgot himself until one of his brothers coughed. Benjamin started laughing and Adelaide blushed.

They retreated into the dining room where the maids had prepared a sumptuous lunch. The judge and his wife sat at the opposite end of the table. Adelaide and Benjamin sat on one side and his two brothers sat on the other side.

After dessert, Benjamin and Adelaide together with the new brothers-in-law said goodbye and the four of them left for Alitagtag.

They got to Benjamin's house and his parents welcomed Adelaide with open arms. Then his father and uncle started getting ready for the trip to Sambat to meet with Adelaide's mother.

In the meantime, back in Sambat, Adelaide's sister, Esmeralda, told her mother what happened. First, her mother, Regina was so angry with her for conspiring with Adelaide. After telling her mother that Adelaide was so afraid to tell her brothers that she wanted to marry Benjamin and also afraid of the Japanese, then her mother finally calmed down. In the end, she thought Benjamin was really a good choice for Adelaide. So by the time Benjamin's father came to the house, she was gracious enough to welcome them.

Regina sat quietly while Benjamin's father did all the talking, apologizing and trying to ask for forgiveness and willing to do everything right for a church wedding. It did not take much convincing because Benjamin's father gave her carte blanche on everything. Benjamin had enough resources to spend on anything Adelaide wanted.

The wedding was set for next week. It will be at Bauan Cathedral. The judge who married them will be the godparents. Benjamin and Adelaide would be back in Sambat the next day. Benjamin's father got back to Alitagtag late that day and told Benjamin what transpired in Sambat. Adelaide was so relieved that her mother was not too upset.

After dinner, some of the relatives started coming over. Somehow, the news leaked out that Benjamin finally took a wife. The whole town was buzzing with the good news that Benjamin's wife was a very pretty girl from the next town and from a prominent family there. Everyone wanted to meet her.

The evening seemed to go on forever. Adelaide did not realize that Benjamin had an enormous family. The relatives came over with all kinds of food and drinks. There was tuba and lambanog, a local drink much like backwoods moonshine. Since it was a special occasion, lambanog was served and there was the traditional *tagayan* or wine-drinking. A single glass was set in the middle of the group and everyone took turns in drinking out of the single glass.

By the time the last of the relatives left, Adelaide was so exhausted, she just collapsed in bed and went right to sleep in an instance. Benjamin looked at her angelic face and left her in peace.

Adelaide woke up the next morning completely disoriented. After she realized she was not in her house anymore, she worried that she had no change of clothes. Then she noticed at the foot of the bed was an open box with new sets of clothes and a note "For my loving wife, Adelaide." Signed, "Benjamin".

She dressed quickly and headed toward the living room looking for Benjamin. He was sitting by the window reading.

"Hello, did you have a nice sleep?" Benjamin asked.

"Yes, I'm sorry. I was so exhausted from yesterday," she replied.

"You must be famished. Let me get you something to eat. Come into the kitchen," Benjamin told her.

She followed him. She just realized that she was now his wife. She should be preparing breakfast for him, instead of the other way around. He was serving breakfast for her.

"What is wrong with me?" Adelaide asked herself. Luckily nobody was around. She wondered where everyone was.

After breakfast, Benjamin took Adelaide to Taal to get her measured for her wedding gown for next Sunday.

Benjamin wanted to buy her the most expensive material the seamstress had and wanted a Maria Clara style with beads of pearls in front of the bodice, the front of the skirt and the sleeves. The train will be long and trailing with roses embroidered at the scalloped edges with a few beads of pearl scattered around. Instead Adelaide reminded him that at this point in time, that kind of wedding dress was not proper. She would have a Maria Clara style of dress but no beads and short veil. After that was settled, they headed to the shoe maker. Here again, Benjamin wanted to order a white satin shoes but Adelaide said no and instead went for a plain white shoes.

After shopping, Benjamin decided to take Adelaide for lunch before they headed home. They went into a nearby sari-sari store, a convenience store which was a small-scale industry in Batangas where you could buy almost anything for everyday living. It was a place where townspeople hung out, caught up on the latest gossip and could provide a secondary income or even a primary income for the family who operated them. The store required a small investment and could be located in front of one's house.

Outside the sari-sari store were wooden benches where you could sit. Adelaide picked one near a corner. Benjamin walked to the counter and looked at what they had. At one end of the store, there was a display case where customers could see all the cooked food for sale that day. The owner asked Benjamin what he wanted.

"What do you recommend?" Benjamin asked back.

Then he pointed to a dish. "That one looks good."

"That is *Tapang* Taal." It was pork jerky and was served with fried garlic rice, sunny side up eggs and *atsara* which is pickled papaya. "It's really good and then you can have hot tablea tsokolate after that," the lady at the counter said.

"I'll take two of that," Benjamin said and the owner started placing some of the dish on two plates. Benjamin paid for the food and took them to where Adelaide was sitting.

When they were alone, Benjamin said to Adelaide, "You're a very sensible young lady and I really love you for that. I would have loved to have you wear the most expensive outfit for your wedding but I guess with the war going on, it was just not right." He smiled and Adelaide smiled back but said nothing.

Back at the house, Benjamin's parents were planning the reception. Since it was still wartime, their best bet was to buy everything in Bauan so they did not have to transport them. At other times, the food would be carried from the groom's house to the bride's house the day before the wedding but the logistics in this case did not warrant this tradition. Instead, Benjamin's parents decided to buy everything in Bauan and brought to Adelaide's house to be cooked there. All the help would come from Benjamin's big pool of relatives.

Enrique informed Adelaide and Benjamin that he promised Adelaide's mother that Adelaide was going back home the next day and prepare for their wedding at her house. They would be coordinating the events. She looked perplexed but did not say a word. Benjamin took Adelaide back home late that afternoon.

The day of the wedding came. Adelaide dressed up at her house. Benjamin waited at the cathedral with his best man, his eldest brother and the sponsors. Benjamin hired the calesa that he always took to Adelaide's house while courting her and decorated it with white crepe paper. Adelaide drove to town to the cathedral with her entourage which comprised of her, her mother and sisters and brothers. There were five calesas.

The Bauan Cathedral was the most artistically built church in Batangas and was started in 1762 and completed in 1881. However, the church burned down during the Philippine revolution against Spain in 1898 and rebuilt and destroyed by fire again in 1938. Then it was restored again.

Adelaide looked radiant in her simple white dress. Her mother always looked regal no matter what outfit she wore. She also wore a simple outfit, not to outshine her daughter. She was a little sad, giving away her favorite daughter but consoling herself that she was gaining a good son-in-law. Adelaide seemed very happy and that was all that mattered.

When Adelaide got married, Regina regretted the fact that she could not share the moment with Eugenio, her late husband. If only she took him to the doctor the moment he got the stomach ache. Maybe he would still be alive. Eugenio would love their new son-in-law. How she wished her husband was here to share this moment. Her mind went back to the time when her husband got very sick, when he was not feeling well for two days. Adelaide was still a little girl, barely five years old. Now, she was leaving the nest and going off and starting her new life with the man she loved.

When Adelaide left with Benjamin for Alitagtag, Regina could not hold her tears anymore. She gave Adelaide a big hug and made her promise to visit as often as she could. Regina also advised her to be a good wife, get along with your in-laws, be generous and kind to everyone but if they take advantage of her all the time and she cannot take it any longer, then learn to fight back and fight back hard. Adelaide and Benjamin left in a rented Packard with a chauffeur taking them to Alitagtag and her new life.

Finally, Benjamin and Adelaide were alone for the first time without a chaperone. She was beaming with happiness. He was very solicitous of her. They were very much in love. They got to Benjamin's house and were given the privacy they longed for. Somehow all his brothers disappeared and Benjamin's parents decided to stay at one of Benjamin's uncle's house.

Benjamin opened a basket full of food from the wedding party. They ate quietly, each with their own thoughts. Afterwards, Benjamin motioned to Adelaide to follow him to the bedroom. Adelaide got up from her chair and followed Benjamin. She was a little nervous. Benjamin picked a wrapped box sitting at the end of the bed and opened it. He got a nice surprise for her. Adelaide sat on the other side of the bed. Benjamin then sat next to her. He ran his fingers up and down her arm. She felt the sensation that she had never felt before. Instinctively, her already excited heart told her something unusual was about to happen.

"I bought you some clothes that you might like," Benjamin said. He pulled out the laced nightgown from the box. She gasped. It was a pretty gown with a laced bodice and a matching peignoir. "Put them on," he asked her softly.

She looked around. It was immediately apparent that there was nowhere to hide, out of the reach of his eyes to take off her clothes. She had never undressed in front of a man before, and she blushed when he handed her the nightdress he had unpacked. Perhaps to help her, he casually took off his coat and vest and hung them in the *aparador* (armoire) nearby, grabbed a magazine from the table nearby, eased his feet out of his shoes and then fell back on the bed, where he pretended to be reading. There was nothing left to do but to get it over with quickly. Her fingers shook from an odd and not entirely unpleasant excitement as she fumbled to unbutton her dress and undo her petticoats. When she stood in her chemise and underwear, shivering slightly, she glanced in the mirror and saw that he was watching her.

"You have the most beautiful neck, Adelaide," he said quietly. It was the first time since their courtship that he had ever mentioned any of her physical attributes, and she blushed so furiously that her body seemed hot all over. "Especially when you blush like that," he said.

"Please turn around," Adelaide instructed him to do. Benjamin smiled inwardly and did what he was told to do. Adelaide quickly got out of her clothes and put the lovely nightgown on.

"Can I turn back now?" Benjamin asked teasingly.

"Yes," she replied.

Benjamin was struck again by her beauty. She looked like a goddess come alive in that nightgown. He had to swallow hard before he forgot himself that he was dealing with a virgin girl here and he had to take it easy. He did not want to scare her.

"You look so beautiful. I believe I won a million pesos by taking you for my wife. Please come over here," he asked her.

Without hesitation, Adelaide came forward. Benjamin kissed her tenderly on her forehead, then turned to the table and blew out the light from the lamp. He came back near the bed and took Adelaide's hand. Then he lifted her face and kissed her again.

Suddenly, he was holding her in his arms and covering her face and neck with kisses. One part of her kept telling her this was wickedness and another told her it's now her duty as his wife. With the darkness in the room, they fell on the bed. She then realized how wonderful it was. "So this is what it is to be in love", she thought to herself.

By morning, it seemed like a dream.

# CHAPTER 21

B y June 1943, Adelaide announced to Benjamin that they were going to have a baby. Benjamin was ecstatic. Adelaide continued her embroidery. She got tired so often and Benjamin was so attentive to her. He would come home early from his travels and they would stroll in the backyard just holding hands. On Mondays when the markets were closed, they would take a calesa and they would go to Sambat and visited Adelaide's mother.

Then the rainy season came. Trips to Sambat were less often and Adelaide was getting bigger every day. She stayed at home but the neighbors and Benjamin's relatives came to visit. She even got friendly with Felicia, Benjamin's old friend. Felicia would come and brought some embroidered outfits and things for the coming baby.

December came and everybody was busy with the coming Christmas. Adelaide's mother wanted her to have the first baby at her house. So Benjamin and Adelaide packed their belongings and headed for Bauan. On their way to Bauan, the calesa that they were riding in had an accident. The horse tripped and bucked which almost threw them off the calesa. Thanks to the cuchero's quick reflexes, he held on to the rein of the horse, kept the calesa upright and they just missed a terrible accident. The horse completely turned around and his head went underneath the front of the calesa. Adelaide was so frightened, she jumped out of the calesa. Luckily she was unharmed. They waited a few minutes and another calesa passed by. Benjamin hired the other calesa. Finally they arrived at Adelaide's mother house. They settled there waiting for the baby to arrive. The doctor said Adelaide might have her baby before Christmas. Benjamin gave a party for Adelaide on her birthday on

Dec. 16, the first day of the Simbang Gabi. All his relatives came to dinner.

Three days later, Adelaide was just finishing her lunch when she experienced a terrible pain in her stomach. Benjamin saw her touching her stomach and the painful expression on her face. He became very concerned.

"Are you all right, Adelaide?" Benjamin asked tenderly.

"I'm having some pains," Adelaide said and held her stomach.

"Just now?"

"Just now," she repeated.

Benjamin called his mother-in-law. "Adelaide is starting to get pains. It just started."

"This might be it. I better get the bed ready," Regina said and stood up and went to the bedroom.

Benjamin didn't quite know what to do and asked his mother-in-law, "Can I help you?"

"No thanks, but I want you to fetch the herbalist. Go now," Regina told Benjamin.

Benjamin took his hat from the hat rack and left to get the herbalist. As Regina was putting the curtain around the four-poster bed, Adelaide came to the bedroom. She sat on the chair next to the dresser as her mother was finishing preparing the bed.

"I'm glad it started. In a little while, it will be over," Adelaide said matter-of-factly.

Regina helped her change into a more comfortable nightgown and helped her into bed. Adelaide laid her head on two pillows.

"I feel another pain."

"It's still far apart. It might take you a while."

In no time, Benjamin came with the herbalist. She was a heavy set woman in her fifties. Regina met them at the door.

"How is Adelaide doing?" The herbalist asked Regina.

"The pains are still far apart."

"Let me go see her."

Benjamin was about to follow her but Regina said, "Benjamin, come with me to the dining room. She will be there awhile."

"Is she all right?"

"She seems to be. But it will take a while. Usually the first labor is protracted."

"Are you sure she's all right?"

"She is. Don't worry. Have something to eat to keep your mind off of these things."

He ate a little of the kalamay that was in front of him and drank some coffee. Then he got up.

"I want to see her," he told his mother-in-law.

He entered the bedroom. The herbalist was sitting next to Adelaide and holding her hand.

"How is she doing?"

"The pain is not coming often enough. She has a long way to go."

He sat down by the bed.

Adelaide smiled at him.

"How are you coming along?"

"I'm fine. It will be over soon."

After four hours of labor Adelaide was having a terrible time. The midwife was called in as well. The herbalist burned an offering in the makeshift pit outside and began reciting some verses in some language that nobody could understand. Then she closed her eyes and began chanting. After her chanting concluded, she told Regina, "Adelaide was *Nanuno*. The *nuno* was playing tricks on her."

"What are we going to do?" Benjamin asked his mother-in-law.

Regina, Adelaide's mother remembered the accident they had on the calesa. "Do you remember the accident you had few weeks ago?" She asked Benjamin.

"What about it?"

"The herbalist said the nuno was playing tricks on Adelaide. Well, there might have been a *"Nuno sa Punso"* (gnome sitting on an anthill) there and he got mad when you disturbed their place. The "Nuno sa Punso" had a magic powers and could cause bad things as well as good things. When passing his anthill, you were supposed to excuse yourself for disturbing his place. Otherwise bad things would happen to you."

"The nuno was the one doing this trick and making Adelaide's childbirth a struggle. Go back to where you tripped and get some soil and apologize to the nuno for disturbing their place," the herbalist told Benjamin.

"But that is in another town. It will take time to go there and back," he protested.

"Benjamin, either you do it or something dreadful might happen to Adelaide," the herbalist told him.

"All right, but please do whatever you can for her. I'll go right now."

"Take one of the boys with you," Regina told him.

In the meantime, Adelaide was getting delirious. She was sweating heavily and the pain wouldn't subside. It would stop one moment and then a stronger pain would follow. The midwife was keeping her company and watching her thoroughly. Regina and Marta, Adelaide's eldest sister, were nearby.

Benjamin left with one of his brother-in-law to get some soil from the place where the horse tripped. They came back about an hour later with the soil. The herbalist did her chanting again and pressed the bags of soil sample on top of Adelaide's stomach.

Five minutes later, Adelaide wailed in pain, the midwife told her, "Push." Adelaide breathed deeply and pushed.

"Keep on pushing. Push. .. Push...."

Adelaide pushed harder and harder. Her hands were holding to the railing behind her head.

"There it goes again."

"Push. Harder. You'll almost there. Good girl."

Adelaide was thoroughly spent. She was breathing hard. Then she felt the pain again.

"You're doing well. Push... Take a breath. Push..."

Then Adelaide felt something. The midwife pulled the baby out. It was over. The midwife held the little thing by the foot upside down and gave it a slapping. The baby started screaming at the top of her lungs. The midwife cut the umbilical cord, took the placenta out, washed the baby and presented it to Adelaide.

"A beautiful girl," the midwife told Adelaide. Adelaide was totally exhausted but brimmed with a smile. Benjamin came rushing to the bedroom, saw his daughter and looked at Adelaide with pride and said, "Thank you. She is a lovely little girl, just like you. I love you so very much."

Benjamin caressed Adelaide's forehead. She was extremely tired and fell right to sleep. Benjamin carried the baby into the living room and laid her down in a little box. She was a little bundle of joy, black raven hair with almond eyes. She was so pretty and tiny.

Five days later was Christmas. There was a big gathering at the house. They had a new member of the family. The baby slept through the festivities. They bundled her in her embroidered outfit and she slept contentedly.

After the baby was born, they decided to stay in Bauan. Benjamin decided to open a business in town. They were able to rent a space and opened a store selling rice and grain. They were getting established and Adelaide was very happy living with her mother and the baby was loved and taken care of by her aunts and grandmother.

By March of 1944, Benjamin's father came and urged them to move back to Alitagtag. He claimed Benjamin was missing all the good fortune of everyone in Alitagtag doing business in Manila. He said Benjamin could do much better than the other fellows in town. Adelaide was reluctant at first but decided later to go along and moved back to his parent's house. They decided to sell their store in Bauan and headed back to Alitagtag.

As the Japanese occupation progressed, things got a little better businesswise. Life went back slowly to normal. The Japanese enticed the people to join them to fight the Americans. There were all sorts of propaganda but the Filipinos were not convinced they were sincere. They were very suspicious of the Japanese. Some Filipinos decided to go underground and join the Philippine guerillas. Still some became Japanese sympathizers. Why would anyone turn into a Makapili and turn on your countrymen and watch as they are tortured? Are they just plain cowards to become a traitor to their countrymen?

One day, Benjamin went to see his *Ninong sa Kasal* (wedding godfather) who he suspected was playing double agent. Benjamin thought he might be able to help him.

Benjamin knocked at the door and the maid answered.

"Who are you sir? Can I help you?" the maid asked when she opened the door.

"My name is Benjamin Maranan and I want to see Ninong."

"Please sit down here sir and I will call him"

"Thank you."

The maid disappeared and after a while, Ninong came downstairs.

"Glad to see you, Benjamin. Come to the sala and we can talk there." Benjamin followed his godfather into the living room.

"Sit down."

"Thank you."

The godfather saw the maid by the door and asked her to bring some refreshments.

"What brought you here?"

Benjamin hesitated for a while. Then he said, "I see everyone is doing a good business lately and I was wondering if you can help me. I know some of the stuff they are selling are stolen from the American bases. I don't want to do that. That is too dangerous and it is not good stealing from the people who are helping us."

His godfather nodded his head and waited.

Benjamin continued, "I want to go back up north. I heard business in Aparri is quite good but traveling up north is a bit dangerous what with all the Japanese sentries you have to go through. I need your help. Is there a way I can get a pass so I can go through the Japanese sentries?" Benjamin knew that his godfather had connections at high places.

Ninong said, "No problem. Come back next week. I'll have it ready for you."

Benjamin thanked his godfather and left.

He then went shopping for some merchandise to sell. The following week, he returned to see his godfather. As promised, the pass was ready. It was made of wood, about a foot long and 6 inches wide.

Benjamin started his new business buying embroidered clothes and selling them in Manila at first. With the help of the pass that he got from his marriage sponsor, he was able to come and go to Manila without any problems at Japanese check points.

When the war broke out, the contractors had inventory that they never returned. These were the ones that were now being sold on the black market. Adelaide told Benjamin that her mother had 18 sacks of embroidered materials when the war broke and she returned most of them to the suppliers. Benjamin said it was unfortunate that he did not know about it by then. Otherwise, he would be able to sell them all.

A lot of Filipinos were now back in business. One day by accident, Benjamin found out where they were getting the products that they were selling. Some got them from American soldiers who got too friendly with the natives before the war and smuggling the supplies from the army and sold the supplies to the natives. Others got them by stealing at the base. One guy was unlucky. He went to the base and was determined to steal some parachutes which were sold at the black market for a premium. The parachutes were somehow wrapped around a 14-ton bomb. The bomb exploded and he got caught. He lost one hand in the process. Another guy stole some mosquito nettings. The American soldiers found out about it and were able to trace where it was. They confiscated the item. But the Americans never filed charges against the Filipino.

Benjamin decided to go up north with Ramon and a couple of friends. He got ready to go up north in a few days. They had a lot of merchandise to sell. This time, the trips were much longer so Adelaide decided to stay at her parents' home with the baby. The baby grew up having all the attention she needed. Teresa grew up surrounded by love on both sides of the family. Her maternal grandmother spoiled her the most. Since Regina was in the jewelry business, Teresa got more jewelry than any one-year old girl could possibly have. In her own little world, everything was great but outside the war was still raging. The Japanese were now dropping propaganda sheets and enticing the natives to join their forces to fight the Americans.

On one of those trips up north, Benjamin decided to visit his store in Mankayan. This time, he took the Naguilian Road. Naguilian was situated on the scenic Bauang-Baguio Road which followed the route of an old foot trail from the coast to Benguet. Bauang is 260 kilometers north of Manila and 60 kilometers west of

Baguio. From San Fernando, La Union, Naguilian road served as the shortest access to Baguio City. The road passed through the towns of Naguilian and Burgos. It then climbed steeply up the Cordillera mountain range in the vicinity of Burgos, Sablan, and Irisan.

From the town of Burgos to Irisan, Naguilian Road followed mountain ridges and the ascent was quite steep. There were a number of sharp hairpin turns and blind curves. The road's surface varied from asphalt to concrete. During inclement weather conditions, it would be touch and go as you climbed in the thickness of the fog that would envelop the mountain. At its higher elevation, vehicles crawled at a snail's pace usually in the afternoon when the fog moved in. However, the road was less affected by landslides than Kennon Road.

There were several stores lined up along the road as you entered towns. They sold all kinds of foods and fresh fruits and vegetables. All varieties of bananas could be seen hanging on a wire as if waving their hands at you to stop by. Travelers stopped and had snacks to break up the trip. The roads were quite scenic and perilous with one side facing the water and the other side facing the steep mountainside.

By the time Benjamin arrived at his store in Mankayan, his cousin and his wife had been there already. Benjamin found out the store was intact but empty. All the merchandise was sold and gone. He was very lucky, the store was not damaged during the outbreak of the war but all the merchandise was gone. He approached his cousin but was told that he got rid of them and would pay him later but his cousin never did.

He went back and forth a few times to Baguio via the Naguilian Road. On one of those trips, he remembered his friend, Mang Sylvestre and decided to look for him. After several inquiries, he found out he died in one of the massacres. He happened to be in Eddet when the Japanese rounded up all the men and sent them to Manenchen in Kabayan where the Japanese massacred Eddet residents. With heavy heart, he decided to leave Mankayan and perhaps never to return again. He lost his business and now lost his friend too. There was no reason for him to go back.

He then traveled to Aparri on the northwestern side of the island. He headed to Aparri in Ilocos Norte, passing through Vigan where several colonial-style homes and ancestral mansions lined the streets.

He traveled with Ramon, his oldest brother. As they passed the sentry, the guards would question them. Benjamin produced their pass. The Japanese soldiers bowed and waved them through. He made several more trips up north. He wanted to settle up in Baguio but Adelaide refused to go. She wanted to stay in Batangas.

One day, a friend approached him to join him to go to Davao in Mindanao. The prospects there looked lucrative. One friend ventured south and ended being a big landowner. Still Adelaide said "No" and Benjamin's parents wouldn't let him move too far away either. Benjamin felt obligated to stay. He was the only one among his brothers making a lot of money and supporting the family so his parents wanted him to stay with them.

Adelaide got settled in her role as the wife of a prominent businessman. She lived with her in-laws in the same house. Benjamin was a very conscientious son and was determined to support the whole family. Adelaide was so happy with her life that she never complained. She kept on doing her embroidery which she loved, going shopping every now and then and finally helping Benjamin in his business. She knew a little about business from her mother since her mother alone was supporting the family. As promised, Benjamin got her two maids immediately after they got married so she did not lift a finger at the house. There were two live-in maids in the house, one to clean the house and the other to cook meals. The laundry was taken care of by another maid who came to the house every other day.

# CHAPTER 22

As the Japanese occupation progressed, it was a time of endurance for all Filipino families. Benjamin's and Adelaide's families were no exception. Benjamin had been traveling to and from the Mountain Province for a long time but with the conditions around deteriorating again and now with his new family, he believed travel up north was a bit dangerous.

Everyday, you heard of something horrendous happening. There was a case when a young girl was grabbed on her way to the market and taken to the field and raped. Men were forced to join them in the raping and if not get killed or worst yet, get beheaded.

During the Japanese occupation, the Japanese appropriated all the farmland in Bauan and several of the rice fields were converted into cotton fields. Adelaide's family who had a large parcel of farm land lost their rice farm to the Japanese. The people were ordered to plant cotton under the watchful eyes of the Japanese soldiers. Under the hot sun, the people planted and took care of the cotton plants. Every morning, the Japanese soldiers rounded up all the young men and women and took them to the farm and assigned them manual work at the farm. Nobody got paid but nobody dared to say no for fear of getting shot or slashed with bayonets. One of Adelaide's neighbors refused, was arrested and was never heard from again. They suspected he was killed by the Japanese.

The cotton grew abundantly and looked beautiful on the field. One could see rows and rows of cotton plants. Nobody planted rice anymore. All the rice and corn fields were used for cotton, hundreds of hectares of them both in Bauan and Batangas. When the cotton plants started blooming, the field looked wonderful with different colors of the blooms – light pink, dark pink, red, and violet. When it was time to harvest them, the Japanese got all women in town to help sort them. They harvested the cotton, took them to their house and then separated the cotton ball from the seed pod. Before Adelaide got married, Adelaide and her sisters used to work sorting the cotton. Then her brothers would put them in sacks provided by the Japanese and then took them to the warehouse located behind the church where the Japanese had converted the back of the church into a big warehouse. The Japanese were exporting all the cotton back to Japan. The sacks of cotton were then shipped to Japan to be manufactured into fabric. Everybody worked the cotton production but nobody got paid.

The Japanese had the superstition that if the cotton turned white from purple, the end was near. Late in the summer of 1944, the cotton fields were now turning the colored cotton into white like the white cloud. They had been watching the cotton produce and one day, its purple color turned to white. It could be the bleaching caused by the sun but the Japanese got this crazy superstition. At the same time, people noticed that the Japanese were getting more tyrannical. They started getting violent. They knew that if they lost the war, it would be a disgrace to their emperor. Their atrocities got worse and worse everyday. On the street, there was talk that the war would soon come into an end. The Filipinos who were also very superstitious people thought the changing color of the cotton must be a bad omen for the Japanese.

One day in Bauan, the people saw the Japanese soldiers go from house to house. You could see them walking up and down the street knocking on doors. Adelaide's brothers found out about what they were doing from a friend so they ran to the fields to hide.

Cayetano heard that there was an order telling people to go to the school or that big house next to the church for a town meeting. The Japanese promised them that they would get some food there. Some people went. The Japanese were able to gather hundreds of people.

The Japanese sent the men to the big empty house next to the church. The men were ushered in the house and guarded with armed Japanese soldiers. The house had been vacant for some time because the owner abandoned it and went into hiding at a remote farm.

The women were sent to the schoolhouse. There was a long line to enter. The Japanese soldiers were watching as women lined up to enter the school. They were only allowing a few women at a time to enter and then the soldiers closed the door. A few minutes passed and a few more women were ushered in. This went on until everyone was brought inside and then the doors closed.

Inside the schoolhouse, the room was big but there were no chairs or tables. When the room was full, the Japanese soldiers who were inside said they would be back, walked out of the school and closed the door. They went to the waiting trucks and left. The women inside the schoolhouse waited and waited. Then, they realized what was happening. They panicked. Luckily for them, the Japanese soldiers all left for the big house. The women started screaming for help. A Philippine scout heard them and ran to the school and frantically broke open the windows and the door and let the women ran out. Everyone escaped.

At the big house, the scene was almost identical. Men were all lined up to enter the building as the Japanese soldiers were watching them with their guns and bayonets at the ready. They let in the men fifty at a time. As soon as they entered, the door was locked. A few minutes later, the door opened and another fifty men were allowed in. This went on for quite a while. Near the end, a couple of men suddenly broke away from the line and ran away. The Japanese soldiers saw them and chased them. They aimed at them and fired. Both fell to the ground. Blood splattered around. The rest of the men in line were so shocked, they froze. They were afraid to move. Nobody dared to challenge the soldiers. Then the soldiers took their bayonets and stabbed the dying men several times. Men in line gasped. They were horror stricken. The door opened and the rest of the men were ushered in and then the soldiers locked the door. Nobody said a word but they were all frightened.

All the rooms in the house were packed to capacity. There was a door in every room and as soon as each room was full, the Japanese soldiers locked the doors. Before the soldiers locked the doors, they told the men they were coming back. There were more than 700 men inside. People started looking at each other and getting nervous. They waited and waited but nobody came. They waited some more and then the men inside realized what was happening but could not get out. The Japanese soldiers poured gasoline at the front of the house and set the house on fire. Then they left. They went across the road and watched the house slowly burning. They turned around and saw the municipal building and decided to pour gas there too and burned it also. There was no one in sight except the Japanese soldiers.

The men inside started smelling the gas and tried to get out. The smoke started seeping in. They tried to open the doors but couldn't. They started screaming and crying for help but to no avail. They started for the window. Everyone was in a state of panic. The windows were tightly shut. They could not get it to budge.

"Does anyone have a hammer?"

"Any tools?"

"Please hurry."

"What are we going to do?"

"Get a chair and smash the window."

"There is no chair here."

"We need strong men to push this window."

"The fire is closing in."

"I can't breathe."

"Hurry, please."

The smoke was getting worse. They were choking from the great amount of smoke generated by the fire. People started fainting. There was no way out. At the far end of the room, the men started for the window. They tried to push the window open. Finally, after pushing hard several times, somebody was able to pry a window open but it was too late. The building was completely engulfed by fire. The Japanese soldiers just stood outside across the street and watched the fire engulf the house. After a while, some of the soldiers left.

The men inside were now frantically trying to get out. Those who were able to escape with severe burns on their bodies dropped dead of smoke inhalation or shot to death. The soldiers who stayed behind saw them escaping and started shooting at them. Very few people escaped. A lot of people died in the flame or from smoke inhalation and some who were lucky to get out were unlucky to get shot.

Later that night, Adelaide's brothers came home. Regina was very worried because they were very late. Apparently, the soldiers were rounding every man at the market too. When the boys found out about it, they gathered their stuff and took off. They had a cousin who lived a couple of blocks from the market so they went by the back roads and hid in the fields near their cousin's house and waited till dark. Then they went to their cousin's house. There they found out what happened.

A week later, Adelaide found out three of her uncles and their sons were at the big house and were all killed. Relatives did not dare look for their missing relatives for fear of getting killed. About 700 people died in that massacre. What was happening in Batangas happened everywhere. The atrocities continued to the end of the war. More so in the big city. It was a system rehearsed in China called *Senko-Seisaku*, a three-part paradigm of 'kill all, burn all, destroy all.'

# CHAPTER 23

On October 20, 1944, MacArthur landed in Leyte, fulfilling his promise to the Filipino people by wading ashore at Leyte, but the evening before the Leyte landing, MacArthur spoke through a radio transmitter announcing.....

*"People of the Philippines, I have returned. By the grace of Almighty God, our forces stand again on Philippine soil... Rally to me! Let the indomitable spirit of Bataan and Corregidor lead... The guidance of divine God points the way. Follow in His name to the Holy Grail of righteous victory!"*

MacArthur, wearing his field marshal's cap, sunglasses and freshly pressed khakis wanted to land on the beach but ran aground in the shallows while still 100 yards from the beach. The commander of the craft could not bring the landing craft in any closer and so an irritated MacArthur accompanied by President Osmena and their staffs had to wade ashore. It became one of the most famous images of World War II. Upon seeing the newsreels of his landing, MacArthur was so stirred by the picture that he ordered his staff to arrange for all subsequent island landings to begin offshore so he could walk through knee-deep water onto the beach.

His troops started the drive to retake the islands, and on October 23, the greatest sea battle in history began, the Battle at Leyte Gulf when out of desperation, the first and coordinated Kamikaze suicide units were used by the Japanese forces on Oct. 25, 1944. Kamikaze means "divine wind" and the word was used for the new Japanese suicide pilots of World War II. It recalled the legend of Ise, the wind god who had saved Japan from an enemy invasion in ancient times. This legend was based on an event that happened on Aug. 14 and 15, 1281 when Japan was saved by a famous typhoon from a Sino-Mongol invasion of 3,500 ships with more than 100,000 warriors under the command of the great Kublai Khan of China to invade Japan.

When Gen. MacArthur returned, the guerillas were in good number. Some Filipinos went underground and joined the guerilla movement. Some joined the American troops.

When Nicolas, Adelaide's youngest brother, reached seventeen, he decided to join the U.S. Army. His brother Julian joined the Philippine Scout two years ago in 1943. Now Nicolas thought it was his turn. He wanted to learn how to drive those army trucks.

Nicolas came to his mother one day and said, "I'm getting a job in the U.S. Army. I want to drive those army trucks and help transport the G.I.'s."

Regina said, "I can't stop you. If you feel strongly about it, then you have my blessing. But be careful."

Nicolas took the driving test. The examiner asked him to drive the army's six-by-six truck between several obstacles. He was determined to get this job and he drove the truck beautifully and after several maneuvers, the examiner gave him his certificate. He got the job right then and there.

The beginning of the year 1945 found Adelaide and Benjamin together with Teresa back in Alitagtag. There was hope that liberation was near. The U.S. troops had taken Mindoro, an island near Batangas on January 1. Batanguenos were expecting the U.S. troops would be in their town soon.

The first of the Sixth Army's 200,000 troops landed at Lingayen Gulf on Jan. 9, 1945 with very little resistance, the same spot where Gen. Homma's troops had landed during the start of the war. MacArthur ordered other amphibious landings at other beaches in Luzon. Landings had been made at Subic Bay and Zambales on January 29, 1945. Two days after the Zambales landing, the 11th Airborne and another regiment of the 24th Division landed at Nasugbu on the Luzon coastline southwest of Corregidor on Jan. 31, 1945. The 11th Airborne Division arrived unopposed at Nasugbu, Batangas about 72 kilometers (45 miles) southwest of Manila and not far from Taal Lake which is only a couple of kilometers north from where Benjamin's family was hiding. Nasugbu was scheduled for heavy navy and air bombardment before the 11th Airborne Division landings but plans were scrapped because intelligence found that the Japanese had abandoned the town. The southern assault was intended as a diversion and an alternative force to seize Manila. The 10 U.S. divisions MacArthur placed on the island outnumbered even the massive landing force that stormed Normandy on D-day and would mark Luzon as the largest campaign of the Pacific War. The U.S. army was now racing inland. In early February they had inched toward Lemery and artillery fire started. The Japanese were now occupying Mt. Makulot in Cuenca, a few kilometers from where Benjamin's family was hiding.

Luzon is 740 kilometers (460 miles) long and 225 kilometers (140 miles) across at its widest. To defend it, Yamashita had about 275,000 men to draw on but most of his men were convalescing wounded, and poorly armed. MacArthur on the other hand brought in 280,000 men to Luzon with new draftees whose average age was nineteen replacing the dead and wounded at the Battle of Leyte Gulf. Since landing on Luzon, the Sixth Army had engaged and defeated the Shimbu and Kembu Groups in the west and south and had pushed Shobu Group into the mountainous northeastern corner of Luzon. Unable to prevent a landing, Yamashita ordered that the beaches would not be defended. Instead, he would fight a battle inland.

Around Manila, there were also about 16,000 naval personnel, mostly sailors whose ships had been sunk in Leyte Gulf in October, under the command of Adm. Sanji Iwabuchi. Yamashita decided Manila was indefensible so he ordered his men out except for a small detachment to guard the supply routes and blow the highway bridges leading from the city. Iwabuchi in defiance to General Yamashita's wishes, ordered his sixteen thousand sailors to defend the city. Fighting was fierce and lasted for a month, devastating the "Pearl of the Orient", especially the Intramuros district where many government buildings were turned into ruins. Day and night the fighting continued. At night, Manila blazed from a raging flame and could be seen from a far distance. Tracers arced through the night sky and the boom of artillery fire could be heard throughout the day.

When the fighting ended, almost all of Iwabuchi's men were dead, and so were as many as 100,000 Filipino civilians dead or wounded caught in the crossfire of the brutal battle.

By late summer in 1945, all of Benjamin's relatives had evacuated to the nipa huts in the midst of bamboo groves and mango trees on the farm where they were hiding far from the main road. Benjamin did not want to join them. He wanted privacy so they stayed at Benjamin's parent's home. They found out later that staying on the main road was not sensible at all. Every so often, there were air raids.

Whenever there was an air raid, Benjamin would grab Teresa and run and hide her inside a 55-gallon drum. He told Adelaide to follow. There were several 55-gallon drums that used to contain diesel oil that the U.S. army left near their house. The drums had supposedly been steam-cleaned and so became a great hiding place during air raids.

One early morning around 4 o'clock, they were awakened by a screeching noise on the road as if a big truck suddenly stopped in front of the house. Benjamin, Adelaide and Teresa were asleep upstairs. Benjamin jolted from his sleep. Adelaide heard it too and grabbed Teresa. Adelaide got very nervous. She held the baby tight and hoped she would not cry. Benjamin signaled to Adelaide to follow him to the corner of the room. They huddled in one corner of the bedroom behind some rolled banig, sleeping mat. They waited as they said a silent prayer.

They heard a Japanese convoy drop some Japanese soldiers in front of the house. The soldiers went under the house. Benjamin's parents' house was built on stilts and the ground floor was wide open. They waited in silence, paralyzed by fear. They heard the soldiers talking and heard them relieving themselves under the house. They could hardly breathe. It seemed like forever. They remained quiet upstairs while the Japanese were blabbering down below them. They hoped the soldiers would leave soon. Finally, they were relieved to hear footsteps leaving the place. There were no people around in town and the whole street was in total darkness so probably the soldiers thought all the houses were empty. Luckily, they didn't go upstairs.

As soon as it quieted down, they knew the Japanese soldiers had gone. They waited awhile. They remained silent, listening intently. There was no sound. The soldiers were gone.

"I think we should join the family at Binukalan," Benjamin told Adelaide, in a voice of quiet concern.

"Yes, definitely tomorrow," Adelaide said still shaking of fright.

"That was a close call."

Adelaide nodded, looked at Teresa who was still asleep.

"It will be safer if we go hide in the woods with my family."

"I tend to agree with you. That is true enough. The Japanese for some reasons don't venture in the woods and so we will be safe there."

So before the sun came up the next day, they sneaked across the street and went out to the field and stayed with Benjamin's family at the farm. It was a drastic change for Adelaide who was used to living in a nice house. Now, she and Benjamin with baby Teresa had to settle in a nipa hut nestled in a small clearing under the protective canopy of huge trees away from the prying eyes of Japanese planes.

When the population grew in Alitagtag, the people had carved great swathes of the forest, cutting down trees and scrub as they made the rich land into open fields where they cultivated crops. It extended for several hundred yards divided by ridges into long strips. Heavy plows pulled by strong carabaos tilled the heavy soil. The village worked the fields and each landowner harvested their crops with the help of the servants.

This was a community of several villages hidden among the trees far from the main road. A kilometer farther away, the woods grew again into a thick jungle before you reached Taal Lake. There was one notable feature near the place: in a small field up a promontory stood a single wooden cross. This served as an open-air church for the people. They called this area Binukalan.

Benjamin and Adelaide were now living in this community in Binukalan. All the citizens of Alitagtag were told to evacuate and settle near Binukalan. Food was getting scarce so here they learned how to live off the land. They fished by the lake which was a couple of kilometers away, cooked them fresh or dried them. They gathered kamote (sweet potatoes) and boiled them. They ate fruits from trees growing nearby. Rice was a precious commodity. Benjamin's parents had property there. They found a ditch on the property and settled down there for a while. Other folks lived in some other ditches not far from there. Enrique built a couple of nipa huts under the canopy of mango trees for his extended family, one to house one family and the other one to house two families and grandparents. Then other cousins came and wanted to move in with the grandparents. It was getting crowded. At night, everyone was sleeping head to head like sardines in one nipa hut.

One morning, Adelaide could not stand it any longer. She went to the other hut and asked her sister-in-law to take in the newcomers.

"We are a bit crowded in our place so can you please take some of the relatives and stay with you."

Dolores, Manuel's wife said, "I cannot take them in."

Adelaide said, "There are only the four of you. We have thirteen people in our place. Why can't you accommodate some of them?"

"I can't."

"Why not?" By this time, Adelaide was getting irritated. "All right. Since you have your own property on the other side, why don't you go there and be on your own? If you cannot be accommodating as I expect you to be, then leave. We are all here through the generosity of Benjamin's parents and we should be at least cooperating with each other. There's a whole family who need help and you think you own this place. Why don't you build your own nipa hut there?"

Adelaide stormed out and went to see her father-in-law. She was seething with anger. She sought the advice of her father-in-law.

"We are so crowded here. There are thirteen people here in this small hut and the other hut only has 4 people. Why can't the newcomers go to the other hut?"

"Yes, that makes a lot of sense."

"I went there and asked Dolores but she said she could not take them."

"She said that?"

"Yes, she did."

"I can't believe her attitude sometimes."

"I tried to reason with her but I could not sway her."

"Let me go there and talk to her. Better yet, I will take the newcomers now and order her to take the newcomers in."

"Thank you. She thinks she owns this place."

"I will show her who owns this place."

One night, they heard a loud explosion. It was dark around where Benjamin and Adelaide were camping in their makeshift village. There were nipa huts scattered under dense mango trees and roofs were covered with leaves. One by one, men came out and looked where the noise was coming from. It was a moonless night. It was total darkness except for the lights coming from the explosion.

Somebody called out, "The Americans are coming! The Americans are coming!" When the people heard that, they all came out of hiding. There was a promontory in the area where they could watch the flashing light. They climbed the little hill and looked out toward the horizon. They could see where the flashing lights were coming from. It looked like they were coming from Lemery. The area was wide open and void of vegetation so the view was panoramic. There were no trees blocking the view. The bamboo trees had been cut down to make nipa huts. One could see all the way to Taal Lake.

When the Americans landed in Lemery and opened a base there, you could see them from where they stood now. When the Americans started shooting at the Japanese, they could hear the artillery shells going back and forth at night. They could hear the start of a flurry of arms fire. Then the shootings got louder and louder.

Then from the distance, you could see the sky light up. Trees and debris were flying high up where the artillery landed. The Americans were not shooting far enough. It could be that they did not know where the Japanese were or the range of the artillery fire was not long enough. The shooting went on all night. In the morning, they found out the shots from the previous night landed in the cemetery nearby where empty shells were everywhere. The

Japanese were now occupying Mt. Makulot in Cuenca on the far side of Lake Taal which was quite a distance from where the shots had landed.

In no time, the American started moving their bases inland to Taal proper. The Americans set up a camp with several tents in Taal at the Plaza across the big Caysasay Catholic Church. The church was built between 1858 and 1878 and stands 95 meters long and 45 meters wide and is considered the biggest church in all of Southeast Asia.

When the Japanese opened their camp at Mt. Makulot, they brought in mining and tunneling engineers to make a military base. The Japanese engineers ransacked the electric plants in nearby towns including Alitagtag and all the equipment and material were brought in to Mt. Makulot where the caves were equipped with electricity, ventilation systems, telephone and radio communications and hidden exits. Caves were dug into the center of the mountain and beyond through a labyrinth of hidden exits. Steel doors covered the entrance and soldiers with big guns were guarding the entrance. In Cuenca, Mt. Makulot became a stronghold for the Japanese troops.

Filipino slave laborers were forced to work day and night building the intricate network of caves and tunnel where they stockpiled their food, supplies and weapons. They hollowed out underground installations and helped install artillery and automatic weapons that were positioned with interlocking fields of firepower, maximizing their killing ability. There was a rumor that a tunnel was built from Mt. Makulot all the way to the mouth of Taal Lake. The Japanese were supposed to use this tunnel as an escape route. There was also a legend that Capt. Yamashita had buried treasure here in the tunnel.

While the Filipino men were building the tunnel, the Japanese also rounded up pretty girls from Aplaya, a suburb of Bauan and brought them to Mt. Makulot for their pleasure and to work in the fields planting, growing and harvesting vegetables for them. The Japanese soldiers had an appetite for unmarried Filipino women and some of them were raped. Once the work was completed, the laborers were ruthlessly murdered so they could not relay the information to the Americans. Eventually one day, some of the female workers escaped while harvesting kamotes and vegetables.

The U.S. soldiers started marching inland toward the Japanese camp. When they reached Alitagtag, some people saw soldiers marching up the road. At first, they were scared thinking they were Japanese, then they realized they were white-skinned and tall. Instantly, they knew it had to be the Americans. Then they got excited. Someone ran to the field and informed everyone. People started coming out running to the street, waving their arms and cheering them on. The American did not expect the kind of reception they were getting and it became very unsettling. The cheering went on for several minutes. Some civilians were asking for food, others just waved and said "Hi Joe." They were deliriously happy to see the Americans.

"Is MacArthur coming?" A man asked.

"Yes," the GIs answered. A big cheering followed.

The soldiers told them to evacuate to the Elementary School and the nearby church. Some evacuees settled in the elementary school. Adelaide and Benjamin decided to stay overnight at the church. There were several evacuees in the church. The little group, huddled together, sat in the pews all night, some praying, some just sitting quietly until their eyes got tired and they dozed off to sleep.

At night, the shooting started again. This time, the Japanese shells started coming in their direction. The Japanese started shooting at the school. Artillery fire was coming from Mt. Makulot. All night long, the shooting never abated. All the evacuees at the school were moved to the church and the rectory in the cover of darkness. It was a long night for the evacuees.

By daybreak, the shooting stopped. The evacuees were told to move again. This time they were told to move to Taal. Benjamin and Adelaide together with Benjamin's two unmarried younger brothers joined the throng evacuating to Taal. The two brothers brought sacks of rice, kamote and some clothing. Benjamin had Teresa on his shoulder as he trod along with Adelaide.

Benjamin suddenly thought of his parents. He dispatched his youngest brother, Antonio to check on their parents.

"They have to be warned. Ask them if they want to join us," Benjamin said to Antonio.

"OK. I'll catch up with you." Antonio sped away and ran as fast as he could to the farm which was only a kilometer away from the main road.

Within an hour, there were thousands of people walking like an exodus of Israelites escaping from the pharaoh. Men, young and old, with their wives and children joined in. Everybody looked scared but nobody protested. They were just following what the American soldiers told them.

Antonio caught up with the group as they were rounding the bend towards Taal.

"They want to stay where they are. I could not force them to join us," Antonio told Benjamin.

"I pray to God they'll be safe there." Benjamin shook his head.

The evacuation ran smoothly with the American soldiers flanking the evacuees and leading the way. However the throng was getting bigger as they reached several villages. More people joined the evacuation as it progressed its way through towns. Some people stopped along the way trying to rest their tired feet. Adelaide and Benjamin kept their pace slowly, rested for a few minutes every now and then. They were totally exhausted when they reached Taal. It took them all day to get there.

At Taal, the evacuees were taken in by the residents of Taal. In the morning, they went to the U.S. Camp to get breakfast. For a week, Benjamin and Adelaide stayed in Taal with the rest of the evacuees. While the evacuees were being housed and fed in Taal, the American soldiers continued their march to Alitagtag and then the shooting continued at night until the American troops reached Cuenca.

By this time, the evacuees at Taal were moved again. People began to scatter around several nearby villages. One of Adelaide's aunts and her family were among the evacuees in Taal. The aunt wanted Adelaide and Benjamin to join them and hide near the sugar cane (sweet grass) fields which were not far from Taal. Benjamin wanted to return to Alitagtag so Adelaide asked her aunt to join them instead. The aunt said they were tired of walking and believed they would be safe in the sugar cane fields.

The cane plant is a form of grass, which belongs to the Poaceae family. The stem produces a juice with high sugar content, which is then made into sugar and its by-product, molasses. The cane plant produces more sugar content during the summer months when there is less rainfall. Batangas' climate which is warm and sunny makes it suitable for growing sugar cane. A well-drained and fertile land with adequate rainfall during the wet season is an ideal condition in planting the crop. The sweet grass is planted using the selected stalk of a mature cane plant. The carefully chosen cane stalks are laid horizontally in a narrow trench in the soil made by a plough. Then, it is covered with soil. Afterwards, roots grow from the base of the new stem of the cane plant. The cane plant can grow as high as four feet, and usually could take 7 to 8 months for it to be available for harvest. The harvest time in Batangas starts in the month of December and ends in the month of May.

In Batangas, the cane plant is harvested employing the traditional way of harvesting the crop manually – a labor-intensive job known around the province as *manggagapak*, or *paggagapak* (sugar cane cutter). Most manggagapak prefer to burn the plant during harvest time for a much easier job and to kill the snake that tends to hide around the sugar cane plants. However, according to most sugar cane growers, burning the cane during harvest reduces the sugar content of the plant.

Benjamin and Adelaide decided to return to Binukalan rather than staying near the sugar cane field. They thought staying at their own property was the best option for them. The American soldiers were now past Alitagtag and on their way to Manila to join MacArthur's force trying to enter Manila.

On the evening of February 3, the 1st Cavalry Division crossed the city limits of Manila to claim the title "First in Manila". By February 4, two U.S. columns were within 15 miles of Manila. General Joe Swing, the 11th Airborne Chief was closing in on the Japanese on southern Luzon. Around Manila, there were about

16,000 Japanese naval personnel, mostly sailors whose ships had been sunk in Leyte Gulf in October under the command of Adm. Sanji Iwabuchi. General Yamashita decided Manila was indefensible so he ordered his men out except for a small detachment to bring supplies and blow the highway bridges leading from the city. Iwabuchi in defiance of General Yamashita's wishes, ordered his sixteen thousand sailors to defend the city. The Japanese started destroying Manila, a city of 800,000 people. Fighting was fierce and lasted for a month, devastating the "Pearl of the Orient", especially the Intramuros district where many government buildings were turned into ruins. Day and night the fighting continued. Downtown Manila was roaring with black billows of smoke. At night, Manila blazed from a raging flame and could be seen from a distance. Tracers arced through the night sky and the boom of artillery fire could be heard across the bay.

As Manila was burning, the Philippine guerillas in Batangas ran into a group of Japanese soldiers. A fierce skirmish with the Japanese soldiers ensued at the junction of Alitagtag and Muzon with arms blazing and men shouting excitedly. The Philippine guerilla group was a ferocious looking group and they were anti-Japanese too. The fight ended with some Japanese casualties.

Benjamin and Adelaide decided to take a chance and leave Binukalan. After dark, they joined another group and moved to another location south of the street. Some of the townspeople were moving to the farm where Pedro lived.

They decided to leave after dark. Benjamin made a papoose bag and carried Teresa in it. Adelaide grabbed a couple of clothes for Teresa, a scarf to cover her head. Benjamin's mother wanted them to stay but Benjamin insisted it was safer to go to Bauan since the Japanese camp was so close to Alitagtag and they might advance to Alitagtag and meet the Americans head on. Luis and Antonio decided to go with them. Benjamin told them to carry the rice and their clothes. Benjamin found a stick to ward of snakes and they left under the cover of darkness.

As they passed the main road, they looked all around to see if there was anyone in sight. Nobody was around. They safely crossed the main road, went quietly through people's yards and began their trek. It was total darkness and not a sound could be heard except their footsteps. As they reached the farm beyond the houses, there was a faint glow from the moon above. They walked at a very fast pace. Benjamin was leading the group. He was following a trail that he knew. They headed south passing through farmland. They reached a small rise then turned east towards the place where a pair of mango trees were and turned south again. Every so often, they would stop and listened for strange sounds. When they thought it was not a Japanese patrol, they kept their steady pace. The quiet of the field was only broken by sounds from the night owl and bats roaming the night. They kept on looking back but could not see a thing. It was total darkness. They didn't even realize they reached the village where Pedro lived until they almost walked into it. In front of them were a group of nipa huts but everything was quiet. No sound was coming from the huts. It was obvious nobody was there. They were thinking of stopping but decided not to.

They veered left through another path which took them to Bauan. This time, the moon disappeared behind the cloud. Everything around them went pitch black. They could not see a thing. It was even impossible to see one's hand in front of one's face, it was so dark. Adelaide got frightened and tightened her grip on Benjamin's arm. Teresa was behaving very well and was sound asleep. Benjamin called out to his brothers and confirmed that they were still behind them. They slowed down their trek, trying to listen to any noise or movement. They had to be alert to any possible danger. Adelaide was silently praying to keep her mind off of negative thoughts. Luckily Benjamin knew the area quite well. With his stick he waved it side to side to clear the pathway. They found a clearing with a little hut and rested for a while. They might have dozed for an hour. Then they saw the moon begin peeking through the clouds again. Benjamin nudged his brothers and Adelaide. He bundled Teresa and they decided to move on. They kept on walking that seemed like forever. They reached Bauan as the dawn was coming up.

When they got to Bauan, they went to their godparents' house in town. The house was located across the market. The town was still quiet. Not a soul was up yet. They knocked at the door. An old man came out and opened the door.

"*Magandang Umaga po.*" "Good Morning sir," Benjamin greeted the old man.

"*Magandang umaga rin sa iyo.*" "Good Morning to you too," the old man replied. He remembered Benjamin from his last visit.

"Is Judge Cordero home? He was expecting me."

"I'm afraid he just left with his family a few hours ago."

"Do you know where they are going?"

"Yes, he said they are taking a boat to Mindoro."

Benjamin looked at Adelaide disappointed. "We just missed them. What are we going to do now?" He asked Adelaide.

"I guess we just have to find my family."

Benjamin turned to the old man and said, "Thank you. We were supposed to join them to evacuate to Mindoro. In case you hear from the judge, you can tell him I came."

"I will. They were in a bit of a hurry. I'm so sorry you missed them. All kinds of rumors are going around and he thinks it is safer in Mindoro."

"I'm not sure it is safer anywhere anymore. The Japanese are killing civilians now, not just soldiers and guerillas. Are you staying here?" Benjamin suddenly asked. "I think you should leave and go to some remote barrio where the Japanese do not venture at all."

"We shall. We are leaving town soon and go into hiding."

Benjamin turned to Adelaide and his brothers who were patiently waiting and said, "We better get going."

"*Adios po.*" Godspeed. Benjamin bid goodbye to the old man.

"*Adios.*" Be careful.

Benjamin and Adelaide decided to go to the barrio of Asis where Adelaide's mother and brothers were hiding. Asis was only a few kilometers away.

While Adelaide and Benjamin got settled in Asis, the Japanese burned the villages between Alitagtag and Taal. Torches were lit and thrown into the houses. Some of the houses which were made mostly of nipa and bamboo were so flimsy that they burned readily. The windows shattered and flames engulfed the interior very quickly. The beams creaked as the ceiling and the whole rooftop fell.

As the fire engulfed the whole town, people who were still in their home started scrambling and ran for their lives. They went running to the sugar cane fields away from the main road. They joined some villagers who were already hiding there. However, the Japanese did not pay much attention to the escaping Filipinos at first but were concentrating on their job of torching the houses. That was their order.

The Japanese ran wild like angry beasts. They went from house to house with torches and set the houses on fire. Then they started on the next town. The sugar plantations which bisected the various villages were not spared. After the Japanese were done with the houses, they went to the fields and burned the sugar plantations. Some villagers who were hiding among the sugar cane were roasted to death. As the flames engulfed the sugar cane, there were cries of agony and desperation. Some people tried to escape but there was no place to go. The fire was engulfing every space around them. People dropped dead as they ran out of their hiding place.

Adelaide and Benjamin were only at Asis a couple of days when Benjamin noticed a black cloud coming from the west.

"Adelaide, look," Benjamin said pointing to the northwest.

"What is that?" She asked, then said after realizing what it could mean, "Oh no. The Japanese?"

Benjamin nodded.

From where they stood, Benjamin and Adelaide could not see the flames but it was definitely a big fire. They saw black smoke shooting up to the sky coupled with bright light on the horizon. They had the suspicion that the Japanese started burning some areas. Benjamin was worried about his parents. Adelaide thought of her aunt and her family who were hiding near Taal at a sugar cane field. How she wished her aunt listened to her. Now, she wondered if they were able to escape. Benjamin suspected it was from Alitagtag where his parents were hiding out in the fields.

"Adelaide, I have to go back to Alitagtag. I have to check it out. I hope to God it is not in Alitagtag and that my parents are safe," Benjamin told Adelaide. She did not know what to say. She was afraid for his safety but Benjamin was so concerned about his parents.

"What about your brothers?" She asked.

"They are staying with you and the baby. You'll all be safe here."

"Be careful."

"I will. Take care of the baby in case I don't come back."

"You will come back. I know you will."

Benjamin made a sign of the cross and left.

As Benjamin took his leave, Adelaide could not help wondering what caused the fire and where it was. She thought for a moment how lucky they were to have left when they did. Some people they knew were so adamant on not leaving. She hoped they were safe. She suddenly thought of her relatives who stayed behind on the sugar cane plantations. That thought gave her a chill and her teeth started chattering and she could not stop it. She crossed her arms in front of her and rubbed her hands to warm herself. After several minutes, when the chills stopped, she plopped down on the ground. She noticed Teresa on the straw mat sound asleep. She came to her baby's side and kissed the baby on the forehead and whispered to Teresa, "Your father will be back. I know he will. God will keep him safe."

Benjamin walked back to Alitagtag. He followed the same path he did a few nights ago. It took him all day. He could smell the smoke as he was getting closer to the main road in Alitagtag but it looked like it was coming from northwest of where his parents were. The air was gray with smoke. He crossed the main road and it was empty. Nobody was around. Looking right and left, he ran across the street into the woods. So far he had not encountered any Japanese soldier.

He reached the area where his parents were hiding. His parents were glad to see him. He found out everything was fine there but found out the Japanese started burning the villages from Muzon about two kilometers from where they were all the way to Taal in retaliation for their losses in Muzon. It started in Muzon where the Philippine guerillas fought the Japanese the week before. He was told tall plumes of smoke began rising in Muzon and at nightfall, the sky to the south of their hiding place was crimsoned by many fires. They could see the fire glow from where his parents were hiding.

The Japanese thought the revolutionaries came from Taal so they set fire to all the houses from Muzon all the way to Taal.

As the fire started to spread out, people did not think it would reach them since it started too far from where they were. But the Japanese made sure they burned the whole perimeter of all sugar cane fields so people had no way of escaping. They also burned all the sugar cane fields which dotted the roadways to Taal. Some of the refugees who were hiding behind the sugar cane fields got caught with the burning fields and succumbed. They had no place to run. People were crying as the fire neared and praying for help. But help was nowhere in sight.

Enrique told Benjamin to go back to Bauan and bring back his family to Alitagtag. So the next day, Benjamin was back on the field going back to Asis to take his family back to Alitagtag. Adelaide insisted on staying for a few more weeks till everything calmed down. They stayed for a couple of months until they got word that Alitagtag was now safe. The American troops were now conquering Cuenca and the Japanese strongholds at Mt. Makulot.

While MacArthur was securing the troops in Corregidor, paratroopers were assigned to help the Sixth Army clear the southern part of Luzon, the Philippines' main island. There were Japanese defensive positions stretched from Laguna Bay to Lake Taal, manned by the fifty thousand men who composed General Tomoyuki Yamashita's formidable Shimbu Group.

The 11th Airborne Division fought a fierce battle against the Japanese defenses on the mountaintop strongholds at Mt. Makulot in Cuenca. The fight was bloody and perilous. The terrain in Cuenca was rugged and inhospitable. The road was narrow with zigzagging hairpin turns around the mountain amidst thick jungle. They met hostile gunfire from the enemy while crossing the bridge at the foot of the mountain. Some bridges were blown up so the troops had to maneuver through ditches to cross while under enemy fire. There was thick, heavy undergrowth along the zigzag pass and mountain sides. Enemy rifle and machine gun fire were met with ferocious intensity as Americans fought back with flamethrowers, grenades and individual combat. Twigs and branches were snapping everywhere. The GIs were crawling as bullets were flying overhead.

There were heavy casualties on both sides. It was jungle warfare. The Americans went after the Japanese retreating to the caves on the western side of Mt. Makulot with flamethrowers and grenade.

From the village in Binukalan, they could hear the explosions and sometimes could see the smoke from fires that had been set. With the fall of Mt. Makulot, large-scale enemy resistance in southern Luzon collapsed.

The American troops continued their march toward Manila to join MacArthur for the final campaign to capture Manila and Yamashita's army. The embattled defense force of Admiral Iwabuchi engaged the American and Filipino troops in a month long intense combat. During the battle, the Americans liberated between three thousand five hundred to four thousand prisoners at the University of Santo Thomas. It was the first American victory in Manila. When the fighting ended, there were heavy casualties, almost all of Iwabuchi's men were dead, and as many as 100,000 Filipino civilians dead or wounded caught in the crossfire of the brutal battle. The city of Manila was totally destroyed.

Meanwhile the Japanese in Batangas unleashed their brutal campaign of torture, rape and butchery against the Filipino civilians. Word spread in Alitagtag that groups of men in Lipa City were rounded up between Feb. 16 -18, 1945 and sent to a building and then the building was doused with kerosene and burned. More than 2,000 Lipa City residents were massacred. Alitagtag was lucky to be spared the wrath of the Japanese because rumors were the Mayor was playing as a Japanese sympathizer. Behind their back, he was also working for the Americans giving them intelligence report on where the Japanese were. There was a saying around *"Pilipino Tagu, Pilipino Turu"* meaning Pilipino Hide, Pilipino Point in that Direction". He was playing both sides thereby gaining good graces from both parties.

On July 5, after much struggle, the Philippine people were finally liberated from Japan. Yet even after Japan suffered a devastating loss, there was no indication of surrender. Therefore, President Harry S. Truman decided to use an atomic bomb, a weapon he told Joseph Stalin at Potsdam Conference, "the like of which has never been seen on this earth". On August 6, 1945, a B-29 named Enola Gay, piloted by Colonel Paul Tibbets dropped the first atomic bomb on the Japanese city of Hiroshima, population 343,000 people. With the blinding light and the mushroom cloud, Tibbets' crew could only say "My God." Something like 120,000 people were killed, obliterated, or wounded.

On August 7, 1945, news from the radio came out that Hiroshima was devastated by an atomic bomb the day before. Two days later, on August 9, 1945, the second atomic bomb hit Nagasaki. Again, there was the great fireball and huge casualties. Finally, on August 14, it was announced that Emperor Hirohito would surrender under Allied terms. The Japanese Supreme War Council decided that the time had come to surrender. The Emperor's radio broadcast did not take place till the following day. Fanatics still resisted and were now retreating to the mountains.

A great rejoicing could be heard everywhere. The Americans soldiers were now marching openly on the streets. However, the folks everywhere were not optimistic that the Japanese would ever surrender.

The next day, August 15, 1945, the Japanese Emperor accepted the demands of the Allies and for the first time the emperor himself went on the radio and announced to his people that the war was over. The Japanese government formally signed the articles of surrender two weeks later on Sept. 2, 1945 on the American battleship, *USS Missouri* in Tokyo Bay. Afterward, by order of Emperor Hirohito, 6,983,000 Japanese soldiers laid down their arms peacefully. Only the emperor who the military considered as a god could have received obeisance to such an order.

The whole country was euphoric. Everybody was cheering the G.I.'s and dancing in the streets. There were festivities everywhere. There was singing in the streets. The Second World War was over.

Benjamin and Adelaide were among those people rejoicing the occasion. The evacuees decided to celebrate at Taal Lake. Young people walked the mile to the beach in a gay mood. They were laughing and singing as they crossed the rugged terrain to the lake. They brought food and drink, set up bonfires around the beach area. Someone brought a banjo and everyone joined in the singing. They were dancing and going wild with the merriment. After a while,

Benjamin took a look at Adelaide who was snuggled in one corner with the baby. They decided to leave the scene and go home. The baby was sound asleep with all the commotion. They slipped out quietly and started walking up the path.

It was a lovely night for celebration. It was a hot night, lit only by the stars. The nearest street-lighting was so far away, so no dull glow marred the perfect beauty of the night sky with millions of stars glowing above. There were more stars than they had ever seen glowed and winked. They saw literally dozens of shooting stars. It must have been the Perseids: mid-August is usually the time for this shower of meteors to pass. But they didn't know about such things then and anyway, their mind was too occupied with everything they'd heard to think of astronomy. "It must always be like this on summer nights," Benjamin thought fancifully.

They walked hand in hand contentedly and decided to go to the house instead of returning to the hut where they used to hide. They passed the street and nobody was there. It was so quiet. Everyone must be at the lake celebrating. They went to the house, opened the door which was unlocked. They put the baby down on the sleeping mat.

"Thank God the war is over and we survived unscathed," Benjamin said.

"Yes, I'm glad. Come to think of it. I'd probably be still single if not for those Japanese. I was so afraid of them."

"I have to thank them for that. Should I?" Benjamin was teasing her.

"You should."

"I don't think so." Benjamin pulled her over and kissed her on her forehead. Adelaide put her arms around his neck. They went to bed that night holding each other arms, thanking their lucky stars.

With a twist of fate, the war that started in the Philippines at Camp John Hay also ended there with General Yamashita returning to Camp John Hay and signing the Japanese surrender to the United States on September 3, 1945.

# CHAPTER 24

Life started getting back to normal slowly until December 19, 1945. Adelaide had planned to have a birthday party for Teresa on her 2ⁿᵈ birthday the next day. They were going to Bauan to get some supplies. They were on their way when suddenly Benjamin started getting a bad headache. The pain was excruciating. He told the cuchero to turn back and head back home.

As soon as they got home, Adelaide called the doctor. She arrived and examined the patient in the bedroom. Benjamin's face was flushed. She put her hand on his forehead. It was too hot and he was getting delirious. She gave him some medication but it did not help.

The doctor turned to Adelaide. "I will not lie to you but he is seriously ill and fighting for his life."

Adelaide opened her mouth to say something but nothing came out of her mouth. She suddenly felt weak.

"It's the fever," the doctor said. "The fever is so bad. If it does not break, he might die."

The doctor gave Adelaide some medications to administer to Benjamin and then the doctor left. Adelaide stayed with Benjamin for a while and then went to the living room. There were some relatives visiting and wanting to know what had happened and wanted to know if the party was still on. Adelaide said since it was planned already and she did not want to disappoint Teresa, the party was still on.

She did not believe Benjamin was going to die. She had to do something. She then called Luis, one of Benjamin's brothers.

"I want you to fetch my mother in Bauan. Tell her to bring an *arbulario* with her. Tell her Benjamin is very sick and I need her and the arbulario here."

Enrique heard this and talked to Adelaide, "What can an arbulario do? The doctor was here already."

"I do not believe the doctor. I don't believe Benjamin is dying," Adelaide retorted.

"I do not believe in quack doctors. The doctor is Benjamin's cousin. She went to medical school. She knows more than a quack doctor," Enrique said.

"But if she can't do anything for my husband, I will go to the next best thing which is to call an herbalist. Benjamin is not dying. I know he is not."

"All right then. If you say so," Enrique conceded.

Adelaide stood abruptly. "I'm going to sit with him now until my mother arrives."

Enrique sighed, shook his head and went to the kitchen.

Regina came with an arbulario in tow. The arbulario made his concoction, closed his eyes and did his prayer. Then he put a piece of paper with some poultice and some writing and put it on Benjamin's forehead. He left it there for a while then he took it out. The paper was all wet with a reddish stain. He turned to Adelaide and said, "Three women were talking about him and playing tricks on him."

Then Adelaide remembered hearing somebody said that Benjamin used to tell some women in Batangas when he came to their store that he was single. But then Benjamin would take Adelaide and Teresa to Batangas and went to the same stores. Teresa would hang on to him and kept on calling him "Daddy." Maybe these women were talking about him behind his back.

On one of those trips, they went shopping and Benjamin bought a doll for Teresa, and later stopped at a restaurant for lunch. At the restaurant, Benjamin went to the bathroom and Adelaide and Teresa were left in a booth. A waitress came to the table.

Seeing the doll, she talked to Teresa, "Did your *Tatay* buy you that doll? Where is your Tatay?" Tatay is the Philippine word for father.

Teresa proudly said, "I have no Tatay."

The waitress looked at Adelaide and Adelaide blushed. Then Teresa added, "Daddy bought me my doll."

The waitress and Adelaide both laughed. At that time, nobody was using Daddy. Everyone was calling their father *"Tatay"* or *"Itay."* Some children called their father "Papa".

Then Adelaide ordered some merienda. She ordered suman. A few minutes later, the food came. The waitress waited for Teresa to start eating. She refused. "I want a spoon," the child said. At this point, Adelaide was getting embarrassed already but Teresa refused to use her hand. So the waitress went back to the kitchen and looked for a spoon.

All afternoon after the arbulario administered to Benjamin, they waited and watched Benjamin. By 6 o'clock, he opened his eyes. He said he was hungry so Adelaide asked one of the cousins who was watching with them to go to the kitchen and get some soup. She placed her hand on his head and felt that he was still hot. She took a piece of young banana leaves, put it on his forehead, tied it with a folded handkerchief. He ate a little of the soup and immediately fell back to sleep. Adelaide breathed a sigh of relief, knowing he was on the mend. For a while, she was worried what would happen to her and Teresa if he died. She did not know any work but she put the thought out of her head. She kept her faith that everything would be okay.

By the next morning, Benjamin was up and about and so the birthday party for Teresa was celebrated that afternoon. All the relatives came by. There were *sotanghon* noodle (clear as cellophane noodle) soup and *mammon* cake (sponge cake) and cookies were served. Teresa was prettily dressed in her new frilly flowered dress and brand new shoes and white socks.

A couple of months later, Adelaide and Barbara, her mother-in-law had an argument regarding the feeding of Teresa. Barbara, her paternal grandmother sometimes took care of her. One day Adelaide saw her mother-in-law feeding Teresa.

"What are you doing?" Adelaide asked her mother-in-law as Barbara spooned out the food that she just spat out from her mouth and gave to Teresa. Barbara was chewing the food first herself before giving it to Teresa.

"I'm feeding the baby. Can't you see?"

"I can see that. But you are chewing the food first."

"Yes, to make it easy for the baby to digest."

Adelaide looked at Barbara in disgust. "Please don't do that. That was unsanitary."

"I'm not sick. What's wrong with it?"

"Even so, I don't want you to do that."

"OK then. You can feed her yourself." Barbara stormed out of the kitchen. Teresa looked at both of them and started crying.

Adelaide hugged the baby and calmed her down.

A week later, Teresa developed a rash on her buttock and started acting strange. Her eyes were shut and she was thrashing her little clenched fists in the air back and forth. She was very sick.

"Teresa, wake up. Wake up. What is wrong with you?" Adelaide felt her forehead. The baby was hot. She looked at Benjamin. "Something is very wrong with her. Let's take her to see her godmother." Teresa's godmother, Cecilia was a doctor. Adelaide knew that Benjamin was not too keen on arbulario. Beside Cecilia lived close by.

Benjamin picked up Teresa wrapped in a cotton blanket. Her head was jerking and her eyes still shut. Benjamin ran out of the house and went to Teresa's godmother's house which was few houses down the road. Adelaide ran after them. They reached the doctor's house and rang the bell. The doctor opened the door and was shocked to see them with the baby wrapped in a blanket.

"What is wrong with Teresa?" Cecilia asked.

"She is very sick," Benjamin said.

"This way," Cecilia guided them inside. They went right into the examining room. Cecilia took the blanket off of Teresa, took a quick look at her and felt Teresa's hot body and said, "She is having convulsion from the fever. Babies come out of convulsions. We can give her a warm bath."

"Will it help?" Benjamin asked.

"Yes, that would help." The doctor went in the back room. "Follow me and bring Teresa," She told Benjamin.

Picking up Teresa, Benjamin followed the doctor to the kitchen. The kitchen maid was there. "We need hot water," Cecilia told the maid.

The maid opened a faucet and poured water into a pot and started the fire on the stove.

"Feel that," the doctor said after a few minutes. "Is it too hot?"

"Adelaide took a dip in the pot. "No. Just right."

The doctor took the baby from Benjamin. She stripped the blanket off and immersed Teresa in the tepid water to the chin. She splashed some on her head too. The stiff arch of the baby's back and neck loosened up and the baby went limp on the doctor's hand.

Teresa eyes opened. Adelaide looked at Teresa and held her hand. Teresa's wan look just wrung her heart.

The doctor gave Teresa a shot of sulfanilamide. "Take her back home and keep her warm," the doctor said. "She should calm down and be able to sleep for hours. I'll come to your house later today and stay with her if I have to."

"Thank you very much. We'll see you later."

Cecilia came to the house late in the afternoon. Adelaide was sitting by Teresa and watching her. The baby was still running a fever.

"How is she doing?"

"I'm not so sure. Her body temperature was shifting from very hot to very cold. Something must be serious."

"Let me examine her again." Cecilia took her stethoscope and started taking the blanket off Teresa. The baby was thrashing her arms, her eyes would open and had a blank stare and then closed them tight. Adelaide was beside herself. All she could think of was that her mother-in-law was instrumental in making Teresa sick.

"I'm afraid she has the symptoms of meningitis," Cecilia told Adelaide and Benjamin.

"Meningitis? How serious is that?" Benjamin asked. Adelaide tugged at Benjamin's arm. She started to cry.

"Meningitis is a very serious illness. I have to be honest with you. I have heard cases that it could easily kill anybody." Adelaide gasped and started crying. Benjamin put his arms around her. He was as upset as she was.

"I love Teresa as much as you do. She is my godchild. I will do anything to keep her alive. I will stay by her bedside till she gets better." Luckily for the family, Teresa's godmother was single and she stayed with her at all hours. She kept her on strong antibiotics and kept vigil over her. She rubbed her with wet hot towels or cold wet towels depending on her temperature. Teresa's eyes would go up and down and she would convulse incessantly. She seemed so helpless.

Benjamin and Adelaide were worried sick. They prayed fervently. They were at their wit's end. They didn't know if their precious little girl would make it. After several days of agony, her body temperature stayed stable. Her godmother said the crisis was not over yet. She watched Teresa for another two days. Then her godmother declared she was out of danger. They watched her as she slowly took some food that was offered to her. She started getting color in her cheeks. Slowly every day, they saw an improvement in her well being. By the following month, she was back on her feet again acting like a 2-year old.

Adelaide and Benjamin decided to visit her mother in Sambat for the town fiesta in May 1946. The people were glad to be resuming their daily routine before the war. It was the first time in a long, long time that they could travel free of worries of seeing Japanese on the road. It was a very good feeling to be free again. Regina was very happy to see her favorite granddaughter.

They were catching up on the news when Adelaide found out from her mother about the fate of some of her relatives. A few of her relatives who went hiding near the sugar cane fields near Taal did not make it. Her Aunt Genoviva, her husband and 7 kids were caught in the fire. They all died in the sugar cane fire. They thought they would be safe there. Adelaide saw them last on their return to Alitagtag from Taal and she encouraged them to join her and Benjamin to go to Alitagtag but they said they would be fine there. Her aunt even asked Adelaide to join them. That thought gave Adelaide goose bumps. She could not imagine what would have happened to her, Benjamin and Teresa if they stayed with her aunt and her family.

They would have stayed with her mother for a few days but Benjamin wanted to go back and spend time with his family for their own town fiesta. They headed back to Alitagtag the next day. Adelaide felt a little tired because of her condition. She was now expecting their second child any moment. But she felt extremely happy. The war was over and here she was with her family all together again and was able to survive the war and a new member of the family was coming soon. A few days later, Teresa's brother was born. They named him Delfin after Benjamin's late brother.

With the new baby, they celebrated their Independence Day on July 4, 1946 as the new dawn of freedom awaits their future and the future generation. They thanked the Holy Cross for keeping them safe and survived the war. As they held their two young children, they pray and hope no war will come their way again.

They heard a plane flying overhead. They looked up. Teresa turned her gaze to her father and said, "Daddy, are we going to hide inside the drum with Delfin?"

"No, Teresa. Not this time. Never again."

"Good."

## ABOUT THE AUTHOR

Rosalinda Rosales Morgan was born and raised in the Philippines, graduated from Adamson University in Manila with a degree in accounting, passed the C.P.A. board exam before moving to New York. Besides accounting, she also practiced real estate while living in Oyster Bay, New York. Tired of the cold weather and high taxes in New York, she and her husband now reside in Charleston, South Carolina. She has written several gardening articles for many years. This is her first novel.

www.ingramcontent.com/pod-product-compliance
Lightning Source LLC
Chambersburg PA
CBHW070324260626

47160CB00003B/937